I0688732

METHOD TO HER MAGIC

AGENTS OF A.S.S.E.T.

KATIE SALIDAS

Method to her Magic
AGENTS OF A.S.S.E.T. Book 4
Copyright © 2019 by Katie Salidas

All rights reserved. No part of this publication may be reproduced, stored in or introduced into a retrieval system, or transmitted, in any form, or by any means (electronic, mechanical, photocopying, recording, or otherwise) without the prior written permission of both the copyright owner and the above publisher of this book.

This is a work of fiction. Names, characters, places, brands, media, and incidents are either the product of the author's imagination or are used fictitiously.

The author acknowledges the trademarked status and trademark owners of various products referenced in this work of fiction, which have been used without permission. The publication/use of these trademarks is not authorized, associated with, or sponsored by the trademark owners.

Cover Art by: Molly Phipps
https://www.wegotyoucoveredbookdesign.com Editing by

Editing: Midnight Library Book Services
http://www.midnightlibrarybookservices.com/

Published by: Rising Sign Books
http://www.risingsignbooks.com

For more information about my books email:
katiesalidas@gmail.com
Autographed Editions of all Katie Salidas books may be purchased at http://www.KatieSalidas.com

OTHER BOOKS BY KATIE SALIDAS

Chronicles of the Uprising
Dissension
Complication
Revolution
Transition
Retribution
Annihilation

Little Werewolf
Pretty Little Werewolf
Curious Little Werewolf
Fearless Little Werewolf

Immortalis
Carpe Noctem
Hunters & Prey
Pandora's Box
Soustone
Dark Salvation

Olde Town Pack
Moonlight
Mated
Being Alpha

The world is full of magical creatures and artifacts. That's where the A.S.S.E.T. agency comes in: Anonymous Supernatural Security and Elimination Taskforce.

The front line, maintaining the balance of power, ensuring humans remain safely oblivious to the danger-ous magic around them.

A Weapon of Magical Destruction
A Taste of Your Own Magic
Magic in Disguise
Method to her Magic
Let Sleeping Magic Lie (2020)
Magic on a Mission (2020)

Acknowledgments

This book was a product of tough love, and I want to thank the team of readers who really put me through my paces.
Martika Cabezas, Jessie Stockton, Anne Loshuk, Jacob Devlin, J.E. Taylor, & Julia Allen!
Thank you for going over multiple drafts, giving me all of your honest feedback, and really paying attention to the small details. You're honesty and critical eye have shaped this story into something special. Beyond the critical, thank you as well for the enthusiasm you've had for this book series. You guys jumped on this project the moment I announced it and devoured each section faster than I could produce them. The late night chats, encouragement, & feedback was just the encouragement I needed to keep this project moving, even when I felt it was all for naught.

**And last, but not least, thank you to my readers!
You are the reason I keep writing!**

ONE

Sage had never realized how much she hated office work until ASSET had freed her from cubical life. Which made medically mandated, light-duty work supremely unbearable. Having her hand carved up like a Thanksgiving turkey hadn't been nearly as painful as the two weeks she'd spent as Ava's personal slave.

She clenched and opened her hand a few times, warming up her still very tight muscles. Scar tissue pulled with each movement. But thanks to the supernaturally fast healing of the Terra people, the bloody ruin had knitted back together, and she'd regained nearly all the function and use of her hand. She was ready for action.

Sage carried her personnel file close to her chest as she scurried down the hallway toward the training room. Devon's domain. His home away from home. She could have sworn he had some kind of magical portal between ASSET and his dojo near her old apartment. No matter which location she looked to find the ogre personal trainer, he seemed to always be there. She prayed that would be the case as she weaved her way through the unusually thick crowd of agents. Clock-in time, at least for her, wasn't for another hour, but already the building was abuzz with an excessive amount of activity.

She rounded the corner and spotted Devon stretching in the training room before she'd crossed the threshold. Fate, it seemed, was on her side.

"Today's the day I get back to real work!" She sauntered into the room in full Captain Trainwreck style.

"You think so?" Devon finished his extended lunge before standing to face her.

She might have thought she was getting an early start to the day, but it was clear by the sweat beading on his brow that Devon had been up and at it for far longer than she. The ogre scrutinized her face, his gaze drawing a straight line down to the file clutched tightly against her chest.

"Let's see, then." He held out his hand.

She passed the file to him with a sly smile, sure of her victory. Nothing was going to ruin her day.

Devon tossed the folder on the bench. "You know what I mean."

She grinned, showing all her teeth to cover any sign of distress that might show on her face as she reached out to Devon. "It might look like a Frankenhand, but it feels just fine."

He manipulated her hand, pressing on different parts of her scar like a bad massage, all the while keeping his eyes on Sage to see if she showed discomfort. She kept her teeth on display, smiling comedically wide and holding that face through all the aches and pains. He pressed down harder, deeper into the muscles that had recently knitted back together. When that did not produce sounds of pain, he began working her fingers, bending and flexing. He balled her hand into a fist and made her bend and flex at the wrist.

"Much better than the last time." He released her hand and held up his own. "Make a fist and punch me, hard as you can."

This was going to hurt, but she had to keep her cool. She balled her fist tight, reared back, and threw everything she had into the punch. The impact nearly took her breath away, but she kept that smile plastered across her face, and breathed through her teeth as she internalized the scream.

"Someone's been doing their physical therapy exercises." He held his hand up again. "High five, Captain Trainwreck."

She slapped his palm before she realized what he was doing. Tender scars threatened to split apart. The burn arced across her hand like lightning. A squeal escaped her lips before she could stop it.

Devon crossed his arms. His eyebrow arched sharply at her as if to say, "Busted."

"I'm good. I'm fine. See." She squeezed and released her hand a few times. Pain faded as quickly as it came, but left an annoying itch that Sage knew she'd never be able to scratch. Her lips twitched with the strain of holding on to her fake smile. "High-five me again. I can take it."

"You don't have to be a hero. I'm not out to get you. I just need to know you're ready to take on normal duty."

"I'm good. I promise." Her voice cracked as she pleaded. "Sign off on the report. You'll see."

"Sure you're ready to go back in the field?" Devon's eyebrow remained arched in disbelief.

She had to convince him. She'd come so far. She was healing. Her hand felt better every day. Today's pain would be cut in half by tomorrow. But she didn't want to wait any longer. She couldn't. "If I have to file one more damn report, I'll slit my throat with a manila folder."

"What good would that do? It would just make a bloody mess that Ava would order you to clean up." Devon chuckled. He released his crossed arms, and that damming eyebrow finally lowered. "And probably earn you more time on medical suspension for Ava to torture you with."

"I take it back." Sage slapped her hand over her mouth.

"You've passed the physical assessments. Range of motion is optimal, though I'd love to see you without pain. But as you're bound and determined to get back out there, I'll let you to it." He picked up the file and opened it. "Before I sign off, I need your word that this time, you'll try to go more than a week before maiming yourself again." He unclipped the pen stashed in the center of the folder and scrawled his name across the bottom of the page.

"Funny." Sage took the paperwork from Devon.

"And that means we're back on your regular training schedule. I want to see you on the mats at least three days a week. Pain or not, you need to train. Your hand-to-hand is acceptable, but you still need to be certified on weapons, and most importantly, we need to work on your concentration under pressure, Miss Shadow Ops."

"Sir, yes, sir!" She saluted him and spun on her heel, prepared to escape in case Devon chose to begin her training immediately as a punishment for her cheek.

Grey's face came into view. Lurking in the hallway. How long had he been there, watching?

"Training. Tomorrow." Devon gave the order as Sage scooted out of the room as fast as her legs would carry her.

Grey stood like a shadow just beyond the threshold. She swatted at him as she walked by. "Spying on me?"

"Someone has to keep watch over you."

Sage swallowed the temptation to invoke the wrath of the gods by asking how much trouble she could get in at ASSET, choosing instead to nod in the direction of Ava's office. "Well, c'mon then, let's get this over with."

The hall leading to the main lobby had swelled to near bursting in the few minutes she'd been in with Devon. She fought to swim upstream against the crowds of agents, all heading the other way. Grey managed it easy enough, keeping pace with her as she made her way toward Ava's office.

"Don't pretend you're not excited to get back out there."

"Oh, I am. Just not the paperwork part of it." Sage waved the file in Grey's face.

"Everything else sorted? New apartment ready and all?"

"I'll have to stay in barracks for another week, but yeah, all sorted everywhere else."

"You don't have to stay there if you don't want to," he offered. "There's plenty of extra space at my place. I'd be willing to bet it's a lot more comfortable than the barracks."

Spending a night or two at his home was a nice gesture, but there was more to it than just the offer of couch surfing. Nerves fluttered in her stomach. They hadn't really explored what their feelings were. Healing and recuperation under the watchful gaze of ASSET and the all-knowing Ava had cooled the heat their previous escapade had kindled between them. Something still simmered there, but Sage wasn't truly sure she was ready to step into the fire.

"Buy a girl dinner first," she threw back playfully. Where was Matt when she needed him? Vampire or not, he was her confidant, and she desperately needed his advice when it came to guys.

"We can do that too." Grey beat her to Ava's office door, opening it with a gentlemanly flourish of his hand to wave her in front of him. "After you."

Sage tripped over her own feet as she crossed the threshold. After the offer he'd just made, the shock of his very un-Grey-like chivalrous behavior robbed her of her senses.

A laptop sat where it always did, in the center of her boss's desk, but no Ava. The one time she welcomed the sharpness of her boss's tone to snap her back to her senses, and the woman wasn't there.

"Maybe we should wait." Sage hugged the file to her chest, not entirely sure where to put it. She scanned the room, her eyes darting all over, everywhere except Grey's face as she searched for a target to hold on to.

"It's just paperwork. Leave it on her keyboard. She knows where to find us when she wants us." The way the word *us* rolled off Grey's tongue sent Sage's stomach into somersaults.

Us. Could there really be an us? She bit her lip, unsure of how to reply.

Grey closed the gap between them and met her eyes as he took the file from her hands.

Her heart fluttered. Sage opened her mouth to speak, but no words came.

"You sure you're okay?" Grey's intense stare softened to curiosity.

"I guess I'm just more nervous than I thought," Sage replied honestly, stepping backwards to give herself breathing room. "You know how it is. Everything must be just so when it comes to her."

"She really does put the fear of the gods into you, doesn't she?" He chuckled and let the folder settle on the keyboard. "Relax. Let's grab something to eat, and we can check in after."

Sage and Grey's phones buzzed at the same time.

All Available Agents, Report to Conference Room 1.

"Going to have to rain check that meal." Grey's expression darkened. His brow crinkled with unease as he stared down at the message on his phone. "I'll bet this explains why it's been all hands on deck here this morning."

Not exactly the distraction Sage had wanted, but it was the perfect excuse to avoid the awkwardness of being alone with Grey. "Let's not stand here waiting. Lead the way."

TWO

"Something major must have happened for Ava to call in the cavalry like this," Grey commented as they waded through the mass of agents in the hallway. Everyone headed toward the conference room, which had filled to standing room only by the time they made it inside.

Ava stood at the head of the room behind a wooden podium. A projector had been set up on the back wall. It silently played clips from the current morning's news. Traffic at a standstill. People crying. Children slapping their hands against the windows of a bright yellow school bus. A strange headline scrolled across the bottom of the screen.

MAGIC SCHOOL BUS OR ELABORATE PRANK?

"That can't be good," Sage whispered to Grey.

His eyes, like all the others in the room, were glued to the ridiculous images being presented on screen. How the hell had she not heard about this? She'd been so preoccupied with getting her paperwork in she hadn't bothered to check in with the news. No wonder Ava had called in every available agent. This was a clear breech of magical security.

Mumbles in the room echoed her thoughts. Fellow agents wondered who would be stupid enough to pull a stunt like this. More discussed loudly about the effect this would have on ASSET's credibility with the magical community. They were supposed to prevent revelations of real magic, like this, from ever reaching human awareness.

Ava stood at the podium, but unlike all the others watching the projector screen in horror, she was watching the room. Her keen eyes absorbed the reactions of her agents, allowing the horror to sink in before she began to address them.

Sage hoped Ava had a plan of attack. She couldn't begin to comprehend how to deal with something this ridiculously damning. If the news was broadcasting it, no doubt it had already gone viral on social media. Real magic out there for all to see.

The most incriminating clip of all came from an eyewitness who captured the video on their cell phone. A school bus, suspended in the air. Traffic was at a standstill all around it. Motorists and pedestrians all stopping to gawk at the sight.

Shocked murmurs continued to rumble through the room.

"Pack it in here. We don't have time to dawdle," Ava addressed the people standing in the conference room doorway. "As of eight thirty this morning, a bus carrying fifty children, en route to its elementary school, lifted six feet off the road. It remained suspended in midair for a full twenty minutes before returning to the ground.

Upon its descent, a message appeared on the side of the bus."

The projector screen next to Ava zoomed in on the side of the bus. The tree of life, the symbol of the Terra race, looked as if it had been die-cut out of the bus.

"I don't need to tell you how dangerous this incident is to ASSET. We all bear the mark, as well as those among us who have not yet been awakened. Our families, your children. We cannot risk the mark being associated with such a public act of magical terrorism." Ava did not have to speak loudly to be heard. The room had gone all but silent as if everyone had taken a collective breath in anticipation of her next words.

The image on the screen froze on the symbol. Sage looked down to the mark on her wrist. The cutout on the side of the bus matched in every single detail. Magic. No question about it. But how? Why? It made no sense.

"Do we know if any Terra children were on that bus?" an agent seated in the front of the room asked.

"Yes," Ava responded quickly. "The parents have been notified, and a team has been dispatched for extraction."

It shouldn't have struck her as odd. She had grown up unaware of ASSET's true nature. But hearing that there were other Terra children surprised Sage more than the images of the bus floating in the air.

Sage leaned in to whisper in Grey's ear, "How many Terra kids live her?"

"A fair few. You'd be surprised."

"This job isn't exactly conducive to raising a family." Sage commented more to herself than in response to Grey, but he'd heard her all the same and shot her a strange look of confusion.

"We have to repopulate somehow," he shrugged.

Maybe to him it wasn't a big deal, but Sage couldn't imagine trying to raise a child while going on dangerous missions and fighting all kinds of crazy magic. Trying to play the loving mother while secretly putting her life on the line. Returning home, helping with homework and social issues, as if those were the most stressful things in the world to worry about. The secrecy had to be maintained even within the confines of the home. Never being able to talk about the cooler aspects of magic. Or prepare one's child for the dangers they might one day face. How the hell had her mother pulled it off? Sage had been none the wiser until her mom died. She'd grown up perfectly normal. Well, as normal as anyone could claim to be.

Grey was still staring at her, as if he expected some kind of response to his previous remark. She had none. He didn't need to be privy to the internal freak-out she was having over the idea of more Terra children being out there.

"You do have a point." He nudged her shoulder. "Children do pose a very interesting problem at the moment."

"You can say that again," Sage mumbled under her breath. She'd never put her own kids through that. Scratch that. She wouldn't have kids. Period.

Another hand shot up from the crowd. "Do we have any suspects at this time?"

"On the record, no. It is our belief that this incident was perpetrated by the organization calling themselves The Order of the Mystics. The use of our symbol accompanying such a public act of magical terrorism is unprecedented. They may simply be attempting to discredit us to the magical community, or this may have a deeper impact by drawing attention of our kind to the humans we interact with on a daily basis. The Order of the Mystics have made no secret of their disdain for the position ASSET and the Terra people play in the magical hierarchy. No matter what their intentions were, the deed is done. It is up to us now to do what we do best. Damage control is our top priority at the moment. We need to get the media off this story in whatever way we can."

Sage watched the screen, paying attention to the faces of the children through the bus windows. She couldn't imagine how scary it must have been for those poor kids. So little. Totally unable to understand what was happening. Some children were crying, but the longer she stared Sage began to notice a surprising majority of the children had expressions of wonder. Little fingers poked through the symbol that had been punched into the side of the bus. Tiny eyes gazed through the cracks, looking more astonished than frightened.

Sage raised her hand. "Any injuries?"

"As of now, no injuries have been reported," Ava replied.

That was a relief. Children were innocents. Harming them would turn this act of magical defiance into a true witch hunt.

How would it have been if they had pulled a stunt like this with adults? People were dangerous when scared. And more often than not, these days, people were walking around armed. Veritable powder keg ready to blow up in the face of the unknown. Maybe that was why the Mystics chose children for their targets. Kids might be scared, but their response to fear would be far less dangerous. Children were often more accepting of magic, still believing in Santa, the Tooth Fairy, and other gift-giving creatures of magical nature.

The act itself was definitely a form of terrorism, but perhaps it had been carefully thought out to avoid casualties. Sage made a mental note of that to look into later.

The news continued to silently play the rescue of the children after the bus had settled back on the road. Sage watched with interest to see if there might be any further clues to the person or persons who had pulled off the stunt. If not for the glaring symbol of her people stamped into the side of the bus, she might have disagreed with Ava's assessment that this was the work of the Mystics. But she knew better. The Mystics had a vendetta with ASSET as the judge, jury, and executioners of magical law. Ava herself had called the Mystics out, very publicly, during Sage's mockery of a trial. Perhaps this was direct retaliation. The Mystics were calling out ASSET in as public a way as they possibly could.

"I need all hands on deck here," Ava continued. "We'll need a team on site to assess the scene as well as teams handling all media outlets. We'll also need spin doctors, so I'm reaching out to the shadow clans for assistance with memory modification and social media campaigns to spin this as a hoax. All remaining agents who are not currently working on cases are to remain in house under our protection. Your families will need to be temporarily relocated as well. You all know what you need to do. Dismissed!"

The assembled group sprang into action as Ava folded her notebook and left the podium.

Her keen eyes zeroed in on Sage with laser-like focus. She made a beeline through the mass of agents toward Sage and Grey. "Shadow Ops. My office, now!"

Sage followed silently behind her boss wondering what part she'd be assigned in this mess.

She was last to enter the room, pulling the door closed behind her.

The moment the lock clicked, Ava pounced. "I need answers. You two, get out there. Find out who did this and why."

Grey stood like a good soldier at attention, his face an emotionless mask. "We'll get names."

"Names… I want their heads on pikes! Gods, I miss the old days!" Ava growled. "We need proof that it was in fact members of the Mystics before we can legally bring anyone in, of course. That is your job, Shadow Ops." She slashed her fisted hand in the air, extending a single finger in Sage's direction. "You are to employ all your resources. Discreetly. Find the people responsible for this."

Needle in a haystack much? Sage sighed but dare not speak those words aloud. Ava would just as soon place her head on a pike. "Yes, ma'am."

"I don't need to tell you how important it is to have this mission zipped up quickly, do I?"

Ava's question needed no answer. Of course she wanted everything handled quickly.

Grey, however, seemed to have an answer Sage did not know existed. "Mabon?" He spoke the word like a prayer.

"They couldn't have picked a worse time to start this little war." Ava nodded.

Sage leaned in closer to Grey and whispered, "Mabon?"

He shook his head, giving her a side-eyed glare that she knew to mean, "Shut up, newbie." When she turned to look at Ava, her boss mirrored the same annoyed expression.

"Do your research, Miss Cynwrig."

"Yes, ma'am." Sage hung her head sheepishly.

"With Mabon upon us, our city will be crawling with magical tourists. I'm already up to my eyeballs in travel notices, and now, thanks to this mess, we have to expend manpower we don't have on damage control. Short-staffed as we are, we cannot afford an international incident."

"We will do all we can," Grey said in his most assuring voice.

"See that you do." Ava slammed her pages down on the desk and yanked open the lid of her laptop. "Dismissed."

THREE

"I've never seen her so stressed out," Sage mumbled as she closed the door to Ava's office.

She weaved her way through the crowded lobby. The frantic pace of earlier had returned with agents buzzing about. Some rushed toward the elevator, ready to take on their missions, while others were on their phones, giving orders to evacuate homes for the time being. Sage followed the flow of traffic heading toward the back office's desks and duty stations.

"She's the Director of Operations in a city that just made international news for a public display of magic. Can you blame her?" Grey spoke with a somberness she'd never expected. "That's the kind of thing that can get someone in her position…re-assigned."

Sage hadn't thought about that side of things. Ava wasn't the nicest of bosses, but she did run a tight ship. She had stuck her neck out for Sage, even if it was after throwing her under the bus.

"We can't let that happen."

"Then we had better come up with answers."

At the trial, Ava had made a complete fool of the magical council while publicly outing the Mystics. No other person in the city had a target as big as Ava on her head. Could she have been the target of this attack somehow? She was supposed to be coming up with answers, but all Sage had were questions.

"Speaking of…" Sage stopped in the middle of the hallway and pulled Grey to the side, so they wouldn't block the flow of traffic. Passersby were too preoccupied with their own tasks they didn't seem to pay her any mind. Still, she waited until the crowd thinned a little before asking, "What the hell is Mabon?"

"Damn newbie." He groaned under his breath. "At some point, you are going to have to do some basic reading."

"I do. All the time. But I can't be expected to learn the entire history of magic in the short time I've been working here. I'm learning as I go." She fought to control the annoyance in her voice. He of all people should cut her some slack. After all they had been through together, he had no right to throw her inexperience back in her face as if she were not working hard to overcome it. "I'm asking you, as my partner, to help explain something I have yet to learn."

Grey's expression softened. "Autumn equinox." He dropped the arrogance in his tone. "It's one of the four main markers of the year. A very big reason to party, in one of the most high-profile cities in North America. All of the magical families celebrate, giving us a logistical nightmare."

"Because we didn't already have enough on our plate, right?"

"It's what we specialize in."

"How long do we have until Mabon?"

"Less than a week. Celebrations and rituals will begin the night before and run for a full twenty-four hours."

Sage resumed her path, heading towards their desk, feeling even more pressure to quickly find the answers Ava needed without a single clue on where to begin the search. "That's a problem."

"What do you mean?" Grey matched her pace walking alongside of her as they entered the large open-air office.

The buzz of agents working in there was accompanied by the roar of fingers frantically typing. Every desk space was in use.

Sage made a beeline toward the desk they shared. "Large gatherings are excellent meeting places. And terror attacks historically happen on special days. What if a big party turns out to be the next target?"

"Entirely plausible." Grey sounded impressed. She caught the hint of a smirk on his face before he turned away from her to take the desk chair. He logged into the computer and immediately pulled up the ASSET search database. "Something we should probably consider. However, if we're working on the assumption that the Mystics are working to discredit ASSET, then they aren't likely to attack their own kind."

She hadn't considered that. But even if Grey were right, that they wouldn't hurt their own kind, it didn't prevent the Mystics' attack from being a non-lethal one. The bus incident proved that. They just wanted to make ASSET look bad.

"Didn't Ava say we've been called in to help chaperone some of these larger gatherings? What better way to show ASSET as inept than to crash a party *we* are securing?"

"We'll have to take that into consideration. Thinking like an agent. I'm impressed."

Score one for Captain Trainwreck. She might be a newbie, but she got things right every now and again. She'd never admit it out loud, but Sage lived for those few moments of praise. Helped her to stave off the little demon that whispered in her mind that she would never be good enough. That she would never live up to Miranda Cynwrig's memory.

"That still leaves us with more questions than answers," she noted as her mind worked to find the thread she needed to tug on to lead her down the path toward an actual clue she could follow.

"True enough." Grey began typing away, entering search parameters into the database. "But we have a place to start looking. We can cross reference the guest lists of the parties our people have been assigned to chaperone with our master database on magical families."

"And see if anyone pings for a prior record of infractions with ASSET?"

"Damn, newbie." He said the words like a cheer. "You're on a roll. I'm so proud of you."

Two atta girls in as many minutes? He was laying it on a bit too thick to be genuine. "Jerk."

"What's that supposed to mean?" He feigned innocence, but she could see something else behind those turquoise eyes. "I was giving you a compliment."

"A backhanded one maybe." She crossed her arms and stared down at him, wondering what his game was.

"I just wanted you to feel you're doing well." He flashed her a comedically wide smile. "You're so cute when you're angry."

"Well then, get ready, partner, because if you keep mocking me like that, I'm going to get really adorable."

"Promise?"

What the hell was he up to? They needed to be on their game, not playing games. Grey was supposed to be the company man. He'd always been the one telling her she needed to be serious.

"Is this you flirting?" she accused more than asked.

"Why, is it working?"

Maybe a little. No. She couldn't say that. They didn't have time to do this right now. She didn't have the mental fortitude to handle all the crazy emotions that came with dating, especially when they had an important job to do.

"Not in the slightest."

"I was trying too hard, wasn't I?" He slumped, defeated in his chair. "What gave me away?"

She hadn't meant to wound him with her words, only to put him off for a little while. She gave him an impish glare, hoping he'd catch on to her playful expression as she spoke. "You complimented me…twice."

"And that's bad?"

"Not bad. Just not…you," she replied honestly.

"I don't understand girls."

"How old are you?" She couldn't help the giggle that bubbled up from her throat. "No. Wait. Better if I don't know." He had her by more than a few years, but their immortality blurred how long those years truly were. Some things were better left unsaid. "My point is, how do you not understand girls at…whatever age you are?"

Grey's smile reappeared. "Now that's a trick question."

"So you're not a complete idiot, then?"

"Now who's being mean?" He feigned shock, but the laughter was there in his words.

"Snark comes easy."

"I think we can both agree on that."

"So, with that in mind, stop trying. Let's just be us… And maybe focus on finding our baddie?"

"I'd say you're right, but I'd be afraid you'd think I was flirting again."

"I'm about to get adorable again," she warned him.

"We wouldn't want that." Grey turned to face the computer screen. "Back to work. Find the bad guys. Travel logs…and, go!"

FOUR

The day dragged on without any answers. The frustration of her failure had given Sage the mother of all headaches, and by the time Grey had asked again if she would like to crash at his place, she felt the walls closing in on her.

She'd do practically anything to escape.

"Tomorrow is a new day," Grey assured her. "I'm sure after a night's rest, we will find a new angle to explore."

She hoped he was right. Searching for a magical miscreant in a city as large as Vegas was harder than searching for a needle in a haystack. The drive to Grey's apartment helped to clear the pressure in her head, but as it faded, she became keenly aware of the nerves building again. Spending a night with Grey. What exactly did that mean? They hadn't actually discussed it. Just like they hadn't discussed their partnership or possibly more. Did he have any…expectations? Shit, why had she agreed to this? She could have crashed at ASSET. She'd have been asleep already. Not stressing over boys.

Grey's apartment was nothing like she'd expected. A converted industrial complex, the sign as they entered the parking lot boasted "Modern Loft Living."

What exactly did that mean?

He was a long-term agent. If this was representative of the kind of lifestyle she could expect to afford on her own, her future looked pretty bleak. The outside was clean enough but definitely didn't give off the warm, homey vibe. *One step away from homeless, maybe.*

Grey pointed a remote at a garage door, it opened, and he rolled his bike inside. She half expected his apartment to be the garage, but thankfully it was exactly what it appeared to be.

The garage door closed behind them.

Grey pulled his helmet off and hung it on the handlebars. "C'mon." He led the way toward an interior door.

Sage followed along, curious to see what the actual living space would be like. "So this is where you live?" It sounded so much cooler in her head, but when the words finally escaped from her mouth, Sage realized how awkwardly cliché they were. *Damn nerves.*

"Yep." He entered through the door into a small hallway and tossed his keys in a bowl on the entryway table. "Come in and make yourself comfortable." He continued on without looking back, heading into the open living room that blew away all of her expectations.

His apartment could have been magicked straight from the pages of a home and garden magazine. Picture perfect with high ceilings, exposed beams, and HVAC vents that gave the ceiling an industrial feel, complemented the sleek lines of his modern furniture.

Grey lived in a freaking palace compared to her two-bedroom shack of an apartment. Jealous as she was, seeing this level of luxury gave her hope that maybe someday she could get out from under all her debts and carve out a nice little life of her own. She did still have her mom's home back in Phoenix. Mental note for later. She needed to get ahold of an agent and turn it into rental income. The sooner the better.

Sage wandered into the open living room slowly, admiring the furnishings and how neatly Grey kept the place. Bachelors weren't always known for being the best housekeepers.

A large couch sat in the center of the room, facing a metal and glass coffee table. The wall across from it, white-painted brick, had a TV mounted to it that could have doubled as a movie screen.

A quartz-topped island separated the living room from the kitchen that continued the industrial feel with stainless-steel everything. No dishes left out, no dirty laundry hanging off the back of chairs, or shoes left stranded in the middle of the floor. How was that possible? Even Matt, her notoriously neat roommate, left the errant shoe next to the couch every now and again. He had to have maid service.

"First time you've ever seen a loft?" Grey sounded more amused than inquisitive. Was he trying to mock her again?

"Sorry, I... Wow." *Sly dog*. Bet he hired a maid to clean this place up, knowing she'd take him up on the offer of a place to crash. He worked his own brand of magic to make sure she'd be impressed. He was right. "How long have you lived here?"

"Can't really remember. It's been a while." Grey walked into the kitchen and opened the refrigerator. "Thirsty?"

"Please." Sage continued her tour strolling through what should have been the dining room. Rather than table and chairs, he'd turned the space into a well-stocked library. Shelves lined the walls, floor to ceiling, each one groaning under the weight of books he'd collected. "This is so not what I expected."

"Appearances can be deceiving." Grey came out of the kitchen, two sodas in his hands, and headed for the coffee table.

"You aren't kidding. Have you read all of these?" She perused the shelves. His tastes were eclectic. His library housed everything from instruction manuals to dystopian fiction, with a few leather-bound classics thrown in for good measure.

"If you want to borrow any, feel free," Grey replied.

Sage returned to the living room, unable to put words to this completely unexpected side Grey had just revealed of himself. Her eyes drifted to the soda he'd brought her, sitting on a coaster. A coaster. Laughter bubbled up from her chest. Bachelors don't have coasters, let alone use them. She couldn't stop herself, nor could she explain to Grey why she was giggling like an idiot. Information overload. Her brain simply short-circuited.

"Take a few breaths. You look like you're going to be sick." Grey hid his amusement behind casual sips from his drink, but the laughter was there in his eyes.

"I just. Wow. This is so unexpected."

"What? A guy can't read? Like nice things?"

"Yeah. Of course. But…" She couldn't finish that sentence without sounding like a jerk. Her roommate was the kind of guy she'd expect to see living in an apartment like this. He and Josh loved that picture-perfect home with all the trimmings, even though they weren't at the income level to afford it. But Grey had always come across as a less-is-more kind of guy.

"You were expecting something closer to your apartment?"

"If I'm being honest…" Sage took a sip from her drink to give her time to finish the rest of that sentence without sticking her foot in her mouth again. "I could never afford a place as nice as this. What does ASSET pay you? No. Sorry, that was a bad question."

"I've been around a while. You'll get there eventually," Grey responded politely.

"Good thing I'm immortal. It's going to take me a lifetime to pay off my student loans. And then there's the whole need-a-car thing. I'm not even sure how I'm going to afford to refurnish my new apartment." She sat next to Grey on the couch, wanting to ask him exactly how old he was, but couldn't bring herself to say the words.

"Hey. You've been through a lot. It sucks losing your place and all. Don't try to focus so much on what you don't have at the moment." He held up his soda as if to toast her. "You've got some good stuff in your corner too."

He could be really sweet when he wanted to. Even if he was totally enjoying showing off to her.

She tipped her soda to him and took a sip. "So then, let's focus on you. What other surprises do you have here?"

"No dead bodies in the closet. No roommates. No pets. Is that what you mean?"

"Good. I was really worried about the pet thing."

"I had a feeling." He snorted. "So. Um. For tonight. I've got a big bed…"

Not the conversation change she had expected. Sage sucked in a breath, a little louder than she'd intended, unsure how to respond to what he'd just said. She wasn't ready for that… Not yet.

Grey opened his mouth but hesitated as if suddenly aware he'd struck a nerve. He had. "You can sleep there. I'll take the couch."

The pressure to perform had been relieved, at least for the moment. But at the same time, they were supposed to be testing things out, and separate beds felt like a step in the opposite direction. Ugh, why did feelings have to be so damn complicated?

"Sure. But I'd be okay on the couch. I'm not going to steal your bed," she replied.

"I insist. You're my guest tonight."

Damn him for being so gentlemanly. She really didn't want to take his bed, but how could she say no after that?

"O…kay." The word left her mouth with the speed of a snail. Distraction. Diversion. She needed some way to change the subject and relieve the pressure.

Dammit, Sage. Get ahold of yourself!

"It's okay to relax." Grey scooted backwards, creating more space between them. "You look like you're about to jump out of your skin."

"I'm fine. Really." She was a terrible liar and even worse with damage control. She'd never been this bad at boys before. Why did Grey turn her into such a blubbering idiot? "It's just I hadn't expected to see this side of you."

Now it was Grey's turn to look uneasy. He tilted his head sideways as he stared at her, silently muttering, "And now you're confused about me?"

Open mouth, insert foot. Maybe she should just stop talking altogether. Might make the night easier on the both of them. But the longer the silence lingered between them, the more she realized she could not escape the moment. She needed to say something. Nice. Reassuring maybe. Truthful.

"No. Well. Not like that. I mean. I like this side of you. A lot actually." Gods, could she sound more stupid? *Get yourself together!* "You're just so closed off and secretive about your life, it's hard to truly know what's going on in your head."

She must have said something right. Grey's expression softened, looking more relaxed than she'd seen him all night. "Don't try and analyze things so much. I'm a person just like you."

"Yeah, but you've already seen all of me." She slapped a hand over her mouth. *Idiot!* "That didn't come out right."

He chuckled at her. "Not quite, but go ahead. This is a much more interesting conversation."

"Let me try that again. You know me. But seeing all of this" — she waved her hand at the room — "shows me that I clearly don't know you at all. The real you. Not the mask you wear at work."

"Interrogation time again?" Grey asked.

"Not like that. Unless you refuse to open up. And then, the rack!" She drew her finger across her throat to make sure he got the joke.

"I don't remember you peeking in my bedroom."

"What?" She stopped short.

"What!" He winked at her playfully.

That disarmed her nerves better than any kind of magic. "See. That's the Grey I know. Snarky and sarcastic."

"I am not snarky. That's all you."

"Whatever." She saw straight through his false outrage. Behind his stern look there was that glint of amusement in his eyes. This was the Grey she liked. "Spill it. Tell me a story. Just be real."

"I don't do monologues." Grey leaned forward and grabbed his soda from the coffee table. He took a long sip, *probably stalling for time*, before setting the can back on its coaster. "Can't we just relax and watch a movie? Have an enjoyable evening without having to do all the backstory?"

Seeing his vulnerability gave Sage the confidence boost she needed. She hadn't considered the big brave warrior might be as nervous about their alone time as she was. Tons of life experience and all. But beyond that, he was just a boy and she was just a girl. She latched on to that courage.

"So you want the first date without the first-date conversation?"

Grey nearly spat his soda, but covered his mouth just in time.

Sage couldn't help the laugh that exploded from her lips. That confirmed her thoughts.

"This is not a date," he said.

"I don't know. Food, drink, and a movie… You've already brought me back to your place." She enjoyed being the teaser so much more than being on the other side of it.

"I would never bring a girl back to my place on a first date."

Spoken like a man well beyond the years his face revealed. He was definitely showing his age with that statement.

"Well, you have me here now," she noted.

"I didn't mean…"

"Neither did I." Sage tripped over her thoughts. She'd meant to be snarky, and somehow, she'd veered into seductive. Whoops. "We're not there yet, right? Wow, this conversation got awkward fast. How about that movie?"

"Good idea." Grey reached across the table for the television remote.

"I mean, you can't tell if you're compatible with someone until you've watched a movie with them anyway," Sage said, trying to save them from the awkwardness.

"How so?" Grey turned toward her, eyebrow cocked with suspicious interest.

"What if you talk through movies?" she asked. "Definite deal breaker."

"Or you crunch your popcorn too loud?" Grey answered.

"Exactly! See? Movies are the truest test of a relationship compatibility." *And provide a few hours of not-sticking-your-foot-in-your-mouth silence.*

"There's one more test we need to get through before we can watch a movie," he teased her, leaving the question to hang in the air.

When he didn't offer the answer to his riddle, she took the bait. "That is?"

"What kind of movie should we watch?" Grey asked. "Genre is an important factor in compatibility."

"Definitely need to watch something thrilling," Sage replied without missing a beat.

"Now you're talking." Grey tossed the remote at her. "Use it wisely."

If the rest of the night could go as smoothly as it had in that moment, there might be hope for them. Sage snuggled in closer to Grey as she pointed the remote at the TV.

FIVE

Sunlight warmed her face. Sage opened her eyes slowly. The room was unfamiliar at first. In the fog of sleep, it took a moment for her to remember she was in Grey's living room. She sat and stretched, trying to loosen up the tense muscles in her back. The couch had been comfortable enough, but the awkward way she'd been lying had left her hips and shoulders stiff. She hadn't remembered falling asleep. Or Grey wrapping her in the plush red blanket. She must have slept like the dead. No wonder she was so stiff. Sage twisted, shifting from one side to the other, working out all the kinks.

Grey was nowhere to be seen, but the sound of running water coming from another room, and the smell of freshly brewed coffee, told her he'd been up and moving for a bit longer than she.

A shower was definitely at the top of her to-do list, but the rich aroma of liquid energy tempted Sage into the kitchen with the silent promise of productivity. She helped herself to a mug and picked up her phone to check messages.

"You're up. Good." Grey startled her with the perkiness of his greeting.

She lifted her eyes to acknowledge him, not quite ready for conversation so early in the morning, but the moment she caught a glimpse of him, wearing only a pair of sweatpants as he walked out of his bedroom, Sage found her spirits perking up to match his tone.

A dark teal towel draped around his neck like an arrow directing her eyes to where she should focus her attention — the firm outline of his abs. She had imagined what he'd been packing under the dark T-shirts he always wore. Now she knew. And knowing was definitely half the battle.

Sage sipped her coffee, enjoying the view as he strolled past her into the kitchen. Her mind not quite fully rebooted from sleep, she was glad to have the excuse not to speak.

"Sleep okay?" Grey moved about the kitchen, prepping a mug for coffee.

Maybe it was the warm infusion of caffeine, or maybe just the thrill of the gorgeous view. Whatever it was, Sage found herself alert and ready for action. "Yeah, thanks."

"You could have taken the bed."

Oh, that would have been a very bad idea. She giggled to herself. "It's your home," she answered politely.

He continued to move around the kitchen, grabbing a bagel for his breakfast.

Sage's phone buzzed. She glanced at the screen, an email alert from her apartment complex. The day had started off on such a good foot, she wondered if she dare open the message and risk Murphy's Law. She stole another glance as Grey walked past her, his breakfast and coffee in hand. The view of him going was just as good as it had been coming. That gave her the courage to tempt fate once more. She opened the message from the apartment complex manager. The stars must have all aligned for her. She needed to hit the casinos with luck like this.

"Speaking of homes," she blurted out excitedly. "Looks like my apartment might be ready sooner than I thought. Can you drop me by the complex for a few hours so I can sign paperwork?"

Grey looked up from his plate, disappointment darkening his eyes. "You don't want me to stay with you?"

"You can if you want to, but I just figured you could better spend that time looking for answers. I'll meet up with you when I'm all done."

"Sure. Of course. I'll finish getting ready." He took a long pull from his mug and headed back into his room.

The sudden shift in his demeanor left Sage confused, wondering if something she'd said rubbed him the wrong way, but what could that have been? They had an important mission to work on. Every moment was precious, and she didn't want to derail any progress just because she had to handle her life issues.

Men were weird. But time was of the essence. She couldn't sit around trying to figure him out.

Sage sent a message to Josh letting him know she was on her way to the apartment complex and needed him to be the second signer on the lease since Matt could no longer be around during daylight hours.

***

Grey dropped her off at the apartment complex front office and drove away before she had even made it through the doors.

Josh sat waiting for her inside. He stood and wrapped her in the biggest hug she'd had in a very long time. "Home sweet home again!"

"You don't know how much I need this. I hate being homeless." Sage sat down to review the rental agreement. Josh had already done his part. Little flags marked all the places where signatures needed to be.

Laura, the apartment manager, had already laid out the keys. She waved at Sage from across the room and mouthed, "On the phone. Be right with you."

Sage scanned through the document and signed the marked places.

"You're all set, Sage. We are so sorry about the delays. If you want, have a peek around your new place." Laura took the papers from her and handed over the keys and a survey form. "Mark off anything you see that needs fixing on this list and turn it in before the office closes at six. I'll leave you to it, then. Welcome back home!"

Just like that, Sage and Josh were ushered out of the office and walked down the path toward their new apartment, another bottom floor unit. All apartments had the same basic floorplan. The only differences were the number of bedrooms.

"You can do the honors," Sage said.

Josh unlocked the door and stepped into the apartment. He wandered around the kitchen opening and closing cabinets and peeking inside drawers.

"This looks like home but doesn't feel like it." She'd expected to feel something more. Finally home again. A place to call her own. But where the emotions should have been, there was nothing. Hollow. Empty. Much like the apartment.

Josh must have picked up on her melancholy. "We will make it feel homey. Give me a few weeks, and I'll have this place looking good as new."

She didn't have time to dwell on her feelings, or lack of, at the moment. She had a home. That would have to be enough. She still had a mission to complete, and this was only meant to be a pit stop. "I'm sure once we all settle in and get our first game night going, all the pieces will fall in line."

"That's the spirit." Josh smiled and headed into the living room. "We could totally maximize the space in here. Get a larger table and do game night here." He waved his hands at the empty expanse where he stood. "Mount a TV to the wall and put two couches on opposite sides here."

She had no doubt he could whip the apartment into shape, and left him to his interior design plans as she wandered into the three-door hallway and peeked into the room that would be hers. It seemed somehow smaller without furniture, but Sage knew a queen bed and bureau would fit easily enough. She really didn't need much else.

Josh came up behind her and opened the next bedroom door, the one he would share with Matt. "I'll get some blackout curtains for that window."

"Might need to do all the windows in the house…to be safe."

Josh's lips tensed. "So many things to remember now that he's…" He hesitated.

Saying the word had been hard for Sage too. She understood. They both shared his secret. But it affected him more than anyone else.

"How's it going between you two?"

Josh winced as if the question wounded him. "Fine."

"Lies."

"This isn't my world. This isn't any real world, and yet it is. But I don't fit in."

"I know exactly what you mean." Sage spoke without any hint of irony.

"How could you?" Josh threw the question at her like an accusation. "This is your world."

"As if I fit in any more than you do?"

"You're not human, as I have been made to understand," Josh said. "And neither is Matt."

She could take his tone at face value and get up in arms over it, but that would only make things worse. He was lashing out in pain. Just as she had when she'd first learned of the other world lying hidden under her very nose. Unfair, unforgiving, and unbelievable on the best of days. And for all the magic surrounding her, she held only the ability to neutralize it. Not exactly a superpower. But it did put her in a unique position. Josh was similar in that respect. An outsider looking into a world he was not supposed to know existed. She owed him some leeway to come to grips.

"Give Matt time. He is still in there. Even if he has changed a bit."

"You make it sound like he has a new wardrobe. He's a…" Josh blew out a sigh.

"I don't know what it is he's going through. But I do know he is still there, deep down. It will show again in time. He loves you."

"Love is not the problem." Josh wrung his hands, averting his eyes as he continued to speak. "Neither is attraction."

"What, then?"

"He bit me!" Josh blurted out.

Sage snorted and immediately reined in her smile when she saw the flesh-toned bandage on his neck. "I'm sorry."

"Nibbling is one thing, but he drew blood…on purpose. It hurts. And not in a good way," Josh said, seeming to defend his outrage. "I mean, I know he thinks it's sexy. I've never seen him so stiff."

"TMI, seriously." Sage's cheeks burned as she fought to keep the vision his words evoked from materializing in her thoughts. No amount of mental bleach could rid her of that. "You guys are like my brothers. I can't go there."

"If I can't talk about it with you, who can I talk to about it?" The desperation in his tone could not be denied, but it was the way he crumpled against the doorframe, needing its strength to keep him standing that really drove the point home.

He was right. Who else could he talk to about these kinds of problems?

"Okay, so he's a bit bitey, and you're not into that." She paused to think of a way to word her thoughts and not die of embarrassment. "How have you handled sexual experimentations in the past? Surely one of you has wanted to try something the other hasn't… Maybe approach it that way. Tell him what turns you off."

"Just like that? He's a vampire. Blood is like crack, right? Like telling an alcoholic he can't have a drink sitting right in front of his face."

Josh had a point. She considered the addict angle as it was so much easier than thinking of her brother as a sexual creature, but that didn't fit either. Vampires weren't addicts. And Josh wasn't a drug. Their situation, much as she hated to consider it, was more akin to BDSM and the need for limits or safe words.

"But you're a person, not a vice. Blood is important to him, and so are you. Make him see that…separately."

"You mean I deny him blood?" Josh's face scrunched in confusion. "Can I do that?"

"Um, yeah. No means no. You have a right to say that."

"No blood for you!" Josh stamped his foot and waggled his finger like a diva.

At least he was taking that well. There was still hope. "Well, maybe don't put it so bluntly. But make sure he knows he's hurting you and you're just not into bloodletting. He can get that elsewhere. You can both enjoy everything else together."

"Worth a try, I guess." Josh scratched at the bandage on his neck.

"I have faith in you both. Besides, you know I can't live without you two, so you have to figure out a way to work it all out."

"I'd hate to be the one that lets you down." The smile returned to Josh's face.

Crisis averted for the moment. She'd find a way to work that into a conversation with Matt next time she saw him. Just to be sure he was playing by the rules where humans were concerned. Especially when it was under their shared roof.

Her phone beeped in her pocket. A text alert. She'd wasted too much time already. It was time to head back to the office before Grey came looking for her. "Good, because I have a favor to ask you."

"And that is?"

"Can you drop me back at the office?"

"We have got to get you a car." Josh rolled his eyes and headed for the kitchen.

Funny how everyone always made it a point to remind her that she need a car, as if it wasn't already painfully obvious. It wasn't like she was actively avoiding having one. "Sure thing. I'll just run out to the money tree."

"Hey, speaking of the office…" Josh pulled his keys and waved her over. "Was that you guys who pulled the whole floating bus trick the other day?"

"That's why I have to get back to work. Still trying to figure out who did that." The fact he'd asked her about it meant that ASSET had not yet managed to get on top of all the media outlets sharing the videos. Not a good sign, and even more reason for her to get back to work, sooner rather than later. "All hands on deck."

"Pretty cool trick though. You have to admit. Better than any magic show I've seen on the strip."

"Part of my job is keeping magic where it's supposed to be. No one was supposed to see, or remember, that bus thing."

"But I'm in the secret club. I can know, right?" Josh asked.

"Best if you stay in the dark as much as possible. Safer that way."

"Safer?" His eyes widened with shock. "Should I be worried?"

"Not if you get me back to work quickly," Sage teased and started for the door before he could argue or ask any more questions.

SIX

She found Grey hunched over his desk, eyes glued to the screen in front of him. Sage jingled her keys as she came up on him. "Mission accomplished. I'm no longer homeless!"

"Congratulations."

"Kind of expected a bit more enthusiasm, but I'll take it." She planted herself on the seat next to the desk and started fingering through papers left in the inbox. "Get any leads for us to check out?"

"The bus was not a random target," Grey said matter-of-factly, his tone offering no hope.

So much for her day of winning. Back to business as usual.

"So the bus was targeted because there was a Terra child on board?" Sage asked, hoping the answer was no.

"At this point..." Grey leaned back with a sigh and raked his hands through his hair. "Looks like it."

"Well, don't just sit there being all secretive. Where is the kid? Are they okay?"

"Yes, the child is fine. He is with his mother and will be relocated."

"Wait. What? They have to move?" She hadn't considered the extended implications of the Mystics' attacks.

"For their own safety, yes. The boy bears the same mark that was stamped into the side of the bus. His mother is an agent here. She knows the way this works. Safer for their family if she relocates to another headquarters. This is standard procedure. Why do you look so bothered by this?" Grey's response was too emotionless, and Sage's rage rose to match the level they both should have been at.

"I never had to move."

That poor kid torn away from all his friends. Starting life over. Not to mention the parents having to start over again in a new place.

"Your mom did a lot of traveling work. And where did she leave you when she did? ASSET headquarters. You were never without protection from your people. This is what we do. Only in this case, their family secret may have been released. We are ensuring their protection by moving them where they will not be known."

"I get it. I just feel bad for the kid. He doesn't know why he's being moved. Losing all his friends because of some magical jerk with a vendetta against ASSET picked him to pick on."

"You're such a bleeding heart. It's cute." Grey smirked.

"Whatever," she sighed. It was clear he didn't see things in the same light she did, and there was no use in trying to argue her bleeding heart. "Why do we think this was a targeted attack? Other than the kid on the bus being one of us?"

"Terra kids don't know who or what they are. We do that for good reason."

"I could argue differently, but go on." As per usual, getting information from Grey was piecemeal at best. She snuck a quick peek at the computer monitor, hoping the screen would give her more to go on, but she couldn't make sense of the variety of windows he had open.

"Finding a Terra child in a city of two million people is like a needle in a haystack," he answered. "The perpetrator would have had to have information on the agent as well as their child, and where that child went to school."

"Couldn't have just been a really big coincidence?" What he was implying took them down a road she did not want to travel on. Not again. Not so soon.

"There are no coincidences," Grey replied. "We questioned the bus driver, and he didn't know the boy was Terra."

"And who or what was the bus driver?"

"Just an old gnome. No active powers. So, no, he couldn't have done this." He answered as if he knew what her next question would be. "He has the sight, of course, and he assured us that no one of fae descent was hiding on board his bus. No kobolds, brownies, goblins, or leprechauns."

"Just one dead end after another." Sage sighed, defeated. How were they supposed to figure this out without a single clue to go on? "No one is claiming responsibility for the bus. No witnesses. No leads."

"Were you expecting the guilty party to just roll out the red carpet?"

Sarcasm for the win. Sage snorted. "Might make our lives easier."

"When has that ever been the case?"

She'd normally feel the need to retaliate when Grey became aloof and snarky, but in this instance, it had a disarming effect on her. "Can't blame a girl for hoping. You know, the occasional softball improves self-confidence."

"You're in the wrong line of work if that's what you're after."

"Don't remind me." She sighed. "So are you thinking we have a mole here in the organization?" She silently prayed that just once, Grey might give her a straight answer. More than that, she hoped that answer, at least in this case, would be no.

His silence offered no consolation, nor did the fact that his brow furrowed. He held her in a prison of worry, hanging on his next words.

"Well?" she blurted out, and at the same time cringed, knowing the answer wasn't going to be what she wanted to hear.

"That's a hard one," he answered. "I'd like to think no, but it wouldn't be the first time."

Sage's thoughts immediately turned to Rina. It hadn't been that long since the little blue-haired girl had duped them all.

"However, active agents are not that hard to find and follow," Grey added before Sage could turn the thought into words. "We're not exactly secret about who we are. The general magical community sees us on a regular basis. So before we go pointing fingers in house, we should exhaust all resources outside."

His words helped a little. At least for the moment, she didn't need to look over her shoulders wondering who might be waiting in the wings to stab her in the back.

"Okay, so we need a new angle. What about the family that was targeted?" Sage asked.

"Now we're on the same page." Grey's furrowed brow relaxed. He pointed a finger toward the computer screen with the multiple windows open into various databases. "That's one of many lines we can look at. I've already requested a team look into the past assignments of the outed agent to see if there might be a connection out there. Someone with a grudge. Anything we can follow."

"Not exactly a smoking gun," Sage said.

"Soon as we get word from the other team, we can follow up. They're swimming through nearly a decade of cases at the moment."

"Do they need help? Shouldn't we be doing that? It's better than the dead ends we've been running into."

"We will. When we have the information to follow up on. But we still have a line to follow."

"Didn't you just say we were out of options?" Sage asked.

"I think that was you who said it." Grey smirked.

Glad he was enjoying himself with this circular logic. She was moments away from a migraine the way things were going.

"Okay, you lost me."

"We're brainstorming. Sound-boarding. Trying to talk our way through a problem. We're not dead in the water yet. We've just exhausted the method we've used to this point."

"Again. I don't follow."

"I still think your idea about the parties is a really strong lead we should follow."

"Our tourist list? Any hits for magic beings with priors?" She prayed that might at least give them some suspects to check up on.

"Registered tourists are all, as you might call them, the grand, high muckety mucks of the magical world."

"Of course they are. Damn. That's two strikeouts."

"We're not dead in the water yet."

"But we will be if we can't find answers for Ava. It will be our heads on pikes." Sage pretended to slit her throat with her finger.

"Honestly, I didn't expect much to show up. We're guarding the most respectable of all magical houses in the city with the cream of the magical crop in attendance. The Mystics would be stupid to attack there, even if their modus operandi is making ASSET look incompetent. Inciting a magical war is not how you make our organization look bad."

"The modus what now?" She'd heard that word before but couldn't place its meaning. And based on the way Grey was glaring at her, she'd accidentally let slip that stupid question out loud.

"I'm going to pretend I didn't hear that."

"Just messing around with you." She smiled sheepishly.

"We're Shadow Ops. Our place is on the street. Reaching out to resources ASSET doesn't have.

"Zack?" Sage had been hoping to avoid dealing with him.

"I was thinking we might check in with Sylvia," Grey said. "She's proven helpful in the past, if not a bit prickly. And she is well connected."

She hadn't wanted to use that connection either. Sylvia had made it known she wanted favors in return for her help. They all did. Being in the pocket of others wasn't exactly a comforting feeling.

"I know," Grey said softly. "I didn't want to have to do it, either, but we've exhausted resources here for the moment. Until we get something of value on the outed agent, we need to reach outside. Even if that means we have to get our hands dirty to do so."

"Can we stop for coffee first?" Sage asked.

SEVEN

"This is beginning to become a regular occurrence with you two." Sylvia did not look shocked to see Grey and Sage sitting in her office. "When I asked you to repair the damage you did to my back door and camera, that did not come with permission to make your own key."

"We didn't want to disturb your workers." Sage grinned sweetly and held out a caramel latte in offering.

"That may be wise considering ASSET's tarnished reputation. No one wants to see your lot skulking around at the moment." Sylvia snatched up the coffee and sniffed it before taking a sip. "Though I do appreciate the peace offering." She nodded to Sage.

"Thought you might like that. I know how early you make it into the office." Sage kept her tone neutral, not wanting to come across too saccharine.

"You looking for a new job? Because I could use an assistant with your level of gumption." Sylvia rounded her desk and took a seat. "With the rest of the magical community starting to lose faith in ASSET, perhaps I can place you in more lucrative employment."

"Word travels fast." Grey's tone was more accusatory than it should have been. "Especially when it is false."

"Yes. It does," Sylvia replied like a viper. "Ava Masters pissed off a lot of people with that stunt she pulled. That mockery of a trial, calling out the High-Class Representatives of our magical families. No respect. No decorum."

"She was doing her job," Sage jumped to defend.

"Tact is just as important as righteousness. Maybe even more so in our world." Black smoke began to swirl around Sylvia. Never a good sign when dealing with a shadowrunner.

"We will have to agree to disagree on that," Grey replied with a noticeably softer tone.

"See. That was tact. Well played." Sylvia's smoke faded as she sipped her coffee. "But as I am assuming you're not here for a lesson in etiquette, perhaps you can get to the point. I have a lot on my plate today."

"Mabon is upon us. As you are probably well aware," Grey began.

"I believe I asked you to get to the point," Sylvia replied.

Sage opened her mouth to speak. Grey silenced her with a look and took the lead. "With the influx of tourism, there will be an increased need for temporary work catering the larger parties."

"Do you want a job, or is there another point you're trying to make?" Sylvia asked.

"We're more concerned with the clientele at these parties being tied to unsavory organizations," Grey answered.

"Isn't ASSET already running security?" Sylvia asked.

Grey's attempt at polite conversation wasn't getting them any closer to an answer. Sage jumped in before either of them could continue talking in circles. "We're not concerned with the parties our people are already booked for. There is bound to be other high-profile engagements where our people have been excluded from attending, for obvious reasons."

"If you think I deal with the Mystics, you're barking up the wrong tree. I don't care how much coffee you try to butter me up with, that kind of accusation I will not stand for." Sylvia's form began to fade into smoke.

Maybe she should have kept her mouth shut. The side-eyed glare Grey was sending her way said as much.

Sage scrambled for the right words. "No. We don't think you'd be involved in something like that. You misunderstand me. What I meant was, with your vast network of associates, maybe you've heard of some parties we were not aware of. That's all."

"More favors? You've not paid up for your last request of assistance." Sylvia stared down her nose at Sage, her cold, calculating eyes offering no hint of the intentions behind them.

She hadn't paid. Not that she could. Sylvia had all but asked for a get-out-of-jail-free card. Sage looked to Grey for answers. For all his tactful talking at the start, he remained oddly distant now, leaving Sage to figure out what the hell she could possibly say. Even if she knew the right words, Sylvia had given no indication that she had any information they needed.

"I was thinking this was less favor and more like we are watching each other's backs. We'd hate for your people to be mistakenly sent to someplace dangerous. These Mystics have already shown they do not care for the safety of magic or magical people. Did you know that the driver of the bus that was attacked was a gnome? If they would attack a magical being with no active powers, what could they possibly do to a large gathering of us?" Sage's throat began to dry as she spoke, but she could see Sylvia's expression softening, so she pushed on, even as her voice cracked. "We want to be sure no one has an unpleasant encounter with any Mystics during this festive occasion."

Sage swallowed the lump that had formed in her parched throat and turned to Grey, hoping he might back her up. He smiled, but offered nothing else.

"I should applaud you for that speech," Sylvia broke the silence. "You keep developing that silver tongue, and you'll get very far in this world. I can make no promises. But if I hear of anything before Mabon, I will let you know."

"Thank you for your time." Sage stood to leave.

Grey came up behind her like a ghost.

"A word of advice," Sylvia called out before they reached the door.

"Yes?"

"Mocha, next time." Sylvia tipped her cup in the air. "I prefer the bitterness of the dark chocolates."

Why does that not surprise me? Sage nodded and took her leave.

"That went better than expected," Grey said with surprising enthusiasm as he swapped his fedora out for his bike helmet.

"How do you figure that?" Sage picked up her helmet, feeling less than enthusiastic about their little field trip. They had learned nothing. Time wasted as far as she saw it. And she was out five dollars for the coffee.

"She likes you." Grey chuckled.

He seemed rather high-spirited after their failure. "Better than you maybe."

"Allies are important. She'll tell us what we need to know if and when she knows it."

"You're sure of this?"

"Can we really be sure of anything in these times?" Grey responded, but with the helmet hiding his face, she couldn't gauge his meaning.

He was supposed to be the grumpy one, grousing defeat when things didn't go as planned. She'd taken his thunder in that regard. Openly admitting defeat.

"You're screwing with me again, aren't you?"

He turned his back on her, mounting his bike. "Am I?"

"Two can play at that game." She mounted the bike, seating herself behind Grey, and wrapped her arms around him.

"You're clearly better at games than me. How about a truce. I suggested this field trip, so let me make it up to you by buying lunch."

Her stomach growled. How long had it been since she'd eaten? The sun was already making its way to the horizon, and she couldn't remember having more than coffee all day. "You mean dinner?"

"What are you, fifty?" Grey laughed openly. "Who eats dinner this early?"

"For all I know, you might be," she replied. "Sure you don't need a nap, old man?"

"You want to know how old I am?"

"Nope." Immortality was a tricky business, and ignorance was bliss in that regard. She'd prefer to think of him as a man in his late twenties at most, not an eighty-year-old man cleverly hidden under taut muscles. "We're not going there. Dinner. Lunch, whatever you want to call it. Let's eat. It's going to be a long night."

"Sounds like you have something up your sleeve. A plan, perhaps?"

"What do you think?" she teased.

"I think dinner sounds good…and then?"

"Don't get your hopes up. We have more work to do. Soon as the sun sets, we have one more pit stop to make."

EIGHT

Sage had been hungrier than she'd thought. After a double steak burger and a pile of fries, she still found room for a cookies n' cream milkshake. More calories than she needed for the day, but all she'd need was a session with Devon to burn it all off.

Grey matched her bite for bite, putting away food like a starving man. "Do I have to wait until after dessert for you to tell me what your plan is?"

"I'd have thought an experienced agent like yourself would have figured it out by now," Sage teased him as she sucked down her shake. "Matt should be up now. I need to talk to him about the new apartment."

Grey's expression darkened slightly.

"And since he's still under newbie jurisdiction, that means Zack won't be too far away. Gives us a perfect excuse to stop in and question him. See if he knows anything."

Grey snatched the shake from her hands as if he might steal a sip. A pretty ballsy move. One she'd normally react to. Not even Matt would dare steal her ice cream, but the joke was on Grey. She'd already finished it and waited for him to learn the truth on his own.

"Thievery gets you nothing." She snickered as defeat wiped away the lopsided grin from Grey's face.

He gave the cup a shove, scooting it across the table. "You really want to head back into a vampire bar? Remember the last time."

Her hand moved on instinct, to the scars on her neck. "I'm hoping that their change of management means they'll be a bit friendlier this time."

"We'd better get to it, then." Grey stood and cleared away the trash on the table. "Don't worry, newbie, I'll protect you."

She didn't need to be told that. Grey had had her back more than enough times to have earned her trust. The memory of her last encounter had left a bad taste in her mouth, but this time would be different. Matt would be there.

Sage followed Grey out to the parking lot and mounted his bike. The more she rode it, the more she found herself enjoying it. Something she'd never thought she could possibly like.

Grey brought the bike to life and tore off out of the parking lot like a madman.

They came up on the Northtown vampire coven headquarters. The building was the same, but the back parking lot had been secured with a gate since her last visit, creating a choke point that had Sage feeling even more nervous as they rode through the opening that could barely fit a single car through.

"What's going on here?" she wondered aloud.

Grey pulled off his helmet. "Added security, it would seem."

"Who's Captain Obvious now?" Sage pulled her phone from her pocket and sent Matt a quick message to let him know they were there. "Should we be concerned?"

"You sure he's here?" Grey looked around, his expression neutral as ever, but Sage could see he was pausing every now and again to note cameras, doors, and any other potential security feature.

"He's been working the bar here all week. I figured he must be sleeping here too."

"Not with his sire?" Grey sounded shocked.

"Not since they came back from the safe house. He said Zack wanted him to integrate with the local coven a little better."

"Sick of babysitting already," Grey scoffed. He stowed his helmet and pointed himself toward the open gate. "Might as well have a look around, then."

Sage followed Grey, keeping pace with him as she took notice of all the cars and the shadows they cast. She'd been ambushed more than a few times by things hiding in dark places, and didn't care to repeat that mistake.

At the main entrance, a bouncer stood guard. Still early in the evening, the queue had yet to form, and they were able to walk straight up to the bouncer.

Grey showed his mark as he approached. "How's it going tonight?" he asked casually.

The vampire guarding the front was built like a football player. Towering over Grey, he had the kind of muscles that made Sage wonder if he had to walk through a doorway sideways just to make it past the threshold. The bouncer's flat expression didn't falter, even after his eyes had fallen to the mark on Grey's wrist.

Sage held her breath.

"We in some kind of trouble?" The guard spoke softly, his voice lighter and higher-pitched than it should have been for a man of his stature.

"My partner here"—Grey angled his head toward Sage—"is the new guy's roommate. She needs a word."

A smile brightened the guard's face. "Matt?"

Sage let go of the breath she'd been holding. Thank the gods for Matty. He could charm the pants off of anyone. "Yeah, he's my best friend."

"That's the strangest thing I've heard all day. Good luck with that." The guard erupted into full-blown laughter as he stepped aside and allowed them through.

Sage whispered into Grey's ear, "Why is he laughing?"

"You remember what happened to your mom, right?"

"That's a low blow, especially from you," she threw back at him. She expected, after all their time together, that he might have some sense of reverence, or at least a little tact when speaking about her mother. But no. Just when she thought she knew what to expect from him, he pulled a jerk move like that.

"Truth hurts sometimes." Grey's reply came quickly and unapologetically sharp.

"Tough words from the man who dated one." It was an equally mean reply, but if he was going to speak so cavalier about her mother being turned darkling, especially after he had to deliver the killing blow, then she refused to feel guilty about reminding him of his own painful losses.

"You're right." Grey stopped short. The look in his eyes shifted between shock and understanding. "That was uncaring of me. I'm sorry."

Not the reply she was expecting. Stealing her anger with his honesty left her with nothing to do but continue to walk silently as they weaved their way through the dance floor. Dark as it was inside, Sage could hardly see the faces of the patrons as she passed them. Many had claimed spaces in the booths which had even less light than the dance floor. If Zack were around, it wasn't obvious.

Matt spotted them before they reached the bar and came around to greet Sage with a bear hug that squeezed the air from her lungs. "You have news for me?"

"Can't breathe. Dying. Dead. My spirit is passing into the nether realm." Sage groaned the words with labored breaths.

Matt set her down with a laugh. "Drama queen." He noticed Grey standing next to her and gave him a curt nod.

"Apartment is ready," she announced happily. "You have time off soon to go have a look around our new home?"

"Let me go check in with the boss first." Matt threw down his bar towel. "You guys good here for a few minutes?"

She expected him to be excited about the apartment, but didn't think he'd drop everything to go look at it right then and there. Poor thing. He had to be feeling as desperate as her to have a home again. It would be a wonderful homecoming for sure when they finally got themselves settled in.

"Zack around tonight?" Sage asked, trying to sound casual. Happy as he was about the apartment, Matt didn't need to know Zack had been her real reason for her showing up at his place of work.

"Uh. Yeah. But." Matt's excitement faltered. His gaze shifted to a place across the room. "Maybe give him a few minutes too."

Sage glanced in the direction Matt had been looking. Bodies were entwined on a couch in a dark corner. She stifled a gasp, immediately looking away. Where was the mental bleach when she needed it?

"Just grab a spot here at the bar. I'll be back in a minute. Promise," Matt said and disappeared from sight as if blinking out of existence.

"You okay?" Grey asked. "You wanted to come here."

"I know. I just can't wrap my head around it sometimes," she admitted. "It's just easier if I pretend like nothing is happening."

"You're going to have to if you live with a vampire." Zack appeared so suddenly Sage squealed and jumped out of her seat.

"Don't do that!" Her hand flew on its own, and before she realized it, her fist connected painfully with his shoulder.

Across the end of the bar, a glass shattered. A bartender, Sage hadn't seen standing there a moment before, was glaring at her with eyes black as the night itself.

Grey jumped to his feet, his hands already gripping the handles of his machetes.

"Sorry, Braxton. It's okay. I should have known better than to sneak up on my friend here. No harm, no foul." Zack held his hands in surrender, a wide smile plastered across his face.

"Never do that again," Sage warned.

"Maybe remember where you are before you go assaulting people. Especially given the drama your organization is in at the moment." Zack popped up on a barstool facing Sage. "Last thing you need is more…problems."

Grey retook his seat next to Sage. "You got a little dinner there in the corner of your mouth."

"Dessert." Zack chuckled and licked his lips.

"What do you know about our drama?" Sage asked, trying to get a hold of her nerves. The faster she got answers, the faster she could get out of there.

"Whatever happened to a friendly hello? You used to be the nice one in this partnership. Now every interaction is a battle of wits," Zack said.

"That was before you threatened to have me for dinner," she replied, anger still on the edge of her voice.

"You? Dinner? Inconceivable!" Zack playfully defended himself. "You know I didn't really mean that. I was trying to teach you. Protect you. Grey boy here has tried to kill you as many times as I have, and you're so much nicer to him. If I didn't know any better, I'd think you were sweet on him. Tell me, was I too much of a bad boy or not enough? I can change, you know. I just have to know your type first."

"You don't give up, do you?" Sage tried to maintain her outrage, but Zack had the market cornered on personality. Even when she wanted to kill him, he never failed to draw the laughter out of her.

"That was a smile. I saw it." He turned around to the rest of the bar and announced, "She's smiling. We have witnesses."

Sage slapped him on the arm. "Stop it. Why are you such an insufferable jerk?"

Zack looked past her and winked at Grey. "Learned from the best."

"We've all had our fun now. Can we have a serious conversation or not?" Grey asked.

"I didn't realize this wasn't a social call." Zack wiped the smile from his face and folded his arms on the bar. "What's going on?"

"As if you didn't know," Grey whispered.

"This is a big city. Lots of things are going on," Zack replied. "It's a never-ending cycle of problems."

"We're all ears," Sage said.

"What's in it for me?" Zack asked.

Always about the payment. The worst part of this job was haggling over information. And Sage, being perpetually bankrupt, had little more than a smile to offer. That would give the insufferable flirt of a vampire too much hope. He'd lost any chance he could ever have with her after the stunt he'd pulled.

"I thought we were friends? Friends tell each other things." Sage spoke sweetly, keeping the conversation on more neutral ground.

Zack stared unblinking at her for a moment. Had she stolen his voice? Or was he calculating his next move? Games, she was good at. A roll of the dice and things would happen. If only that worked here.

"Was I mistaken?" she asked, breaking their prolonged silence. "Are we not friends?"

"Oh, she is getting so good," Zack said to Grey. "I'm proud of her. Are you proud? Look at how fast she threw that out there."

Grey's jaw tightened. He had less patience for Zack's game than she did. And that gave Sage her next move.

"You were right, Grey. He wouldn't have information for us." She maintained her sweet tone as she turned to face her partner. "I should have listened to you."

"Ouch. Next level mastery. Emotional manipulation." Zack covered his grin with his hands. "I could cry. I'm just so impressed."

It took all Sage had not to punch him again. That damn vampire was enjoying their little tête-à-tête way too much and at the same time adamantly refusing to give her anything to work with.

Sage hopped off the barstool and peeked around Zack, hoping to see Matt emerge from the back room. "I'm so glad I could brighten up your evening."

"That's it? You give up so quickly?" The amusement in Zack's voice soured. "C'mon, Sage, you were on a roll there. Keep going. You're so close to breaking me."

"I'm bored with games, Zack. I need friends I can trust." Sage spotted Matt and waved him over. "Like this guy right here."

Matt's expression shifted. He looked like a man walking before a firing squad, the moment she'd drawn attention to him. "Did I miss something?"

"Just Zack toying with us, as always," she answered. "You have time off to go see the apartment?"

"Not fair," Zack groused. "You're pulling my strings just as hard, Sage!"

"You keep using that word," she fired back. "I do not think it means what you think it means."

"Crafty little thing, you." Zack saluted her with a flourish. Clearly, he'd gotten her nerdy reference, and even if he hadn't given her the information she'd wanted, that was enough to concede her as the victor in their battle of wits.

Grey groaned loud enough for the bartender on the other end of the bar to hear. "Both of you are giving me a headache. We're done here, right?"

"So done!" Sage winked at her partner. "I'll ride with Matt to the apartment if you want to take off..."

"I'm going to stay and have a conversation with Zack." Grey turned an evil eye on the mischievous vampire. "You two go ahead."

"Is that a good idea?" Not even a moment earlier, he'd acted as if he were ready to escape this place. Why stay now? Alone without backup or a partner. That couldn't be a safe plan. "We can stay."

"You have my word as a gentleman, he will make it back to ASSET alive." Zack held his hand over his heart.

Sage stared deep into Grey's eyes. "Are you sure?"

If he was worried, she couldn't see it.

Grey wore the mask of neutrality well as he waved her off. "Go. I'll call you later. Proof of life. Okay?"

Sage didn't like that one bit, but Matt urged her toward the door. "I've only got a few hours off. Let's do this."

NINE

"Here we are," Sage exclaimed as she opened the door. "Care to do the honors, or should I invite you in first?"

"You think you're pretty funny, don't you?"

She waved a hand to let Matt cross the threshold. "I'll be here all week."

His face held the same lackluster expression that Sage imagined she'd had when she first entered the apartment earlier that day. "A bit empty." He passed through the eat-in kitchen into the living room. "At least we got the upgraded flooring. Love the wood look."

Sage followed him inside but gave him enough space to explore without getting in his way. "Josh is already picking out curtains."

Matt's eyes were drawn like a magnet toward the two windows. He nodded at each one as if keeping a mental tally. "Good. He needs a project. Helps keep his mind focused on fixing things rather than dwelling on the things he can't change. Might be a good idea to let him take on the design of the whole place. Make the transition easier on us all."

That was more honesty than Sage had been prepared for. But after the conversation she'd had with Josh earlier, she should have expected it. They were knee deep in relationship troubles. Both clearly loved the other, but the tension between them since Matt had become a vampire was so thick it choked out all of the good.

"Men are such complicated creatures," Sage mumbled in solidarity. Her—she couldn't call it a relationship—thing with Grey was a constant mix of hot and cold. At least ASSET was never in short supply of world-ending magical problems to fix. "And a busy mind has no time to dwell on issues, that's for sure."

"Hold on. Have I missed something?" Matt narrowed his eyes and planted his hands on his hips. "Has Sage Cynwrig dipped her toe into the dating pool without telling me?"

"I wouldn't call it dating, really." Sage wasn't sure what she'd call it. They hadn't done much more than a little flirting between fights. Though seeing him earlier that morning, freshly showered, wearing only a pair of sweatpants had definitely perked her up more than the coffee she'd been drinking. She couldn't deny the attraction. "I mean, it's Grey we're talking about. We work together. That's kind of off-limits, right?"

"Let me get this straight. The fedora? Now you like him?" Matt's mouth hung open.

She understood his shocked expression. Those two guys hadn't really gotten along. And even she had to admit, Grey's tendency to rub people the wrong way had her cringing at the prospect of being tethered to him as a partner. But he'd shown her a whole other side of himself while they were on the run.

"He's not so bad when you spend time with him."

"Is what people with Stockholm syndrome say," Matt shot back without missing a beat.

Heat rose to her cheeks. She tried to hide the blush with her hand. "Damn. That's mean even for you."

"Can you blame me? The few times I've spent with him, he's been a complete tool. Excuse me for being protective of you. You deserve only the best."

He had a good point. And looked appropriately sorry for his initial outrage. "Fair enough. I've gotten to see more of his…"

Matt's eyebrow arched sharply with devious interest. "Do tell?"

"Stop it." She playfully swatted Matt's arm. How long had it been since they'd shared a moment like this? Both of them. Their world had been turned completely upside down. Sage missed this more than she realized. At that moment, they weren't Terra and vampire trying to live among humans. They were back to being best friends and talking about boys. "You know what I mean. He puts on a front. He's not as bad as he wants people to think."

"If you're defending him so hard, why are you acting like you're on the fence about crossing the boundary between partners and…something with a few more benefits?"

"That's just it. We work together, for one thing. If it ends badly, that makes life hell."

Matt glared at her with sarcastic disbelief. "If you're an immature baby about it, sure. Next."

"My life is a train wreck right now. I guess… I mean… I'm just not sure…"

"Honey, your life is always a train wreck. You've adopted that as your nickname. Embrace it. Next."

She blew out a defeated breath and threw her hands up in surrender. He was right. She was making more of this than it should be. "Fine. I haven't…you know…in well, forever."

"Feeling a bit rusty, are we?" Matt giggled.

Not exactly the response she had been hoping for. She was serious, and he was laughing? "Thanks. I needed that."

He must have realized he'd crossed the line. In a blink, he'd closed the gap between them and took her face in his hands.

He urged her to look up at him. "Listen, hon, you are gorgeous, strong, smart, and sexy as hell. You have no reason to be self-conscious. And even if you didn't have all that going for you, he'd still be lucky as hell to have you. He doesn't deserve you."

She pulled out of his grip, turning her head away to hide the burn of her cheeks.

"Hey, I get it." Matt softened his tone. "First time jitters and all. And I'm assuming you've had way too much time to think about it, so you've built it all up to be more than it is."

"Ding, ding, ding. We have a winner!" Sage snarked.

"Stop worrying about it. And if it does happen, remember that the first time with anyone new is a complete train wreck. You don't know each other's bodies yet. So have a drink or two to calm the nerves, and just fake it."

"Um, hello… Terra!" She held up her wrists with the tree of life in full view. "Alcohol no longer has any effect on me."

"Oh, you poor thing." He patted her head playfully, but the worried look in his eyes said she'd stumped him.

If Matt didn't have answers or advice, it was hopeless. He was her guru.

Silence passed between them as Sage struggled with a way to get the conversation going again.

Matt's expression shifted suddenly, his eyebrow arched deviously again. "Plan B," he said proudly.

"There's a plan B?"

"Yep."

"And that is?"

"Take charge yourself. Beat him to the punch and lead the charge. Be assertive and school him in the ways of your body."

"Easy as that, right?" She scoffed at his total non-solution.

"Confidence is so hot. Trust me. You tell him what you like, and watch him perform." Matt winked. "And if he does something you don't like, make sure he knows that too. Just between you and me, guys like to be the best at whatever we do. Knowledge is power."

"Speaking of." Sage hesitated, wondering if she should break the news to him before Josh had the chance.

"Yes?" Matt asked eagerly.

"Word of advice, from someone who's felt a vampire's bite. Maybe leave that out of the bedroom. I know it's your thing now, but it really hurts." She rubbed her neck, remembering the feel of teeth tearing her skin open.

Confidence faded from Matt's eyes. "Josh say something?"

"I guessed, seeing his bandages," she lied. "He loves you so much, so he might not want to rock the boat with this. You know, keep you feeling like the best. And you are the best for him. But odd as it is to say, I know how those teeth feel. It's not sexy. So maybe just leave biting out of the bedroom."

Matt nodded and let out a sigh. "Probably right."

"So hey. I've got an idea. Double date?"

"For real? You think that's wise?"

"Might take the pressure off both of us." Sage begged silently with her eyes for him to agree.

"Would give me a chance to see this other side of Grey." Matt shrugged.

Sage threw her arms around him. "Thank you!"

Matt's whole body stiffened. He sucked in a breath and held it. He'd been so normal she'd almost forgotten how much he was fighting to keep control.

She released his neck and stepped back. "Sorry."

"No. You're good. I'm good. Getting better at this every day!"

"Ready to come home, then? We can move you in tonight if you like."

"More than you know, hon. I'm ready to get back to some sense of normalcy."

"How's the new job?"

"A bar is a bar, I guess. Still getting used to the clientele."

"And Zack?"

"He's pretty cool, actually. We're definitely adding him to the game night rotation."

"I can't wait!" Sage rubbed her hands eagerly. Game night was definitely something they needed to get back into, quickly. Even if it meant adding the insufferable flirt. Nothing beat the stress relief of stepping into another life and becoming a character, even if it was only for a few hours.

"But before then, we need to take you shopping and get you ready for your date," he teased.

"Jerk. I was almost feeling good, and then you had to go remind me."

"Alcohol really doesn't work?"

"Nope."

"Damn."

"Thanks for the vote of confidence."

"When I'm through with you, you won't need mine. You'll be full up on your own."

"We'll see." Sage sighed.

"You staying here tonight? Or do you need a ride back to ASSET?" Matt asked.

"Better take me back to work. It's not like I can sleep here on the floor."

TEN

ASSET was busier than usual considering the lateness of the hour Sage returned. She ran through the conference rooms, around agents' desks, and peeked into the break area, looking for Grey, but he was nowhere to be found. She'd texted him at least ten times, past the point of sounding like an annoying ex-girlfriend. Where the hell was he?

Zack wouldn't have been stupid enough to attack him, but that didn't mean others in the bar were as intelligent.

"Burning the midnight oil?" Devon poked his head out of the training room.

"Have you seen Grey this evening?" she asked.

"Can't say that I have, but I haven't been here all night myself."

She sighed. "He's not answering his texts."

"Probably sleeping."

"Yeah, that would be the reasonable thing."

"But you're not that reasonable," Devon joked.

"Am I ever?"

"Go grab your workout clothes. I'll tire you out."

She knew she'd walked into a trap, but it was too late. "Planning to beat some sense into me?"

"Tonight I think we need to help you learn to center yourself. Find your calm." Devon pointed back toward his training room. "Be here in five minutes."

She'd much rather punch out her frustration than center herself. That sounded too much like yoga, and she hated all that bending into a pretzel while remembering her breath stuff. *Namaste home!* She wouldn't dare say that out loud. Devon would definitely kill her for that remark. Or at least make her wish she was dead.

She jogged to her room and threw on a sports bra, tank top, and leggings, and returned to the training room to find Devon standing on his head, stiff as a board, pointing his toes to the ceiling.

"That looks painful."

Devon had his eyes closed, meditating as he maintained his perfect balance.

"If done correctly, it is quite relaxing." His voice came calmly.

He brought his legs down slowly—with more control than Sage felt she would ever be able to muster—and then somersaulted out of the pose.

"Is that what you had in mind?" Sage asked.

"You're not ready for that." Devon chuckled. "Tonight, we're going to get into some nice deep stretches to unwind your muscles and help you clear your head."

Sage came to meet him on the mat. "You lead. I'll attempt to follow."

"You're familiar with yoga poses, yes?" Devon asked.

"Unfortunately."

"Don't take that tone. Stretching is important. Those poses, when done correctly, not only help the muscles but the nervous system as well, and that, Captain Trainwreck, is where you need the most help."

"Sorry."

"Don't be. Just drop the attitude. That's one of your biggest failings. You have a good heart, you are strong, and you are determined, but you tend to always see the negative in things before finding the positive. That will always cause you to act without reason. You need to learn to calm your mind and see all sides of the picture before making decisions."

Of course there would be a lesson in there.

"You've come a long way, in a very short time," Devon continued. "That is an achievement in its own right. But you're recent promotion—something I argued against, if you really want to know—is going to put you in situations where the decisions you make can truly be life or death."

His words smacked painfully hard of betrayal. She shouldn't have let him get to her, but Sage let her mouth run before she could stop it. "You argued against me getting this promotion?"

"You've just made my point. Of everything I said, what did you focus on?"

She turned away sheepishly. *Dammit.*

"I did not argue against your promotion because I felt you couldn't do it. You have more potential than most agents I see come through these doors. However, you haven't grown enough into your own abilities. You're not ready. That point is moot now. You are Shadow Ops. Congratulations. The time for training wheels is over." Devon planted his feet and bent forward, folding his body as he reached his hands for the mat.

"I can handle anything." Sage followed Devon's lead, moving as he did from forward fold into downward dog.

"You can, yes. But will you?" Devon countered.

"I will." She kept her tone neutral as the stretch burned all the way up her legs.

"Don't say it. Do it." Devon lowered himself from downward dog, resting on his knees, and sent his arms out across the floor. "This is called Uttana Shishosana. Great for your arms and shoulders. Especially when they're sore after a fight. You'll do good to remember it."

She moved with him, holding the pose, enduring the slow burn traveling up her protesting muscles, moving up her arms into her shoulders. Not nearly as painful as the last pose she'd held, this one worked like a kind of magic, untangling knots in her muscles that had formed without her knowledge.

"You know something I don't?" Sage asked. "Should I be preparing for some fights?"

"You should always be prepared. But as to your specific mission, no. Shadow Ops is a special level of agent. What I do know is you will need both mental and physical preparation to do your job properly. You work off the grid, and that can mean surviving on your wits and skills alone until someone can extract you."

"Undercover super spy type stuff," she joked.

"Torture, starvation, interrogation, and blackmail." Devon lifted out of the pose, extending his legs as he planted his palms to the floor.

"You're really selling it with that pitch." Sage followed into the plank position. She always hated this one. No matter how many times she had trained, she found her whole body shaking violently after a few moments of trying to hold herself stiff as a board.

"That was the plan." Devon flowed through plank into a deep lunge.

Sage followed and settled into position, breathing through the more intense burn.

"What if you are caught behind enemy lines and your cover is blown? What then?" he asked.

She found it hard to talk as she concentrated on her breath to help maintain the stretch.

"You have to be able to think under pressure. Look at the situation calmly and make smart choices if you want to stay alive," he continued.

A minute had gone by, and her legs and hips were on fire from holding the position. Devon, however, didn't seem bothered at all. Nor did he appear to be planning to move anytime soon.

"You're not thinking now." He pointed out. "You're so focused on how much your legs are burning, and struggling to maintain. The reality is you could ease up, take the pressure off, or simply come out of the stretch. But because you feel you're stuck, forced to do exactly what I'm doing, that you're not willing to do what you *need* to do. That is exactly what I am talking about."

"But I'm just following your lead." She breathed through the pain, attempting to keep her voice level.

"No one said you had to go down as deeply as I do. I have much more flexibility than you do. Pushing your muscles past the burn and into pain will not gain you anything. In fact, I'd hate to be you in the morning. You'll feel the damage you've done tomorrow."

"Dammit!" Sage fell onto the mat, clutching her inner thighs. "But I thought…"

"Don't assume things. You could have asked for clarification. But, knowing you, all you wanted to do was prove you could do it, rather than learning how to do it right."

He was right. He knew exactly why she'd forced herself into a lunge so deep she was practically doing the splits. Her legs and inner thighs screamed for relief. Her hips felt as if they had been pulled from their sockets and roughly shoved back in.

"You tricked yourself, Sage. I want you to remember this lesson." Devon stood over her and held his hand out.

She wasn't sure she had the strength to stand, let alone walk back to her room. "Can't I just lay right here?"

"No. You need to get up and move those joints and muscles. Take a few laps before you go to bed," he said. "You're going to feel it in the morning. Let that be a reminder to you. Don't be in such a hurry to prove yourself that you don't think a situation through."

ELEVEN

"Plan on getting up today?" Grey's voice pulled Sage from her slumber.

She tried to roll over, but her muscles screamed in protest. Devon had been right. Muscles on fire, joints aching at the slightest motion. She couldn't help the groan of pain that escaped her lips.

"You okay?" Grey came into the room, closing the door behind him.

"Training with Devon last night. I'll be fine." She threw her legs over the side of the bed, clenching her jaw to prevent any more cries of pain from revealing her weakness. "Where the hell were you? I called."

"I know. I saw." He chuckled. "Drama queen much?"

"I was worried the vampires had a little too much fun with you, but if you're going to be a jerk about it, then I take it all back. They can have whatever fun they want."

"Someone needs their coffee," Grey teased.

Smug as he was acting, he was right about that. Sage never claimed to be a morning person, even less so with her muscles screaming as she pushed herself to stand.

"Someone is about to get a punch in his face if he doesn't shut up."

"Brave words for someone moving slow as a granny." Grey chuckled.

He had her there. She pushed through the first few aching steps, finding her muscles easing as she continued to force them to work. "Don't have to be fast. You can't hide. I know where you live now. I'll get you eventually." Teasing came as naturally as breathing. Grumpy as she'd felt upon waking, their verbal sparring session had begun to brighten her mood.

"But then I wouldn't be able to tell you the news I learned," Grey continued, taking a step backwards for every step forward she took.

"Out with it." Sage stopped before she'd pinned Grey against the wall. "I have not had the requisite amount of caffeine needed to deal with teasers."

"We're going on a field trip." Grey reached behind himself and grabbed hold of the door. He pulled it open and slipped out saying, "Get ready and meet me in the lobby."

"Dammit! What about my coffee?" *And maybe a bottle of muscle relaxers?* It was too late. He was gone. Out of earshot. The jerk.

Sage dressed as quickly as she could, and stopped into the break room to guzzle down a quick cuppa before she met him.

"Planning on telling me where we are going, or are you just going to keep me guessing?"

Grey looked smugly self-satisfied. "I don't know. It's more fun to make you guess."

"Whatever." She wouldn't admit aloud that he'd bested her this morning. She'd have another chance later. "Let's go."

"That's not what you were supposed to say." He eyed her suspiciously.

Maybe he hadn't bested her after all. She smirked, seeing another opportunity to play. "Sorry, did I ruin your moment?"

"Nice try. But no. I'm thoroughly enjoying teasing you."

"You do you," she said casually.

"Playing the *I don't care* card?"

Amazing what a little bit of caffeine can do to get the mind working. If things kept going the way they were, this was shaping up to be a fun day.

Sage continued to play it cool, shrugging as she brushed past him to press the button to call the elevator up. "Frankly, I'm too damn tired to care. Let's just get this over with."

Grey kept silent about where they were headed. Down the elevator, through the parking garage, and all the miles he drove them toward the southwest part of town. Properties there were older, spread farther apart, and came with a lot more land. Like driving through a portal, they left the glitz and glamour of the modern city behind, and managed to arrive back in the old west.

They pulled into a long dirt driveway and came to a stop at a ranch-style home. He finally broke his silence after taking off his helmet. "Before we go in... We're going to be meeting with a Púca. Please..."

"Let you do the talking while I keep my mouth shut?" After the time and missions they had shared, she hoped he'd trust her a little more, but still, every damn time. This stupid warning. Her annoyance slipped out in the tone of her voice. No doubt he could see it plastered across her face. Maybe that was why he looked at her as if she had struck him.

"I was actually going to say be nice." He delivered the words deadpan.

Maybe she should have had that second cup of coffee. *Open mouth, insert foot. As always.*

She took a breath and tried to blow out the remainder of her negativity. "Yeah. Will do."

"Púca are sensitive to emotional vibrations. They can be a little skittish."

Sage pasted a smile across her face.

"There you go." Grey led the way. "Just smile and nod, and let me do the talking."

She couldn't see the expression on his face, but she could imagine the shit-eating grin. Of course he had to throw that last little jab at her. It worked like a charm though. Sage laughed softly as she followed his lead.

The house was on a few acres of land with gorgeous wood post fencing. They bypassed the front door as Grey led them around to the back of the property.

Horses stood grazing in a large field. Among them was a beautiful black stallion, standing taller than the rest. His long silky mane reflected the sun's light, glistening like a thousand specks of glitter as he trotted up to the fence line.

"That's our guy?" she asked. Just as with the shifters she'd met before, she found the closer she got, the more she could see the other form of the Púca taking over.

"How could you tell?" Grey asked, ribbing her with more playful sarcasm.

They approached slowly, meeting the true form of the Púca at the fence. His glamour was the best she'd seen. A very tiny man, no bigger than a garden gnome, stood atop the fence post.

"We hope we're not intruding." Grey extended his hand, offering it to shake, but quickly pulled back as if realizing how awkward that might be considering their size difference.

"The vampire said you'd be by today." The Púca spoke with a slow southern drawl. "Shame what they're saying on the news. Hope those kids are all right." The Púca looked up, meeting Sage's eyes. "Now where are my manners, miss? I'm sorry. The name's Travis." He tipped his tiny hat to her.

"Sage. Pleased to meet you," she offered sweetly. "And this is my partner, Grey."

"Thank you for being willing to talk to us," Grey said, using his best nice-guy voice.

"I'm not sure how much help I'm going to be to you. I got no problem with ASSET. I want that on the record." Travis glanced around behind him, out into the pasture.

"Anything you can tell us would be appreciated. ASSET's mission is to protect our magical community." Grey sounded as if he were reading lines from a card.

"I reckon that you're after the guilty party who pulled that little bus prank. That's why you're here?" Travis asked.

"Do you know of anyone bragging about pulling off that little stunt?" Sage asked hopefully.

Travis turned around again, paying particular interest in a chestnut-colored horse slowly strolling up behind him. "You can see through the glamour, right?"

"It's just a horse," Grey confirmed.

"Right. Of course. See." Travis glanced back again. The horse stopped and lowered its head to graze at the grass. "The thing is, that's not my horse. Not sure how I ended up with her."

"Does it belong to a neighbor?" Sage stared hard, trying to see what wasn't there.

"Naw. It's not one of theirs," Travis replied.

"Did you do any favors recently? Could this be a payment?" Grey asked.

"I do favors all the time for my friends. Just the kind of guy I am," Travis said with no hint of irony. "You sure that's just a horse?"

Sage rubbed her eyes, struggling to see anything that shouldn't be there. Nothing about the horse appeared otherworldly. Not that one, or any other grazing in the field. "Yeah, just a standard horse."

"Make any enemies recently?" Grey asked.

"No, sir," Travis answered sharply, as if he'd been accused. "I try to keep my nose clean."

Grey had said to be nice, but Sage could see his last question had rattled the Púca. She didn't want to scare him off before they could glean anything of value from the conversation. "What's your occupation?"

"I run a riding school. Got a nice bit of land here," Travis replied proudly. "Rodeo stuff, trick riding, horse jumping. That kind of thing."

"Do you ever board other's horses?" Grey asked.

"Strictly my own here." Travis's gaze turned back to the horse. It lifted its head as if realizing it was being watched.

"How about new clients?" Grey asked. "Any fae learning to ride horses?"

"There was this one fella who came in about a week ago. Rich as the day is long. Called himself Raynor. Big Scandinavian-looking guy." Travis rubbed at his chin thoughtfully. "He rented me out for a whole week to learn how to ride. Just for the fun of it. Now, he was definitely something else. Never did ask. It's impolite and all. But my poor horses wouldn't go near him. Scared, they were. I apologized and refunded him his money. That was that."

"Raynor sound familiar to you?" Sage looked to Grey.

He shook his head.

"Do you think that Raynor might have gifted this horse to you?" Sage asked. "Perhaps as an apology for costing you a week of work?"

"Don't see how that would help me at all," Travis groused. "Now I have an extra mouth to feed with less money in my pocket to do it."

"Would you like us to have a chat with this Raynor guy?" Grey asked.

"Oh no. That would be terribly rude." Travis's little eyes went wide as saucers. "I didn't mean to point the finger. It's just you asked and I remembered. Not trying to cause any trouble."

"We would not do anything to besmirch your good name," Grey assured him.

"Can I ask a question?" Sage jumped in before Grey could push the topic further.

"Ask whatever you need to." Travis leaned in, giving her all of his attention.

"The vampires." Sage hesitated for a moment, not entirely sure how to broach the topic tactfully. She found it odd for a gentle, seemingly good-natured creature like Travis to be dealing with the likes of them. And just as she let that thought cross her mind, she remembered Matt. He was one of them too. She couldn't allow prejudice to creep into her thoughts and color this investigation. Especially ones she knew were wrong. "Sorry. Collecting my thoughts here. What kind of dealings do you have with them?"

"I'm in the business of making friends, not enemies. I don't judge."

She'd insulted him again. Not intentionally, but it was clear by the sour tone in his voice. "I didn't mean it like that. It's just an odd friendship."

"Hardly." Travis looked annoyed. "Their mental capabilities are quite handy when you've got an animal that just won't calm down and listen."

"That would be handy, yes," Sage noted, still wondering what the connection was. And why Zack would send him here of all places. It didn't add up at all.

"Well, thank you so much for your time," Grey said cheerfully.

Had he given up, or had he picked up something in the Púca's conversation that she hadn't?

"My pleasure, though I'm not sure what information I gave you." Travis looked relieved to be done with the conversation.

"You've been extremely helpful," Grey replied.

"Thanks again," Sage said, confused, but trying to be as polite as possible.

Travis tipped his hat, and they turned away, taking their leave of him.

"Did we learn anything here?" Sage asked when they reached Grey's bike, still completely confused.

"We need to look up this Raynor character. That's our clue. Someone with money doesn't have anonymity. They are a person of very much interest. Why don't we know about them?"

"If Zack knew this, why didn't he tell us?" Sage asked, annoyed.

"Because he is Zack." Grey sighed. "Or because he didn't have the name. Maybe he'd just heard the story and figured we should investigate."

TWELVE

Sage slammed her fist down on the desktop. Every time they had a potential lead to follow, it lead them straight to a dead end. "The name isn't coming up in our databases."

"Scoot over. Let me have a look." Grey swapped seats with her, taking over the keyboard, and began typing. "That means he's either not registered or goes by a different name than we have on file."

"Sign of a super bad guy, like the kind we need to locate?" Sage dared to hope.

"Or someone who values their anonymity. For good reason," Grey commented, his eyes riveted on the screen as he tapped the keys furiously. "He's wealthy. That often brings the wrong kind of attention."

Damn the searches and the database. They'd already failed at that multiple times. "So how do we track him down?"

"What were the clues that Travis gave us?" Grey asked.

"His horse wouldn't calm down. He was big, but appeared in human form. I'm guessing we're looking for a werewolf, maybe?"

"That's not a bad guess." Grey turned to face Sage, a glimmer of excitement reflected in his eyes. She was onto something. "They do spook horses."

But the light faded just as quickly as it had come. Grey tapped his finger to his lips and shook his head as if having a private argument. Point and counterpoint, she could see the workings of it, though Grey had not yet given his words voice. She waited, hoping the right argument would emerge victorious.

He turned again to the computer, typing again into the search form. Moments passed, and Grey's brow furrowed once more. "Shifters and werewolves run in packs. Packs share resources. Less chance of individual wealth. Less anonymity too."

While he'd refuted the option she'd suggested, he didn't sound as utterly crushed as she'd expected. If anything, he sounded like he was still trying to pull victory from the jaws of defeat.

"You have something better in mind, don't you?" she asked. "Well? Don't play games with me now."

Grey moved away from the computer screen, offering Sage a seat front and center to his revelation.

"A dragon? For real?" She read the file on a man by the name of Brurdur, a fire drake shifter believed to live in the mountains on the extreme western border of the city. An Elemental with no clan affiliations or public records of dealings with ASSET. All their databases had on him was a registration notice when he came to the city thirty years prior, and a few notes on high-profile events where his name appeared as a guest. Hardly a damning paper trail.

"Honestly, it sounds like a longshot, but as much as Zack vexes me," —Grey sighed loudly—"the fact he made sure we knew this guy exists means we should at the very least look into it."

Whether it took them down another dead end or not, the prospect of meeting a dragon would be well worth it. "Let's go meet a dragon."

"Slow your roll there, sparky."

"I'd prefer newbie if you're going to give me a nickname. Sparky is too…"

"Childish? I wonder why I'd think to use that?" Grey snarked.

"Still better than your nickname," she quipped.

"I'm not even going to ask."

Better he didn't. She snickered to herself. "So why can't we pay a visit?"

"He's on the list for a Mabon party. A masked ball." Grey pointed to the screen.

"You thinking what I'm thinking?" She took a closer look at the listing for the party. It had been registered with ASSET but did not appear to be one they had on their security roster. Knowing what she did, that made sense. Why would they if there was a dragon in attendance?

Grey had a mischievous look in his eye. "Can you dance?"

"Nope."

"Good. Neither can I. But I do look damn good in a suit." He ran his fingers along the edge of his fedora. "And I have just the hat!"

"Don't mean to burst your bubble but can't just go waltzing into a party ASSET wasn't invited to."

"Masked ball. The easiest undercover assignment we could hope for."

"Well, you're half right." Sage snickered.

"What?"

"If we're going undercover, you're going to have to do it hatless." She flicked the edge of his fedora playfully.

"Don't you dare!" He jerked away from her and reached up to make sure his hat remained firmly on his head. For all his playfulness through the day, this was the one joke he didn't appear to enjoy. "It's my trademark."

"Exactly. You're too easy a mark with that on. Even with a mask." She tried to flick the brim of his hat again, but he was too fast for her.

"I don't like you right now."

Of all the things in the world to get bent out of shape about, the hat was an oddity. She giggled. "I know. But you'll still look damn good without it."

"What?"

"What?" She winked.

"Thanks. I think."

She didn't need to imagine him looking damn good. She'd seen enough of him earlier to know for a fact that he did. "So. Hey. Let's do that thing we said we were going to try to do."

"That was oddly cryptic."

"You know." She leaned in close and whispered into his ear, "The D A T E."

"Did we say we were going to do that?" He smirked.

"Yeah." She slapped his arm. "But I want to make it a little more interesting."

"Oh really?" His eyebrow shot up with a glimmer of excitement lighting up his eyes.

"Yeah, so…uh…Matt and Josh have been needing a little normalcy with their relationship." She sucked in a breath, feeling the overwhelming awkwardness of what she was proposing. The room suddenly felt ten degrees hotter. Sweat began to bead on her forehead. Dammit! She'd already opened her mouth. Best stick her foot in it. Maintain expectations. There was no way to save the conversation anyway. "So, I was thinking we could, you know, try and double up to help keep the conversation light and fun."

"That was…not…what I thought you were going to say." He chuckled.

"It could be fun," she offered, "and a good way for us to get to know each other off the clock."

"Me and your roommate?" He sounded more worried than intrigued. "That guy hates me."

"What better reason for him to learn to like you."

"I really don't care if he likes me," Grey said.

"I do. He's family. And since you and I spend a lot of time together, then I want to make sure everyone in my life gets along."

"Sounds like I have no choice in the matter," he groused, turning his attention back to the computer screen.

Maybe she should have waited to broach that topic. But now that it was out there, she felt obligated to see it through. Besides, she couldn't date someone her brother didn't approve of, so they were better off getting this kind of thing out of the way early, before they got too close and it became a problem.

"Say no if you want to. I'm not trying to play games here. I just thought it would be a nice way to spend an evening."

"Sorry. I didn't mean it like that." He sighed loudly and rested his head in his hands. "I don't do the whole big social gathering thing. That's all."

"It's fine. Really. Forget I asked." They could argue over dates later. He'd inadvertently given her an idea. A possible way to follow up on their new lead. She needed to go alone, and quickly, before she lost her train of thought. She picked up her purse and headed for the door. "I'm going to head off. I need to work on getting my apartment put together. Let me know what I need to get for the party."

"Stop." Grey was on his feet and caught up to her in a flash. "Don't do this."

"What am I doing?" *Besides avoiding this totally awkward situation?*

"You're storming out because I rejected your offer."

"It's fine. Really. There are way more things to get stressed over at the moment. So let's just focus on what we need to do to investigate Mr. Dragon man."

His eyes all but screamed disbelief, but when he spoke, his words came with calm assurance. "Glad to see your head is in the game."

"Totally." She started down the hallway again, waving behind her. "Divide and conquer. You figure out how we get into that party. I'll work on wardrobe."

THIRTEEN

"I'm surprised to see you here so soon, Miss Cynwrig." Sylvia floated into her office. She glanced past Sage to the empty seat. "Alone. Especially since I have not summoned you."

It was a gamble on Sage's part, but she'd made a decent impression on the shadowrunner in her earlier dealings, so speaking one-on-one might work to her favor.

"Sorry to intrude. I had a theory I wanted to run past you." She leaned in close to the desk as Sylvia took her seat, and whispered, "Without the opinion of others clouding my judgement."

"Trouble in paradise with Mr. Maddox?" Sylvia chuckled. "How…unexpected."

That man did have a knack for rubbing people the wrong way. "No. Nothing like that. I just want to be sure I'm heading in the right direction before bringing up something." A few minutes earlier, she knew exactly what she had planned to say, but as Sage stared into the coal black eyes of the shadowrunner, she found herself tongue-tied. "I like to…uh…"

"Appear intelligent?" Sylvia sharply finished what Sage had struggled to say.

"Sure. Let's go with that."

"Don't sell yourself short. You might be wet behind the ears, but you've got a head on your shoulders. I've seen what you are capable of. And don't you ever let a man make you feel less than you are."

Heat bloomed across Sage's cheeks. She hadn't expected to hear such praise, least of all from Sylvia. How was she supposed to respond to that? Should she thank her? Should she make a defense for Grey? He wasn't the misogynistic jerk everyone painted him to be. Sure, he was a bit rough around the edges, and had little patience for her newbie questions at times, but he'd also been equally generous with his praise. More so lately. In that moment, however, Sylvia's loaded compliment carried more weight than it should, and Sage couldn't reason why that was. She opened her mouth to speak but found that no words wanted to escape.

"Don't let it go to your head. I said you had potential." Sylvia's sharp tone brought her back to reality. "So what is your theory?"

Sage cleared her throat, testing her voice to see if it might cooperate. "There's a person of interest whom I think would make a possible ally in our investigation. Someone who has a philanthropic spirit, but likes to remain anonymous."

"I know a few people who match that description," Sylvia replied, casually perusing the stack of papers in her inbox.

"I'm sure you do. You know everyone," Sage said, throwing in a quick compliment of her own. "I don't want to come right out and scare this potential…friend…by approaching as ASSET in an official capacity."

"A smart idea."

"I have it on good authority that this person is planning to attend a specific party for Mabon." She hoped Sylvia might pick up on the connection to what she was truly asking.

"You want to attend this party, or work the party in order to better understand this potential ally before approaching them?" Sylvia asked.

"That's where I get hung up." Sage picked at her nails and sent her gaze around the room as she worked out how to make her thoughts come out clearly. "Both plans allow for close proximity."

"But one reveals your true nature." Sylvia wasted no time in her reply. "If you attend a party as yourself, you are blatantly stating that ASSET is involved. Your people are pretty easy to spot." She pointed to Sage's arm. "And if that weren't a giveaway, your eyes are also a very unique and revealing color."

That had been Sage's fear. Masked ball or not, there were still ways she could be spotted as a Terra. "I would run into similar issues as a worker, then, too?"

Sylvia's gaze returned to the papers on her desk. She made a good show of moving them around as she quietly contemplated her answer. That gave Sage confidence. The shadowrunner would have answered immediately otherwise.

"On the one hand," —Sylvia tapped her fingernail against the wood of the desk—"workers are often in uniform. Your mark could easily be concealed. And hardly anyone pays attention to the staff, so I'd be willing to wager that no one would pay attention to your eyes."

"That helps me a lot."

"If I may ask. Whose party are you planning to crash?"

"Wish I could say."

"Of course. ASSET being ASSET."

"Thank you." Sage pushed herself up from the seat, ready to leave, confident in the direction she'd take for this mission.

"On the other hand…"

Sylvia's words stopped her in her tracks.

"If you were thinking of attending any of the more upscale parties, I should warn you their catering service and wait staff are all employed from within the specific families hosting the event."

Dammit. There was always a catch. And if what Sylvia had said were true, which it most likely was, then she'd just killed the plan before Sage could get it off the ground. Sage retook her seat.

"Better you figure that out now, rather than find out the hard way."

There had to be another way. If ASSET had not been invited to a party, there was a reason. She couldn't count on Grey to get them in. Working that kind of magic was not something she thought him capable of. Not with the way he seemed to repel people. She had to approach this from another angle.

"Why would these host families make their people work the event rather than enjoy the celebration themselves?"

"Serving is an honor." Sylvia appeared as if she were shocked to hear Sage ask such an obvious question. "Especially for those who wish to rise in the ranks."

"Ranks?"

"Think of the four families of magic like big corporations. One must first begin as an intern, then maybe they can be hired on for seasonal work, and if they prove themselves competent, they may be given a full-time position."

"Sounds less like business and more like the mob."

"We don't go around taking out members of other families." Smoke began to form around Sylvia. She replied with a sharpness in her tone that confirmed Sage had taken it a teensy bit far with her last little quip. "Our aim is always the betterment of magic as well as our people."

"Purely altruistic intentions, eh?" Sage didn't believe that for a minute. "Then how do the Mystics fit in?"

Smoke thickened as Sylvia's body faded into it. Her voice, however, remained sharp as a blade. "The Mystics are not a family. They operate independently, and against the natural order."

She'd already stuck her foot in her mouth and pissed Sylvia off, so no point in backpedaling. Sage continued to press for clarification. "You mean to tell me there is no mixing of the magical families? What happens if an ethereal and an elemental fall in love?"

"They get married," Sylvia said without any hint of irony.

"And any children they might have?"

"What are you hoping I will reveal with this line of questioning?" Sylvia met Sage's eyes with a determined glare. "Do you know how mixed magic is these days?

No one is purely one thing or another. Our people go where they can best use their skills."

"Innocent questioning, I assure you." Sage held her hands in surrender as she stood again, ready to leave before she really angered the shadowrunner. "I'm still new, as everyone points out to me. I should be entitled to ask a few dumb questions every now and again."

"You're fast running out of time for that excuse, Miss Cynwrig. Crack a book every now and again. ASSET has plenty to choose from."

"Yes, ma'am." Sage turned to the door. "Thank you again for your counsel."

"Sage," Sylvia called.

Hearing her name spoken so calmly after the heat of their conversation stopped Sage in her tracks.

"Yes?" She turned her head enough to make eye contact but kept herself pointed at the door just in case she needed to make a break for it.

"If you can keep these talks between you and me, you are welcome to my counsel anytime you need."

Not the response Sage had expected to hear, but better than she could have hoped for. The shadowrunner was a well-connected ally to have. Sage nodded and quickly took her leave.

Mabon would be here before she knew it, and Sage still needed to find a way into that party.

FOURTEEN

Home sweet home. Sage unlocked the door to her new apartment, not sure what she'd really intended to do there. It was still empty. She hadn't even begun to look at furniture, not that she'd had much time to do that. She'd been so wrapped up in the mystery of the Mystics, nothing else seemed to matter. But as she opened the door into her dark and empty home, she realized taking time to settle her life needed to be a priority. And who didn't love a little online binge shopping. Put that renter's insurance money to good use and pick out some nice things.

The moment she stepped into the apartment, Sage knew someone else had been there…or maybe still was. A brown paper bag sat on the kitchen counter.

"Hello?" Sage called out softly.

"I didn't expect to see you here," Matt called out from the back bedroom.

The day had gotten away from her. How long had she spent riding the bus from ASSET to Sortilege and back home? Getting a car really did need to be added to her list of priorities.

"Nor I you." Hearing his voice brought a smile to her face. She pranced toward the hallway, eager for companionship after the day she'd had.

Matt came out of his room and wrapped her in his arms before Sage had the chance to utter another word. The warmth of his affection contrasted the cool kiss of his skin as he held her close. She rested her head against his chest, listening for the deathly slow beat of his heart.

"I think you needed that." Matt held her gently, allowing Sage to be the one to choose when to break their connection. "Want to talk about it?"

He always knew exactly what to say or do. No perfect man ever existed before him. The mold had been broken when he was born. Thank the gods he was chosen to be her best friend. She needed him. Probably more than he needed her.

Sage held tightly for a moment more before she pulled back and met his icy eyes. "Not sure I can talk. Even if I could, I'm not sure what to say."

"Sorry, I don't speak cryptic. You're going to have to translate," he teased.

"I was never meant to be a detective. I studied accounting. This job is so beyond me, at times I feel like I'm going to drown."

"And the drama queen award goes to…"

"Shut up."

"You were born for this. So you didn't study to be a detective directly. You chose one of the most analytical if not boring fields of education. So analyze the data you have. Solve for x."

"That's algebra."

"Whatever. It's numbers. If you can do that, you can do this. You just need to have all the variables."

"That's just it. I don't have variables. I have clues that go nowhere. I feel like I've been running into brick walls all day."

"Yeah, that was so much less cryptic. Thanks for explaining." Matt chuckled.

"Everything I do takes me down a dead end. I change directions but always end up in the same place. It's frustrating."

"I disagree."

"What would you call it, then?"

"Your job is action and adventure. At least as far as I've seen. You're living like The Doctor. Without all the timey-wimey business. Every day is some new kind of crazy, and you get to make sense of it."

"That's one way to put it. But am I The Doctor? I can't make sense of it. I'm just the companion riding along and trying not to die."

"You know better than most never to discredit the companion. They play more than just a witnessing role. Some have saved the universe… Many, in fact."

"Because they have the knowledge given to them to do so."

"And you do too. You just have to piece it together properly."

Sage sighed, allowing her shoulders to slump. No need to hide her feelings from Matt. "Maybe if I had a space time machine."

"You don't need one. You have a ton of excellent resources," Matt suggested, a little too strongly for Sage to ignore.

"More of these elusive variables you think I can make sense of. Do you know something you aren't telling me?" She narrowed her eyes, daring the vampire to lie. "Don't make me tickle it out of you."

A full belly laugh erupted from Matt's lips. She hadn't heard that sound from him in a while. It worked like a salve on her mood, lifting her ever-so-slightly from the doldrums.

Still giggling at her threat, Matt lifted his hands in mock surrender. "I know nothing, I swear. I'm not yet invested enough into the coven for them to start letting me in on their secrets."

"You're a bartender. Secrets are your business." She lifted her hands, but unlike Matt, hers were poised and wiggling, ready to strike at his most ticklish spot.

"Mercy. I beg you. I know nothing." He backed away, feigning fear, but laughter remained at the edge of his voice. "Zack did ask me something odd the other day. Maybe it has to do with your brick wall. Or maybe he is planning to whisk you off your feet in another attempt to woo you."

"Okay…" She dropped her hands. "Out with it."

"Do you dance?" Matt eyed her curiously, as if hanging on her next words.

Matt knew very well that she had two left feet. He could have answered that question for Zack. For a man claiming to not speak cryptic, he made a pretty good messenger. "What does that vampire know that he's not telling me?" *And why hadn't he come out and said say something when they were at the bar last night?*

"Maybe we go ask him," Matt offered.

"Do you know what he's doing?"

"Officially, no."

"Unofficially?" Why was Matt being so evasive? That annoyed Sage more than the wild goose chase Zack seemed to be sending her on. How dare he use her best friend against her?

"He appears to be distancing himself publicly," Matt suggested. "Not just from you and Grey. He's hardly been by the bar. The other night when you guys came by had been the first and last I'd seen him in more than a week."

"Did he say why?" That wasn't like Zack at all. He might as well have been a public figure as much time as he spent mingling in the magical community. "You're his ward or whatever."

"He's not really said anything. This is just my observation." Matt shrugged, but Sage wasn't buying his attempt at looking casual. Either Matt knew more than he was letting on, or he was truly as in the dark as he claimed and was powerless to do anything but play messenger. "He sent me to stay at the coven. With the thin excuse of needing to bond with them." He rolled his eyes as he made air quotes with his fingers.

"He's distancing himself from you, then, too," she observed.

"Physically, yes. But he's been in constant contact with me as my sire." Matt held up his phone as proof. "Keeping tabs, so I don't think he's trying to avoid me. Maybe just the people I am most likely to be around... You."

How could one little floating bus have such a wide ripple effect in the magical community? ASSET weren't the ones who magicked that bus into the air? They couldn't have known it was going to happen? Even the best spy networks in the world couldn't have predicted something so asinine. But somehow they were being blamed, and everywhere Sage went, she found members of the magical community pulling away as if being associated with ASSET were some kind of contagious disease. Zack of all people. Slippery as he was, she'd have never expected to hear him being one of those now hiding from her.

"Where is he now?" she asked.

Matt picked up his phone and sent a message. "Give me a few minutes to find out."

Maybe there was a way to salvage the day after all. She might not have all the answers, but getting at least one was better than the constant stream of failures she'd been experiencing.

"Hey, don't look so worried. I'll get ahold of him." Matt nudged her shoulder. "Have I ever let you down?"

Matt's phone buzzed before Sage had the opportunity to respond. She turned her gaze to the tiny screen.

Is she with you? I'm on my way.

"He's coming here?" Sage asked, confused.

"No one knows where we live. Best place for anonymity." Matt replied.

He was right. Mostly. With their apartment burned to the ground, she and Matt had been rendered homeless. Looking around the empty space where they both were standing, the feeling of homelessness still seemed to be the case. But they did have a roof over their heads.

New to them as it was, Sage was willing to bet, aside from Grey and Josh, there was at least one other person aware of the magical realm who knew where they lived. If he had survived their last encounter. She could kick herself for not visiting him sooner. She owed him more than a simple thank you. If not for his sacrifice, Sage's adventure might have ended in that burned-out husk that was her old apartment. The craziness of the last few weeks had made it all but impossible to stop in for a visit, but now she had no excuse. Times like these, she needed to keep all her allies close.

"Do I have time to pop out for a quick minute?" Sage asked.

Matt stared down at her like a lost little puppy. "Somewhere better to be?"

"Kind of. Sorry. I just had an idea and need to see it through really quickly." Sage made a break for the front door. "I won't be long. I promise. If Zack gets here before I get back, keep him busy."

FIFTEEN

She sprinted down the path heading toward the barricaded construction site where her old apartment had once stood. Stuck somewhere between demolition and reconstruction, the building was an eyesore that couldn't be hidden, even under the cloak of night.

Up a flight of stairs across from her old home, Sage spotted lights in a familiar apartment, and a lone figure standing in the shadows of the balcony smoking a cigarette.

"I always know where to find you." Sage approached cautiously, keeping her tone light and friendly.

"Glad to see you're still alive as well." Luke stepped forward into the light. "Pretty close call last time."

"Don't pretend you didn't already know that." She closed in, wanting to give him a hug, but their friendship had never quite reached that level of familiarity. "You deal in information, don't you?"

Luke didn't look much like he wanted a hug from her. He stood stiffly, keeping his cigarette close to his lips. "When the right client comes along." He took a long drag from his cigarette. Burning embers briefly cast his face in an orange glow.

"Any of those clients lately?"

"Sadly, no." He flicked his cigarette to the ground and stamped it out with his boot.

"At least you're up and walking." She softened her tone, hoping to shift the mood of the conversation.

"Had a bit of help there." Luke patted his thigh.

Sage noticed the ring. Dark metal. His old talisman, on the third finger of his left hand. "Wishes?"

"I'm not in that business any longer. You saw to that personally, remember?" He held up his hand, showing the ring proudly. "All that remains from that part of my life are memories and trinkets."

She'd expected him to be a little grumpy with her for not visiting sooner, but the frosty reception she was getting from the former Djinn seemed a little over the top. Was he, too, among those actively avoiding ASSET association? Even if that were true, why here of all places?

"You still have friends." She tried again to turn the conversation, hoping that by claiming that friendship, he might relax.

"Not nearly as many as you might think." Luke sighed.

"So who helped you with the leg?"

"EMTs were very nice. Doctors too. But the nurses…" A satisfied grin cracked through the stony expression Luke had been wearing. "Ahh, they were the best part. Still aches a bit when I walk around too much, but it's healing."

"No magical help?"

"I have no magic."

Talking with Luke used to be a lot easier. Something was going on. He couldn't be that mad at her for not visiting sooner. He knew the kind of trouble she had been in. She'd tried nice. That had got her nowhere, and she only had a few minutes before the vampire would arrive. Plan B.

"Why are you being so evasive?"

Luke crossed his arms, and stared down his nose at her. "What are you after?"

"A little banter with my friendly neighborhood djinn." She groaned with frustration. "Look, I just came to say thank you for helping, and to see how you were doing. But clearly I've made myself a pariah, so I'll go and let you rest."

"I didn't mean to be rude." Luke blew out a breath and let his arms fall to his sides. "I think it's time for my next dose of pain meds. I get cranky. Don't take offense."

"Do you want me to see if ASSET can help you? After all, without you, I'd have never made it. I owe you."

"I told you we were even, and I meant it." His tone softened, and it seemed his entire body relaxed. "But thanks for the offer."

He was hiding something. Even relaxed as he appeared at that moment, Sage saw through the ruse. She wasn't going to get him to say it out loud, either, that much she was sure of. But maybe with a little time, he'd reveal what was causing him to close up.

"I mean it." She used her most reassuring voice. "I have your back, when you need it. And I hope I can still count on you in the future, to have my back."

"Of course. We're neighbors." He smiled but the sincerity wasn't there in his eyes. "I'll stop by next time I need a cup of sugar."

"You do that." Sage turned to leave with yet another question to ponder. She'd have to add Luke's recent frostiness to her list of dead ends. But in the spirit of giving off a friendly vibe, she offered a, "Happy Mabon to you," as she turned to wander back to her new apartment.

"Your people celebrate that?" Luke asked.

"So I've been told." She glanced over her shoulder. "Been invited to a party, but I'm having a bit of a Cinderella problem."

"What kind of party?" he asked.

"Masked ball."

"Oh, that is fancy."

He seemed more interested in the Mabon party than anything else she had asked him. Sage had to wonder if there was a connection.

"Yeah, but I might not be able to go. You know… Apartment burned down and all my clothes with it."

Luke started to laugh. A sound she did not expect to hear, nor appreciated given the reason he was laughing. She turned on him, all pretense of playing nice fading with each step as she closed in.

"Something funny about that?" she growled.

"Actually, yes." He chuckled again despite the angry glare she'd given him. "I might actually be able to grant that wish."

Her eyes flew open, wide as they could. Had she heard him right? "You have your magic back? But you just said…"

"No, silly." The smile that stretched across his face was more than genuine. "You do remember my…girlfriend?"

"How could I forget?" she answered suspiciously, not quite understanding his meaning.

"She had a thing for fancy designers and pretty trinkets. It's actually how she lured me into service. Or maybe it was the other way round."

"Get to the point, if there is one?"

"Small wishes don't eat up much of one's soul, but they start the magical contract." He shrugged. "Want to come in and have a peek around the closet? See the spoils of your victory over her?"

"Are you kidding me? That would be amazing." It was Sage's turn to smile. She might not be going home with information, but she wouldn't leave empty-handed. Small victories.

He led her into his apartment, opening up what should have been a bedroom door. Inside had been converted to a walk-in closet, stocked like an upscale thrift shop. Racks of clothes, purses, shoes, and all manner of girly things had been neatly arranged by color and size.

"She was a shifter of sorts, so she had a wide variety of sizes. You're about what? Six?" Luke asked without the usual hesitation men showed when commenting on a lady's size.

"Sure. Let's go with that," she agreed, gawking at the luxuries she could have never afforded herself. All hanging there, just begging to be worn.

"Grab anything you like, as much as you want. You deserve it after losing your home."

"Why are you still holding on to all of this?"

"When I don't have active clients to…ah…watch out for…" He cleared his throat. "I've been selling it off bit by bit to pay the bills. That pair of shoes right there. The strappy gold things. I just sold the same ones in silver to cover this month's rent."

Based on the stock he had in the apartment, Luke could be set for quite a few years.

"You sure?" she asked, already eyeing a few dresses.

"Whatever you want." Luke held out a duffel bag. "We are friends, after all, aren't we?"

Djinn were tricksters. With or without magic. A small part of her wondered what repercussions might come from accepting his generosity. "Friends. Yes."

SIXTEEN

Sage returned to her apartment, her arms weighed down with two duffel bags of designer clothes and shoes. Zack had gotten there before her. She found him standing with Matt in the middle of the empty living room. Their sudden silence as she opened the door rendered her instantly suspicious. She'd been doing that with everyone, it seemed, and stopped herself from uttering something pissy. What if that had been part of the Mystics' plan all along? Turn everyone against her kind and force all Terras to become suspicious of everyone they crossed paths with. Zack had come for a reason. And starting off the conversation with negative words wasn't going to help matters.

"Killer. I've been looking forward to a private visit with you." The look Zack gave her bordered on hungry as he strutted across the room toward Sage, his hand held out.

Burdened as she was with her new treasures, she could not accept his offered hand.

Matt moved in a blur behind Zack, escaping into the safety of his room, leaving her to fend for herself with the rogue vampire. *Damn him.*

"You're still a little mad at me. I get it. Please, what can I do to make it up to you?" Zack asked, his hand still hanging in the air.

"Excuse me for a moment." She brushed past him as she headed to her bedroom to set down the bags. "What was the wild goose chase you sent us on all about?"

"That was a gift of information," Zack said flippantly. "Did you not open it?"

"Oh, we talked to the little man, but I fail to see how that was supposed to help our case," Sage grumbled, hoping her annoyed tone would push him to be more forthcoming. "He went on and on about some silly horse."

"Where did that horse come from? Did you figure it out?" Zack chuckled, the riddle-maker reveling in his victory of subterfuge.

"How am I supposed to know if we figured it out? We had nothing to go on."

"You had plenty if you read between the lines. But if you'd like a little help, I am at your service." Zack narrowed his eyes, his brow crinkled, giving a sense of unnatural age to his immortal face. "And what is with all of those shopping bags?"

"My clothes burned up in the fire," she said gruffly.

"No time to decipher clues, but you had time to go shopping?"

"Don't be stupid. A friend donated some items for me to wear."

"I saw the sparkle in the depths of those bags. Those are not street clothes. Whatever could you need with fancy dresses?"

"Well, well, aren't we nosy?" She allowed a little snark to seep into her voice. "Mabon, if you must know."

"Which party are we attending?" Zack hit the nail on the head. Damn him, he always knew what was going on. Of course he would know about the parties for Mabon.

"There is no *we*. And I don't need to tell you that my job requires a certain level of anonymity."

"You have every reason not to want to trust me, Sage, but I have only ever acted with your best interest in mind. I wouldn't dream of damaging your anonymity."

Zack sounded sincere. She wanted to believe him, but that was his game, and he was an expert-level player.

"Thanks for that," Sage replied politely.

"What party are you attending?" Zack asked again, a little stronger.

"I can't divulge."

"This isn't general curiosity. I know you're on the trail of the Mystics. That was the reason I sent you to Travis."

"Then be helpful and explain your reasons because I learned nothing from the little Púca."

"Distrust I can accept, but there is no need to be rude." Zack's voice turned dark.

She had been a tiny bit rude. "Sorry. Stress." She hoped the excuse would be enough. Weak as it was, it was better than admitting she was deliberately venting her anger.

"I've heard word of some recruitment happening at a special party. One hosted by the richest of the rich.

And damn near impossible to get into unless you know the right people."

"Was Travis one of those right people?" she asked.

"No."

"Then who? Because I fail to see the connection."

"You're not that dumb, so stop playing like you are. Do you want a ticket into this party or not?"

"If you were able to get me into the right party, then why all the subterfuge?"

"Because I can't be seen with you right now. The same people who would invite me to such parties would frown upon my continued association with those they are working against."

"Forget the party. Give me names. That's really all I need."

"If I had names, I would give them to you."

"But you were invited by someone."

"And you assume that someone is part of the organization?"

"Wouldn't they be?"

"Not necessarily. As I understand it, they are a curious party willing to host an event."

"I don't really see the difference."

"Then you should not go."

"I could just have you brought in and questioned at ASSET."

"Is that how you operate now? Perhaps I was right after all in distancing myself."

"What am I supposed to do? I have Ava breathing down my neck. The whole city is in a state of unease, and until we can figure out who these Mystics are, it's not going to get better."

"It's not going to get better if you show the people that ASSET is willing to lock up the innocent in an effort to cover their asses."

"That's not what I'm doing."

"Are you? You ask for names so you can go in guns blazing without proof."

"No one said anything about guns. I would never. I just want to…investigate."

"Which is why I made the offer to help you get into the party."

"But you won't tell me who your contact is? Someone actively gathering people outside of ASSET's gaze."

"You want to see what is going on under your organization's nose, I will help you do that. Learn the true intentions of these people."

"Even if that means putting myself at risk to do so?"

"There is minimal risk in observing. This is a masked ball," Zack said. "With the right amount of cloaking, no one will recognize you. And as long as you are simply observing and learning the truth, no one will have reason to suspect otherwise."

She understood his reasoning, though she didn't exactly agree with it. He'd painted a bleak picture of the ASSET organization. One she'd heard echoed multiple times in her short career. Almost from day one on the job, she'd witnessed the grousing of those in the various magical families regarding her people acting like tyrannical rulers rather than upholding the law as they had been charged to do. Even if Zack did make the tiniest bit of sense, his plan left all the risk on her side of the table. But it did come with the invitation she had been seeking.

"Is there a reason you have been invited to such a gathering?" Sage asked. More to the point, could she trust that Zack wasn't leading her into a trap? What was in it for him to make such an offer?

"I'm well-known around the city as one who lives in the gray places of society." He shrugged. "Perhaps this is meant to lure me over to their side."

"And you're entertaining this option?"

"Who am I to pass up an exclusive gathering?" Zack waggled his eyebrows with mischievous excitement. "Mixing and mingling with potential new clients. Yes, please."

"Who are you really?"

"I assure you, I am not entertaining joining the Mystics or anything like that. Anarchy is bad for business," he said. "I just love a good party."

"How many people can you bring in?" She wasn't about to go in alone. He had to know that. And yet, the look on his face said otherwise. Zack might have promised himself as an ally, but she needed more security than words.

"I… Wait… What?" He stood with wide-eyed surprise for a moment. Brief as it was, Sage enjoyed seeing the vampire off his game. "That is not where I thought the conversation would be going, but I could certainly get you in if that's what you need."

"Grey too," Sage demanded.

Zack's expression darkened, and the smile that stretched across his face appeared more strained than genuine. "Of course he'd be joining us too. Your partner. How is Grey boy?"

"Don't pretend you're best buddies. Can you do it?"

"As you wish." Zack bowed with a flourish. "But when I do this, you must agree to wipe the slate clean between us. Friends again." He stepped in close enough to whisper in her ear, "Second chances."

His proximity and the daggers that came with it sent a shiver down her spine. She tried to force the unease at bay. The last time he'd gotten this close, he'd been threatening to bleed her and drink her blood. The time before that, he had. The memory of his tongue gliding across her open wounds resurfaced with another cold chill.

She moved away quickly, backing against the wall. "Friends, yeah."

Matt's bedroom door opened. He poked his head out and met Sage's wary eyes. "Are we ready for a fashion show?"

His smile was infectious, melting away some of her unease. Though she'd rather have had him with her during that awkward conversation rather than hiding in his room.

Zack backed away. "Let me make some calls."

"You do your work. I'll do mine." Matt ushered Sage into her room and closed the door behind them.

An hour and fifteen dresses later, Sage emerged from the bedroom wearing a red two-piece dress that hugged every one of her curves. She ran toward the bathroom mirror and admired the way the elaborate crystal beading woven through the halter-style bodice picked up and reflected the small amount of light in the room. Beading continued in an intricate, lacy pattern around the waist and curves of her hips on the floor-length skirt. A slit high enough to make her nervous about a wardrobe malfunction allowed her leg to peek out as she walked.

"Are you sure about this?" Sage asked. Never in her life had she dared to wear something so blatantly sexy.

Matt's expression said plenty. But it was a whistle from the doorway that sealed the deal.

She turned to see Zack, fangs on full display.

"It will be a very happy Mabon, indeed," the vampire said.

"I'll take that as a compliment."

"You should." He stepped into the hallway outside of the bathroom and handed her a silver masquerade mask. "You're going to need this for the party."

"Incognito accomplished." The mask was a relief. Naked as she felt in the dress, at least she'd be able to maintain some anonymity with her features concealed.

"Feel free to congratulate me. I have arranged for two friends to attend with me."

"Together, then?"

"Is that a problem?" Zack asked.

"This should be fun."

"Took the words out of my mouth," he agreed. "But I can't be seen strolling in with two Terras. You'll need to hide your birthmark, for obvious reasons."

"Leave that to me. With the right makeup, I can hide anything," Matt offered. "And I have a perfect idea for your hair.'"

"My work here is done. And as a sign of my enduring friendship, I'll make the night even more special and pick you up in a limo." Zack quickly took hold of her hand and pulled it to his lips. "Perhaps a corsage too? It will be like prom. That's a thing, right?"

"Don't forget Grey." Sage yanked her hand away.

"Who could forget him?" Zack turned toward the door. "Third wheel," he mumbled as he made his exit.

"Glad I'm not going with you two." Matt chuckled. "Awkward."

"You can say that again."

"Don't worry. When I'm through with you, every man at that party will be wanting a dance. You won't have time for Zack's antics."

"You might want to tone it down a bit. Remember, this is a covert operation. I don't necessarily want every man in the room trying to figure out who I am."

"Right. Well, I do have standards to maintain, but I'll make sure you're not totally irresistible."

"My life is in your hands," Sage said. "No pressure."

SEVENTEEN

Sleeping on the floor had given Sage a stiff back and a neck ache she never wanted to experience again. She spent her morning bus ride into ASSET ordering herself a new pillow-top mattress and feather pillows, thanking the gods for the miracle of next day delivery! Might not be instantaneous, but it was magic enough for her.

Aching as she was, Sage knew she'd get no sympathy from anyone at ASSET. Devon least of all. He'd ordered her in for training, and that always ended with screaming muscles. Breakfast of coffee and painkillers would have to suffice. But even with that looming over her head, Sage came into ASSET with a smile.

She planned to start her day with positivity. Her serendipitous success with Zack was well worth a little celebration. She searched for Grey to tell him the good news before she hit the mats with Devon, and he knocked the happy right out of her.

She expected to find him hunched over the computer, where he had been nearly every day of the past week. But he wasn't there, or in the breakroom, or the infirmary. Sage made a pass by Ava's office, listening at the closed door to see if she recognized the voices within.

Finally she pulled out her phone and sent him a message, demanding he reply quickly. Her excitement waning, Sage headed to her temporary room in the barracks and grabbed her workout clothes.

A knock came seconds before her door opened.

"Hey," Sage screamed, struggling to pull her pants on before the whole of ASSET saw her in her underwear. Her foot slipped and sent her crashing into the bed.

Grey erupted into laughter as he slipped in and closed the door behind him.

Sage scrambled to get to her feet and finish dressing with what was left of her dignity.

"Wait for me to say come in next time." She growled the words at first, but couldn't maintain the angry tone. If she had been in his shoes, watching him tumble ass over feet, clothes flying through the air, she'd have died of laughter.

Grey cleared his throat and wiped the grin from his face. "Sorry. I didn't know you were getting dressed. The message you sent me sounded urgent."

She forced herself to face him despite embarrassment burning her cheeks.

Grey looked out of place. No. Not that. Different. His clothes were far too casual. She'd never seen him wear a tank top and sweat pants. At least not at the office. Where was his leather jacket and jeans? Or his steel-toe boots? And why wasn't he wearing his hat? Casual wasn't a bad look on him, but it was a curiosity.

"Where have you been?"

"You're not the only one with a training schedule. We all have to maintain our physique and combat skills." He crossed his arms as he stared down at her. She'd never noticed before how well-defined his biceps were. Muscles he'd always managed to keep hidden behind sleeves were now on full display. He'd clearly been keeping up on that part of his physique.

If only she could have been a fly on the wall during his training session. Grey was a proven warrior. Watching him go toe-to-toe with Devon would make for quite a show.

"That's me next," she said.

"I know. Devon's waiting." Grey sat down on her bed and rested his back against the wall. "But first, what is your urgent news?"

"I've got us a way into the Mabon party," she announced proudly.

She'd expected a reaction of some kind. A smile, an atta girl… Hell, she'd take a snarky reply, something to indicate he'd heard her, but Grey just sat there, staring blankly. The wheels might be turning inside his head, but nothing was happening on the outside. She might as well have been speaking to him in a foreign language for all the reaction he'd given her.

"Aren't you going to ask me how?"

"Nope. Don't need to."

"Killjoy." She wasn't going to let his sour mood ruin her proud moment. "I had a speech and everything planned."

"Last time we talked, you had tasked me with that, if I recall."

Not the reaction she'd expected at all. He should have been happy hearing her news. Instead, he sounded as if she'd kicked his puppy.

"And now you come back saying you've taken care of it yourself? We're supposed to be partners, Sage."

She softened her tone, hoping to smooth away his disappointment with the truth. "I wasn't trying to undermine you. Call it serendipity or whatever. Right place, right time, right people, and all the puzzle pieces came together."

"Somehow I doubt that."

"Really? That's the attitude you're taking?" Sage threw her hands on her hips.

"I wish you hadn't gone to the vampire without me." His disappointed tone smacked of jealousy from where Sage was standing. And this was not the time to get all bent out of shape over Zack of all people.

"If I'm being honest, it wasn't my idea. It just sort of happened."

"Which is why you don't deserve the praise you're so eager to claim."

"Someone piss in your cereal this morning? Devon hit you a little too hard? Why are you being such an ass today?"

Springs under the mattress creaked and groaned under Grey's weight as he leaned forward. "You do understand we're supposed to operate undercover, right?"

She'd had the same thought, but without Zack's assistance, they'd have never found their way into the party. Sometimes undercover work meant using one's resources wisely, and the vampire was one of the best connected weasels in the magical community.

"This is Zack we're talking about."

"He deals in information for profit," Grey reminded her.

"Thank you, Captain Obvious." This was not how she'd expected this conversation to go at all. Nor did she see a way to shift the tone of it.

Sage eyed the door. If she was going to get beaten up, better she was on the mats in the training hall with Devon than taking her lumps with her temperamental partner.

"While we're on the subject… You didn't think it odd that he not only knew the exact party we were trying to get into, but also that the Mystics were involved?"

"I'm not an idiot despite your current attempt to paint me so." Sage fought to control her temper.

"And how is it that Zack, of all people, can not only attend, but request personal invites to such a party?" Grey asked.

"Why don't you ask him yourself? You're coming with us." She threw the words at him.

"That's not very secretive, now is it? Waltzing in with him of all people. We're supposed to be going undercover, Sage!"

"If you're going to keep speaking to me like I'm stupid, you can leave." She slashed a finger toward the door. "I'm doing the best I can with the resources I have. Tell me, could you have done better?"

Grey opened his mouth as if to argue, but no words came out.

She stared him down, seething in anger, well aware that this would be a dangerous mission without his constant insistence she lacked the mental fortitude to handle herself. She'd been ready to lay her whole plan out for him. Proud of the angles she'd already factored in. But now, more than anything, she wanted to shove that plan down her partner's throat with the hope he'd choke on it and his pride as well. So much for her day starting on the right foot.

"Are you ready to listen? Or are you going to continue being a pig-headed jerk bent on steamrolling over me before I have a chance to explain my plan?"

He waved his hand as if giving her permission to speak.

"This is a masked ball," she began. "Our faces will be hidden. No one should know who we are by sight. We can use makeup to hide our marks." She held up her hand and covered her wrist with the other as a visual aid in case Grey wanted to continue acting as thick as a brick wall. "No one should spot us as Terras. The same can be done with our eyes. We just need a pair of color-changing lenses to wear. You can buy those just about anywhere these days. With that, we will keep our identities secret. As for Zack, he did not give our names. He simply requested invites. We are his plus two. Anonymous," she said the word loud and slow, so there could be no reason for him to claim he didn't hear it. "And if we are there to simply observe and learn, there is no need for this party to become dangerous. We just have to blend in."

Grey nodded; his stern scowl softened. "As plans go, it's not terrible."

"You really want me to pop you upside your head, don't you?" She sneered. "How hard is it for you to say something nice?"

"But you're so cute when you're angry."

"Shut up." She wasn't about to fall for Grey's weak attempt to flirt his way out of her anger.

"Sorry if I upset you." He met her eyes, daring to hold her gaze. "I don't think you're an idiot."

He at least sounded sincere that time. She let herself relax and took a seat next to him on her bed. "Thanks."

"You have to admit, you do a lot of stupid things."

So much for his short-lived attempt at being nice. "Quit while you're ahead."

"Admit it, you don't always listen to advice." He nudged her with his elbow, but she wasn't ready to be playful. Not yet.

"Careful now," she grumbled. *Here we go again.* "I'm getting more adorable by the minute."

"Despite all of that, your instincts are good, and your heart is in the right place."

"Not really making good on your original statement, are you? It really is impossible for you to just say something nice. Isn't it?"

"I am. Are you listening?"

"To you, pointing out every one of my flaws, yeah. That's making me feel so much better about our conversation."

"I'm trying to point out your strengths. You have a way of seeing things from a different perspective, which, while difficult at times, is extremely important."

"Just stop with the backhanded compliments. I'm getting a headache."

"I feel the same way about you dealing one-on-one with Zack."

There it was. Jealousy rearing its head. He would never admit to it, but she could see how much it burned him that she spoke with Zack without him there to chaperone.

"Don't get all worried. Matt was there. He came to my apartment."

"I really don't like that." Grey's jaw tightened.

"He's Matt's sire."

"He doesn't have to be that close. What's his angle?"

"Aside from making sure his charge is behaving? He's got to get in his daily quota for flirting. He claims to have a soft spot for me and wants to be friends." She turned away, snickering silently, knowing she'd just poked the bear.

"Nothing soft about his feelings for you."

"So your objection to him is testosterone-based, then?" she teased, having no intention of acting on the vampire's flirtations. She couldn't pass up the opportunity to needle Grey about it since he'd all but confirmed his jealousy though.

"Do we have to remain with Zack the entire party?"

Finally a real question. She hadn't actually figured that part out, but it was worth confirming next time she had the chance to speak with Zack. "He's getting us through the doors, as far as I know."

"I still don't like it."

"Of course you don't, but we do what we have to do, right? Use whatever resources we have available. Get in, learn what we can. Get out."

Grey blew out a breath in frustration. "Atta girl. There. You happy?"

"Next time, try and make it sound a little more convincing, okay?" She smirked.

"No promises."

"You don't always have to be a jerk. It would be comforting, on occasion, to see a softer side of you."

"Now you're onto something." Grey jumped to his feet. A mischievous smirk stretched across his face. Of all the things she'd said, that got a rise out of him?

"You planning to embrace your gentler side?"

"Masks aren't enough to completely hide us from scrutiny. We need to adopt totally new personas. A cover story. New name, new family, and some believable form of magic if we need to prove ourselves."

He was onto something. Sage hadn't thought that part through. And she had to admit, pretending to be someone she wasn't sounded kind of exciting. But that brought its own complications to the table.

"We have no magic, so how can we fake it?"

"Might not have to. We could adopt a persona of someone with non-active powers." He pulled out his phone and started tapping out a message. "We'll have to look into the recent additions to our prison to see if we can match anyone."

"I love it when a plan comes together."

"Don't love it yet. We still have a little work to do if we're going to make your plan a success, starting with a plausible cover story, or we won't make it much past the front door."

"I have faith in you." That's the attitude she'd been hoping for. Planning and cooperation. She'd have loved to continue that spirit of camaraderie, but Devon was waiting and he'd make her pay for every moment of his time she wasted. "I expect when I get back from my training session, you'll have wrapped up all the loose ends."

He angled his head toward her suspiciously. "Buttering me up for something? What else haven't you told me?"

"Can't a girl just offer positive reinforcement?"

"No. Not when that girl is you."

"I was hoping to lead by example." She huffed. "Remind me not to do that again. Being nice is wasted on you."

"Did you miss your morning cup of coffee today?"

She headed for the door. "Three cups and I'm still not one hundred percent. But when has that ever stopped me?"

"Where do you think you're going?" he asked. "We're not done with our plan."

"Training with Devon, remember?"

A clown-like grin stretched across Grey's face. He chuckled as if reaching the punchline of a joke only he knew. "It's a good thing you'll be wearing a mask at the party."

"Why?"

"It's black tie, not black eye."

"That was bad. Even for you." She left the room shaking her head at his pathetic attempt at humor.

He had a point though. The party was a day away, and she didn't need any fresh bruises for Matt to try and cover with makeup. He already had enough magic to work getting her party-ready.

EIGHTEEN

Devon sat cross-legged in the center of the room, waiting for her.

"Grey says you should go easy on me today." Sage couldn't even get the words out with a straight face.

Devon chuckled right along with her. "You want easy?"

Smiles and laughter were the last thing she had expected. She tried to look innocent as she came to stand in front of her trainer. "If it's an option, yes, please."

His amused expression turned sinister as he pointed to the floor. "Drop and give me twenty."

Push-ups? Of all the exercises she could have been forced to do. Arms were the weakest part of her body. But she had no choice. She'd asked for this. Sage placed her palms on the mats and set herself into a plank position. Her weight stretched the scars on her hand. Not quite pain, but the sensation reminded her that she was not yet at her full strength, even if she wanted everyone else to think she was. Just like the scars on her neck, this would forever be a reminder of the damage that had been done to her in the line of duty.

"These will not be normal push-ups. I don't want you racing to the finish." Devon circled her as he spoke. "You will go slowly. Concentrate on your movement. Be purposeful, controlled, and most of all, silent. I don't want to hear grunting. Any sounds of effort."

One, two…three. Muscles strained as she struggled to slow herself. *Four…five.* She kept the silent tally of each rep as her muscles began to burn.

"Embrace the pain. Don't fight it. You can do nothing to prevent it. Endure…until it's over," he ordered.

Six…seven… Her arms vibrated with the strain. She pushed through each rep with a deep breath in and out. *Eight…nine.*

"Slower," Devon demanded. "This is an exercise in control, Sage, not a race to the finish."

Damn him. If she'd been allowed to go at a normal pace, she'd have been done. No. Damn her. She'd asked for it. She shouldn't have said anything, even in jest. This was her punishment. She had only herself to blame for the fire spreading across her chest.

Ten. Halfway through. Sage focused on that to give her the strength to finish. *All downhill from here. Eleven.*

"Do you hate me yet?" Devon taunted.

Twelve. Answering him would require breath she needed to keep her laborious pace. And anything she might think to say would only earn her more pain. *Thirteen, fourteen…fifteen.*

"Hold there. Plank position," Devon demanded.

Oh, for fucks sake, really? Sage nearly let slip the grunt of frustration, but held her breath. Somewhere in the back of her mind, she wondered if this was a test or if he was teaching her another lesson about knowing her limits. Their last training session he'd chided her for not easing into positions she was not ready for. Her arms shook violently as she fought to hold herself away from the ground. Fire spread from her chest down through her stomach, licking all the way to her thighs as she forced every muscle to work, holding her in place until Devon gave her permission to move again. No, this wasn't like the last lesson. This was a real test. He'd given her the order to hold. She'd better damn well do it. Failure would only make things worse. The tender spots on her hand began to ache as if the skin might split again. Still, she held.

"Good. Silence is the key here. Don't fight the pain. Don't count down the moments until it is over. Embrace it. Stay in the moment." Devon knelt in front of her. He lifted her chin and met her eyes. "When you are on an undercover assignment, you are at risk of being caught across enemy lines. That can mean facing unknown pain and torture. Should that be the case, you are required to keep your tongue."

Her arms threatened to go out from under her. She didn't know what was worse—holding the plank knowing she still had five more push-ups to do when he finally did tell her to go again, or the ominous truth of his words. She was going undercover…quite soon. Did he know more than he was willing to let on? When it came to Devon, the answer was almost always a yes. She clamped her jaw tight, gritting her teeth, fighting the groan trying to claw its way out of her throat.

"Mind over matter. Your arms are strong enough to hold your weight, even if your mind is telling you it can't be done."

If she could just hold for a few more minutes. She clenched her core muscles to try and stop the shakes, but her whole body trembled beyond control. All she could do was let it happen, and pray for Devon to release her quickly.

"Continue."

She let slip a sigh of relief, but it was short-lived. The moment she put her muscles into use, another sound came, ripping its way up her throat. Groaning, she pushed faster than intended, completing the last five before Devon could tell her to stop.

"What did I say about silence? Where is your control?"

Sage collapsed after the last push-up, crashing to the ground, welcoming the solid support of it as her entire body went still, and rested.

"Repeat the entire exercise, again. And this time, silently."

She gnashed her teeth, struggling to push herself back up. He had to be joking. Her arms were already jelly. She turned to face him, hoping he'd recant, but the stern look he gave her said enough. Get it done, or worse would follow.

Twenty push-ups didn't sound like all that much, until she was the one doing them. They might as well be a hundred or a million. Her muscles had already passed the point of fatigue. The tremors as she moved shook her entire body so violently she wasn't even sure if she were actually pushing herself up or down. Fire spread to every part of her body, lungs, arms, stomach—it all burned. Sage pushed on, groaning through the pain, not caring if Devon wanted silence. And when she collapsed the second time, she prayed he would release her.

"Two sets of twenty push-ups have nearly killed you." Devon didn't bother to hide the disappointment in his voice. "You lack stamina. But we'll get you there. I shouldn't see fatigue like this from you until you've at least hit one hundred push-ups."

That number was unfathomable. Even on her best day, she'd never done that many push-ups. Maybe if she worked up to it, sure. She wasn't even sure how she'd managed forty. What could she say? Words would do her no good. Begging, pleading, apologizing—none of it mattered. He wanted silence. His goading her to respond was just that, a test to see if she could hold her tongue under duress. It had to be.

"Again," he ordered.

Sage nearly let slip the curse dancing at the edge of her tongue. She couldn't hold back the groan, however, as she pushed herself back up.

She tried. Gave it her best effort, but after one strained press against the floor, gravity won the battle and she collapsed.

"Uttana Shishosana. You need to stretch your arms and back."

That required a level of flexibility she hadn't yet achieved, but dammit, she had to. He was right—her muscles needed to be stretched. If for nothing else, it might stop them from trembling. She moaned loudly with the effort it took to push herself into position.

"Silently. You want everyone around to know how big a baby you are? If you were injured and in enemy territory with no backup, would you give away your position?"

She held her breath, reaching out her arms as if grasping for freedom.

"Breathe!" Devon ordered. "Your muscles need air."

In and out, she filled her lungs and released her breath, fighting the pain until it eased into a deep stretch. She'd need more than a few yoga poses and deep breathing to quell the fire in her arms. But this was a start.

"As you may have guessed," — Devon came around and stood next to her — "we are beginning a new phase of your training. You've proven yourself a decent fighter. We continue to spar weekly to maintain practice, but considering your current assignment and going forward, I need you to learn how to overcome pain."

"Am I allowed to talk now?" Sage continued to hold her position. Her muscles felt looser now, still tender, but the fire had died down.

"Only if what you say will add to the conversation. I don't want to hear any bellyaching."

"Thank you." Not the words she had intended to say, but they came out before other choice phrases.

"Was that meant to be funny?" Devon asked.

"I wouldn't dare."

"Yes, you would, Captain Trainwreck. But this time, I think you've learned at least one part of my lesson, so I'll let it slide."

"Not quite the kind of lesson I expected to learn here," Sage said.

"Your current assignment requires improvement on your current skill set. You've dealt with pain. I have no doubt about your ability to withstand quite a bit of it. Now you must learn how to be silent and keep your wits about you while you do it. Next week, I want you to be able to do sixty without complaint."

Of course he would order her to do that. "Yes, sir."

"And you were worried about physical scars hurting your mission." He stared down at her. She could have sworn she saw a twinkle of excitement in his eyes.

"I might still need the use of my arms, you know," she fired back before she could stop herself.

"You want twenty more, right now?"

Sage clamped a hand over her mouth before she dared utter another word that might tempt Devon to make good on that threat.

"Learn how to deal with pain…silently." He held a hand out to help her up. "Have I ever given you something you couldn't handle?"

Sage shook her head as she took his hand. Standing took much more effort than it should have, and the pressure of her hand in his rekindled the fire in her muscles. She bit her tongue and refused to let the sound of her anguish escape.

"Tough love, Trainwreck. I know you can do this. It will not be easy. If it were, you'd never appreciate how much you've accomplished."

"Do I get a merit badge if I do?"

"A shiny gold patch for your cape." Devon laughed. It sounded genuine that time, but Sage wasn't going to fall for any more tricks.

She kept still, politely waiting for his next words to come.

"How are your arms feeling now?"

"String beans, if I'm honest, but I'll manage."

"A nice hot soak will work wonders," he suggested. "Use magnesium flakes and some lavender. Make it part of your beauty regimen before the ball."

Had Grey told him their plan? He must have. They had not even filed their report with Ava yet. She opened her mouth to ask as much, but Devon stopped her, putting a finger to his lips. He lifted an eyebrow deviously and shook his head. She might be Shadow Ops, but he was something else entirely.

"Yes, sir." She fought the urge to give him a cheeky salute as she slowly backed away from him, knowing it would only end in more pain.

"Off you go." Devon pointed to the door. "You have work to do."

NINETEEN

Showered and changed, Sage met Grey back at their desk. "What did you tell Devon?"

He spun around to face her, attempting to look shocked, but the laughter in his eyes gave him away. "A bit sore from training, are we?"

"Not at all." She folded her arms behind her back and stood tall. Two could play the lying game. "Easiest training session I've ever had."

"You really are a bad liar." Grey tossed a glass paperweight at her. She caught it, groaning as her muscles protested the sudden jerky movement. "Might want to work on that."

"What gave me away?"

"Really? Devon, easy?" He snickered.

The paperweight felt like a million pounds, tired as her muscles were. She searched for a clear spot on the overloaded desk to set the small glass dome back down. "You'll pay for that."

"Add it to my tab." He pulled out her chair, a gentlemanly peace offering, and waited for her to sit before taking his own. "I've got some news on that agent whose kid was on the bus."

"Really? A connection?" Finally, a little good news.

"A loose thread maybe, but it's the best we've got at this point. According to her case log, she was on security detail during the council meeting to discuss your hand."

"You mean that mockery of a trial?"

"It doesn't mean we have a smoking gun or anything yet, but there were many high-profile people who attended that…meeting. And many of those people are also on the guest list for a certain party you want us to crash."

"Ding, ding, ding! We have a winner." That loose thread, as he called it, was the best lead they had, and meant they were on the right trail.

"You're so cute when you're optimistic."

"And you're insufferable. You want me to get adorable again?"

"Don't make promises you can't keep." He nudged the glass paperweight on the desk as a subtle reminder. Not that she needed a reminder. Her arms were still aching. "You should feel lucky to have me as your partner."

"Really? Cocky much?"

"Confident. Don't confuse the two. While you were getting your ass handed to you with Devon, I've found our cover stories. You're going to be taking on the persona of Liliana, a Succubus we brought in a little bit ago. I've got medical crafting a pair of color-corrected contacts for you. Amethyst eyes. You think you can pull it off?"

"Never worn 'em before, but I'll do what I have to do."

"I meant being a succubus."

"You don't think I can be sexy? Are you really asking me this?" She narrowed her eyes, daring him to say something stupid.

Grey threw his hands up in surrender. "I think you're sexy as hell…in a clumsy, awkward…"

She threw a punch aimed at his chest. He dodged and her fist landed on his bony shoulder instead, causing more pain to herself.

"Jerk!" she sniped at him.

"You wouldn't have me any other way."

His taunting and laughter made her want to strike at him again, but she resisted the urge. "And who exactly are you pretending to be?"

"Wouldn't you like to know?"

"You know what? Nope. I don't. Just send me the file on Liliana, and I will study my part while I prepare for the party." By her count, she had a good twenty-four hours to get herself ready for this mission. Hopefully that would be enough for her to accurately take on another person's life. She'd done a bit of acting in high school. That had been fun.

"Now who's being a jerk?" he teased.

"Takes one to know one."

"Is this the kind of professionalism I can expect on your mission?" Ava snarled behind them.

Sage hadn't even heard her approach. "Sorry, ma'am. We were just blowing a little steam." She was on her feet in a second, standing at attention. Grey too.

"I don't need to tell you how important your mission is. Bickering like this threatens to break your cover. You two need to pull your heads out of your asses and start acting like you belong in Shadow Ops before I bust you down to prison guards. Understood?"

"Yes, ma'am," Grey answered.

"There is no margin for error in this mission," Ava continued. "Failure to infiltrate undetected can result in death. And there is nothing that the agency can do to assist you. You are acting alone. ASSET cannot be implicated, and if you are caught, your actions will be publicly disavowed."

Her warning, coupled with what Devon had said earlier, came down on Sage with a weight she had not expected. She opened her mouth to say she understood, but the words dried in the back of her throat, forming a lump she struggled to swallow.

"We will do all that is expected of us. You can count on us," Grey answered for the both of them. If he was worried, Sage would never know. Some people have resting bitch face, but Grey… His neutral expression worked like a mask of indifference. Someday she needed to learn how to don it herself.

"I expect a full report upon completion of the party," Ava demanded. "Not the following day. Not after you have had time to go home and change. You are to immediately report here for debriefing. Is that fully understood?"

Ava was scary on a normal day, and this was far from normal. To see her boss so stressed out really drove home how imperative it was that she and Grey needed to get concrete evidence, and fast.

"Yes, ma'am." Grey's voice cracked as he answered.

Ava narrowed her eyes, zeroing in on Sage. "Miss Cynwrig. Do not forget to check in with medical to have temporary tattoos applied and to pick up your prosthesis."

Sage struggled for words, her voice refusing to come, leaving her with no choice but to nod like an idiot. She couldn't blame Ava for sneering as she turned to march away. Sage wanted to say how important this mission was and that she and Grey would do their very best, but that was expected. She had nothing more to offer to assure her boss, and by the time Sage finally mustered some sound from her throat, Ava had rounded the corner out of earshot.

Sage turned her next question to Grey. "Prosthesis? Something you didn't tell me about Liliana?"

"Contact lenses." Grey chuckled. His expression had softened in the wake of Ava's departure.

"Oh. Good. For a minute there, I was wondering if I'd have a third leg or something." She took a deep breath and let it out, trying to relieve the pressure that had suddenly developed in her chest.

"'Didn't you tell me you wanted a new hand?" Grey teased.

"All the better to smack you with."

"I'd probably deserve it."

His admission shocked her into silence, but the moment passed quickly. "Better me than Ava, right?"

"If someone is going to hit me, I'd take anyone over Ava."

"She is stressed!" Sage peeked around to make sure her boss wasn't lurking around eavesdropping. "I've never seen her come here. She usually calls us into her office."

"She feeds on stress." Grey shrugged. "It's her superpower."

He could play casual all he wanted. She'd seen the way he stood stiffly at attention, and heard the crack of his voice when he replied. He understood how much was riding on them ferreting out the members of the Mystics. How dangerous it was for them to go in under-cover with no backup from ASSET. Ava was a hard ass, but she did care for the welfare of her team.

"I think she might actually be more worried than she's letting on."

"Because you know her so well." Grey arched an eyebrow in disbelief.

"She always threatens to throw us under the bus when she's worried."

Grey burst into laughter. "I'll remember that. When women threaten to have you killed, it means they are stressed.

"In your case, it could just be they actually want to kill you," she teased.

"Noted." He retook his seat and started typing on the keyboard. "I'm sending the information on Liliana to your email. Don't forget to stop by medical on your way out. I'll see you tonight."

"You're really not going to tell me who you are im-personating?"

"Now you want to know?" He tilted his head, giving her a side-eyed glare.

She matched his look, putting her hands on her hips impatiently.

He spun out of his chair, winked, and picked up his fedora. "Get used to disappointment." He slapped the hat on top of his head and ran his fingers along the brim as he breezed past her on his way out of the office.

"Jerk!" she called after him, tempted to follow, but refusing to play his game. She had her own things to do to get ready for the party, and the clock was already running down.

TWENTY

"I have to admit, purple is a good color on you." Matt took her face in his hands, staring at her like an artist preparing to mold a lump of clay into his next masterpiece. "We can't have any stray hair hiding those gorgeous eyes."

"I'll be wearing a mask." *Thank the gods for small mercies.*

"Even more reason for me to keep the hair from your face." Matt released her face and took up his brush. He moved around behind her and started working his magic. He tugged a little harder than necessary as he pulled the brush through her hair. She squirmed, earning a snippy, "Sit still," as he grasped a fistful of her hair.

"Hope it's enough." She hadn't meant to say it out loud, not that it mattered. A vampire could hear a whisper across the room if they wanted. But as she'd already opened her mouth, Sage figured she might as well stick her foot in. "This whole disguise. I mean... Fancy dress. Fancy hair. Makeup." She waved a hand around her face like a frame. She wore a bit of lipstick every now and again, but Matt practically pulled out a trowel and spackle for her this time. "All the window dressing."

"Have I ever let you down? Trust me. You look the part." Matt still had her hair clenched in his hand as he came round to face her. "But I doubt that's what you're worried about."

As usual, he'd hit the nail on the head. Nerves had her more wound up than the hair wrapped around her roommate's hand. "It's not the danger. I've got Grey with me. Zack too. No matter what happens, I've got backup."

"That you do." Matt tied her hair into a severe ponytail atop her head then began to section out strands as he moved in a circle around her. "You and Zack might not be the best of friends right now, but he's definitely got your back tonight."

"I hope you're right."

"Even if I'm wrong, your new boy toy isn't going to let you get into too much trouble. I doubt he'll leave your side."

"Boy toy?" She giggled at the thought of what Grey's face would look like if he ever heard someone call him that.

"Speaking of… Have you two figured things out?"

He would have to ask her that question. She'd practically chickened out when she had the perfect opportunity. Alone time, in Grey's apartment. Her stomach still tickled with nerves thinking about it after the fact. Snuggled up on the couch with him, watching movies late into the night. If any time would have been perfect for figuring out where they were heading, that would have been it.

"Not yet. I…uh…haven't had time."

Matt tugged her hair a little harder than necessary. "Bullshit."

She yelped but kept still, knowing better than to try and pull against him as he weaved her hair. "I've got so much on my plate right now. And this assignment…"

"Stop being such a baby."

"I've been studying…working… This is an important mission."

"You're doing it wrong." He chuckled, clearly not buying her excuses, but she wouldn't give him the satisfaction of admitting he was right. Giving herself over to the duller parts of this assignment ensured she hadn't had time to entertain thoughts about her partner. Every time those thoughts crept in, nerves followed.

"I have to know the type of person I'm trying to impersonate."

"A succubus? Nothing more to know. They are sensual creatures who feed on sexual energy. So, in order to attract their prey, they must be sexy." He'd spent less time in the magical world and yet somehow knew more about it than she. How was that even possible? "That's not something you can learn from a report. You just have to be." Matt continued working around her, wrapping braided sections of her hair and pinning them into his masterpiece.

"I can be sexy." Sage realized the irony of that comment even as she tried her hardest to deliver it confidently. The truth was, she'd been actively avoiding getting close to Grey for that exact reason.

"Save your lies for someone who doesn't know you better."

"Damn you." He was right. She could pretend to be mad, but that's all it would be—acting.

"You are sexy. You just don't remember it." He continued to pin, working behind her to secure every tress in its rightful place. "I recall a younger version of yourself who truly knew the power she held."

"Lies."

"Should I recite the names?"

"You kept a list?"

Matt came around, smiling as he tapped a finger to his head. "It's all up here. Names as well as walk of shame stories saved for future blackmail."

"Hey!" She threw a punch at his arm.

He retaliated, thwacking her in the shoulder with his brush. "My point is, you were once able to command your sexiness like a five-star general. And damned if every guy you came across didn't stand at attention."

She blushed, trying to look away, but Matt took her face again and forced her to look him in the eye. "You know how you did it?"

"Enlighten me."

"Confidence."

She pushed his hands from her face and stood, desperate to escape the conversation, her cheeks burning with embarrassment. "Don't give me that bullshit."

"You have everything you had back then. Every asset is still there, and thanks to all your training with the ogre" — he swatted at her again, slapping her hip with the flat of his brush, playfully illustrating his point — "honed into much firmer shape."

She spun around and threw another punch at him, but Matt dodged.

"That the best you got?" he taunted, brandishing his weapon of choice — her wooden brush.

"Don't make me destroy you!" she fired back with a sneer.

"Yes. That's the missing piece. Right there."

His words caught her off guard. She didn't know how to respond.

"Confidence." He punctuated his word, thwacking her once more in the side. "You've forgotten the power you once wielded. Lost your edge. Why?"

Sage dropped her defenses with a sigh. "That always leads to complications."

Boys had never been hard to find. They simply never stuck around long. The minute she'd let her heart get involved, they'd disappear, for one reason or another. Sex became something that led to heartache. Desires she could take care of herself without risking emotional damage. Sage struggled to remember the last time she'd gone on a date. Somehow over the years, Josh and Matt had become her surrogate boyfriends, filling in the emotional gaps. She had never needed anyone else.

"You need to get this in order." Matt tapped her forehead. "You're making too big a deal out of sex. And in this case, it might cause a problem with your mission considering you're supposed to be impersonating someone who eats and breathes sex. Literally."

"What do you suggest, then?'

"Deal with your Grey issues. Tonight, you are a succubus. He is your prey. Let everything fall into place. Stop thinking." Matt handed her a mirror. "And put your assets to good use!"

The face she saw in the mirror was her own, but at the same time, she barely recognized herself. "Damn, you're good."

"I did nothing but highlight what was already there."

"You did more and you know it." He was right. She was more than capable of playing the part. Whether it was his pep talk or his makeup magic, he'd ignited the spark. Confidence had begun to kindle within her. She could do this.

"I did create a masterpiece, and I will now accept your praise and gratitude for it." Matt held out his hand.

She took the offered hand and let Matt spin her around where she stood. "You, sir, are the best. No better man ever lived."

"Be sure to tell Josh that when he gets here."

"Date night?"

"With a possible sleepover." He winked.

"Remember what we talked about," she warned him. "Have you fed?"

"Juice boxes are in the fridge. I've taken care of all that. I promise to be a good boy. No biting. Vampire's honor."

Sage shuddered at the idea of storing blood bags in the house. Not exactly something you expected to find when reaching into the fridge for a cold one, but compromises had to be made. This was his apartment as much as it was hers, and if that was the price she had to pay for keeping her best friend close, it was a bargain.

"Night in? Or will you boys be heading out for the evening?"

"Dinner, a movie, and perhaps something more." Matt waggled an eyebrow. "Nothing as fancy as your little soiree this evening, but it's got me with butterflies in my stomach."

"You just make sure you behave yourself."

Keys jingled at the door.

Matt caught the sound a moment before Sage, and his head snapped to attention. "Speaking of."

"Go finish getting ready. I'll stall for your grand entrance." She headed toward the kitchen, leaving Matt to finish his own prep.

Josh opened the door just as she stepped into the kitchen. His eyes landed on her, and a gasp escaped from his throat. "Damn!"

Sage took a spin, letting him admire the whole ensemble, sparkles to spackle.

"Who's the lucky man? Grey?" he asked.

"If he plays his cards right," she replied with a sly smile stretching across her face. That thought became more enticing the longer she let it roll around her mind.

Matt snuck up behind her, quiet as a ghost. "Well, then. We'll leave you to it."

Josh's eyes shifted from Sage, widening as Matt closed in on him. He looked as if he wanted to say something, but Matt swallowed any words before they could escape in a passionate kiss. Sage couldn't remember the last time she'd kissed someone like that, if ever.

"You boys better get moving," Sage said loudly. "My date should be here soon."

Matt looked as if he were ready to devour Josh, but he paused long enough to come up for air and give Sage one final moment of his attention. "I want a full report when you get back tonight."

"Only if you're good." She hoped he caught the weight of her words.

Matt put an arm around Josh and strutted toward the door. "I'll be good if you will."

TWENTY-ONE

The knock at her door came faster than Sage had been prepared for. She gave herself a moment to calm her nerves before opening it.

He stood on the other side, the perfect gentleman, dressed to the nines.

"You clean up nicely!" She stepped aside to let him enter the apartment.

Grey said nothing. He didn't need to. His eyes lingered long past the point of admiration, as if he'd never truly looked at her before. Slowly, he staggered across the threshold, as if drawn towards her like a magnet. His lips parted, releasing a ragged breath as his gaze roamed lazily down the length of her body, tracing the curves of her form-hugging dress to the tips of her glittering stiletto heels.

"Say something. You're making me nervous." Despite the layers of satin and silk covering her body, Sage felt naked and exposed, but at the same time a rush of exhilaration quickened her heart. Whatever Grey was seeing, he liked it. Heat bloomed across her cheeks; the truth of her feelings remained safely hidden behind her silver mask.

"Wow." Grey blinked once, twice; each time his eyes opened, they fixed again on her.

"I'll take that as approval," she said nervously. "This outfit is acceptable for the evening?"

"So much for incognito." He chuckled. "All eyes will definitely be on you…" Grey raked his fingers through his hair. "Not that I'm complaining." He coughed and sent his gaze skyward.

She hadn't noticed until that moment, but he had lost the fedora. She always laughed at that stupid hat, but now that it was gone, she wondered how hard it had been for him to leave it home. Though the way he'd slicked his hair into a high pompadour gave his head a whole new shape. She could get used to that too. The eyes were all wrong. The contacts masked the true beauty of his natural color. A temporary change, thank goodness. The suit, however, she could get used to. Purple was definitely his color. He'd matched the tie and his shirt to the color of her eyes and topped it off with a jacket of slate grey and the clean lines of thin pinstripes to pull the outfit together.

"This is meant to be a high-class party, right?" She spoke just to break the awkward silence. "Matt helped me."

"I love it. You look… Damn… I mean… I'm just…"

"Rendered stupid in the face of four-inch heels and a bare midriff?" She giggled, enjoying the way he struggled to speak in full sentences.

"Guilty," he admitted readily with a laugh to match hers.

Laughter helped to break the tension. Every time his eyes landed on her, she felt them. An unseen weight that tugged at her heart and released butterflies into her stomach. At any moment, her knees might go out from under her, and she'd come crashing to the ground in a great big sparkly puddle of chiffon and silk.

"The feeling is mutual." She turned away sheepishly.

"You're rendered stupid at the sight of bare stomach?"

She knew all too well the memory-melting abs he had hidden under his clothes. She'd spent more than a few nights cuddled up next to him. Never daring to explore, though she'd been more than tempted. Business first. Emotions weren't a luxury when they were on the job.

With that reminder, she turned her thoughts back to the mission. "Speaking of that. Where will I put my weapons?"

"In a dress like that?" Again came the weight of his eyes, scrutinizing every inch of her. "Not many places to hide them. What are you planning on bringing?"

"Just a few of Mom's shiny pointy things. In case of emergency."

"Where we are going, you're best served by using Faith and Courage." He taunted her with the names Devon had given her fists. "But if you really want to be creative..." Grey knelt down in front of her, his face inches from her bare stomach. His breath tickled her skin as he spoke, sending a wave of goose bumps erupting across her body. "I can show you how to use those garters for something a little better than keeping up your nylons."

"S...sure." She struggled to keep her knees from turning to jelly.

He opened his jacket and pulled a slender throwing dagger from an inside pocket. "With your permission." His eyebrow arched mischievously.

She all but melted into a puddle. Sage reached out, steadied her hand on his shoulder, and nodded.

Grey's fingertips breeched the flimsy barrier of her skirt. Soft as a whisper, he caressed her leg, slowly making his way up to her inner thigh.

She held on to his shoulder, tightening her fingers, afraid at any moment she'd collapse. His touch was pure heat, warming her to the core. And then it came. The cold kiss of metal. She hissed as the blade sank under her nylons, all the way in until the tiny handle caught on the hemline where her garter clipped to the stockings.

"Won't be able to carry much here. But you've never needed much." Grey's voice pulled her attention down to his face. "You're sharper than any weapon I've ever seen."

Her world narrowed to the gap separating his deliciously kissable lips. Before she could overthink and stop herself, she reached for his face, and closed the gap between them. The moment came instantaneous and urgent. His tongue breeched the barrier of her quivering lips, tasting like sweet peppermint as he swept into her mouth.

She'd longed for this. Wild tremors awoke every nerve in her body, and the rushing warmth that followed threatened to steal what remained of her strength.

As if he knew she'd melt, Grey's arms wrapped around her, taking all her weight as he urged her tongue to dance with his. All their flirting, never crossing the boundary of their partnership no matter how close they stepped to the line—this confirmed it. No matter how much they argued, there was something very real between them. Something very much worth exploring.

Wild and thrilling as the moment was, Sage would drown if she didn't take a breath. She had to come up for air. They still had a mission. They couldn't lose their heads no matter how badly they wanted to. Sage broke the connection, gasping as she pulled away long enough to find his eyes.

He stared at her blankly, as if his brain had short-circuited. She understood that feeling all too well.

"We've got a bit of time before…" Grey whispered, and a mischievous smirk stretched across his delicious lips.

"Matt would kill me if I messed up his masterpiece. Do you know how long he spent creating this?" She waved a hand at herself, drawing Grey's attention to the strip of bare stomach separating the two halves of her curve-hugging outfit.

"Worth it."

A shiver of excitement raced up her spine. Tempting. So very tempting. Gods, why did he have to be such a jerk? They had a mission. She needed her head in the game. This was uncharted territory, real secret agent shit. She couldn't risk screwing it up. Grey licked his lips, and she nearly lost her nerve.

"Dammit, we have a mission!" she blurted out, not meaning to sound angry, but the words flew out faster than she could pull them back.

"Now who's the company man, er, woman?" He turned on his heel and reached for the door handle.

"You're such a jerk, you know that?"

"And you've got a thing for bad boys, so it all works out," Grey teased as held the door open for her. "After you."

TWENTY-TWO

For all his posturing, Grey wasn't the bad boy he pretended to be. He put on a good show around others, acting aloof and snarky. It was only when she had him alone that the truth was revealed. Grey hooked his arm with hers and escorted Sage down the lighted path. A limo waited just beyond the night gate, with Zack leaning against its door.

She and Grey had dressed up for the occasion, but Zack looked his typical self. Clean button-down shirt and trousers, with a sports jacket over the top. Not quite formal, but definitely not street clothes. The only real difference in his look was the addition of a tiny superhero-style mask. Hardly more than a strip of black across his face.

"Did you know he was waiting?" Sage asked.

"The vampire? Yeah."

"And you planned on making him wait for…uh…longer?" What would Zack have done if she had entertained Grey's suggestion back in her apartment? Had he planned for the vampire to tire of waiting and come knocking, and find them together? A dick move as far as she was concerned. Sage wasn't exactly

Zack's biggest fan, but he didn't deserve to stumble in on something like that.

"Just a few minutes, maybe." Grey's cocky attitude soured her mood.

She refused to be a pawn in whatever game those boys were playing with each other. "Was that supposed to be a glowing endorsement of your…skills?"

Grey stopped short, as if realizing his mistake, but Sage urged him forward toward the gate.

Zack stood at attention as they approached him, a broad smile allowing his fangs to peek out from between his lips. His eyes fell on her with a mix of shock and awe.

"You are stunning this evening." Lust oozed from his voice as Zack offered her his hand.

"Thank you." The chill of his touch sent a shiver all the way to her heart.

He tugged her forward as he bent to kiss her hand. If not for the shoes she'd chosen, Sage might have been able to counterbalance the vampire's strength. High heels were hard enough to stand in without the added pressure of someone trying to pull her down. She faltered, her right ankle sagging. Sage threw out her free hand to steady herself against Zack's shoulder.

"Feeling a bit light-headed?" He kept hold of her hand as he lifted his head to meet her gaze. "I have that effect on women."

The attention of such a dangerous man, especially when he glared hungrily at her like a treat to be devoured, was more than unnerving. How the hell was she going to play a sensual man-eater if she couldn't handle Zack? At least the vampire's eyes were still blue. She was reasonably safe with his beast in check, even if his fangs were out there for all to see. She wouldn't fare so well with the unknown attendants at the party. No excuses. She had to get her head in the game.

Confidence. Matt's voice echoed in her mind. He believed she had all the right assets to get the job done. If he believed in her, then she should too.

Grey cleared his throat, reminding them that he was still standing there, waiting. His prickish nature worked in her favor, giving Sage the chance to pull her hand back while Zack was distracted.

"Don't expect me to kiss your hand," Zack teased. "Though you do look very lovely."

"Can we get moving?" Grey replied humorlessly.

"Yes. We should. Thank you, Zack, for all the help you have provided," she said politely, remembering her manners. He was, after all, the reason they were attending the party. She ducked into the limo before the vampire twisted her words into some kind of flirtation and found yet another way to make her squirm.

"You are too kind, m'lady." He scooted into the car.

Of all the seats available, Zack chose the space next to Sage. Because of course he would.

"You will remember to be professional, vampire." Grey took his seat. The moment the door closed, the car began to roll out of the parking lot.

"I am always a professional," Zack replied. "So, who do I have the pleasure of escorting this evening?"

"Liliana, my dearest love," Grey replied.

"She is a naughty thing," Zack said with a little too much enthusiasm. "If she is Liliana, then I can only assume you're the infamous Mr. Rathburn?"

"You would know the criminals of this city, wouldn't you?" Grey's teasing only seemed to excite Zack further.

"Intimately," the vampire replied. "I've never known Rathburn to turn down a good show." Zack shifted toward Sage, hunger clouding his icy eyes, the beast within him rising to the surface. "Should we give him a show, Liliana? How far are you willing to go to play the part?"

Was he being extra creepy on purpose? He was an insufferable flirt on the best of days, but surely Zack had sense enough to know when he was crossing the line.

"If you mean killing those who are stupid enough to get close to me?" She stared deep into the vampire's eyes despite the chill rolling down her spine. "You're well on your way to being my first victim tonight."

Darkness stole what little color the vampire had left in his eyes. "You can feed on my essence anytime you'd like." He moved like the wind, one moment at her side, and the next she found him kneeling in front of her, hands like claws gripping her knees, pulling them apart. "Perhaps you might let me return the favor?"

Her breath caught in her chest, refusing to come out. She fought against the pressure of his hands, squeezing her thighs tight, but Zack proved too strong. Her skirt was all that shielded her from the vampire as he filled the gap he'd created.

"Too far, vampire," Grey warned, his posture tight, like a predator rearing back, ready to strike. He made a show of cracking his knuckles, but despite looking deadly, he remained where he sat.

"Would you prefer to go first?" Zack taunted. "You can warm her up. I'll finish when you're done… Wouldn't be the first time."

"What the hell is going on with you two? What the hell kind of game are you playing at?" She tried to squirm away, but in such tight quarters, where could she go? Even if she wanted to, she couldn't escape. At least, not until the limo came to a stop. "Zack, I swear if you don't back the hell away and leave me alone, I will make sure this is the last night you ever see."

"Feisty is my favorite flavor." He might look like Zack, but in that moment, he was no more than a creature of desire and hunger. "Your threats are empty. We both know this. If you were truly Liliana, you'd have the power to send me into the next life with a smile on my face." He had her exactly where he wanted her. His body pressed against hers, hard as stone, excitement clear in more than just his beastly eyes. "But you're only pretending. I, however, can promise you a satisfying end."

"Grey! Don't just sit there. Do something!" She pressed trembling hands against Zack's chest, hoping to hold him at bay long enough to reach for one of her knives.

"Don't spoil the show. Not when it's about to get good." Zack laughed at her feeble attempt, pinning her hands as he lowered his head.

She knew what was coming. Sage closed her eyes, preparing for the vampire's bite.

The kiss of his breath tickled her skin before the soft touch of his lips. Where she expected pain, he came in like a gentle lover, seeking the pulse at her neck. A moan escaped from her lips on the back of a relieved sigh.

Damn him.

"If I can see through your ruse, so will others. If they catch you, you're as good as dead." He punctuated each sentence with a kiss. "They won't be as kind about it as I can be." His tongue followed, tasting her skin.

Her heart thundered in her chest as if it meant to punch a hole through her ribs. Why was he doing this? Why wasn't Grey stopping him?

The gentle scrape of his teeth came next.

"Enough, dammit," she demanded.

"Screaming is no fun. Wouldn't you rather be moaning my name?" He nipped her earlobe and chuckled at her squeak of a response. "Save yourself the inevitable pain," he whispered like a prayer, "and let me finish you off."

"I may be pretending to be someone else…" Her voice cracked. She squirmed as much as space would allow, freeing her hands, and quietly reached for a small dagger she'd hidden between her breasts. "But I'm still just as deadly." She pulled the knife, swift as she could, and set the blade against the vampire's neck. "Last warning. Back off before I end you!"

"Wrong. That's what he's supposed to do." Zack retreated with his hands held in surrender and retook his seat.

"Wait. What?" She clutched the knife, her hand trembling with terror and rage, and turned to Grey for answers.

"The vampire is right." All signs of aggression had faded from Grey's face. If she didn't know better, she'd think he'd been amused by that little show. "You're supposed to enjoy all the advances and attention. I'm the violent one that makes threats and ensures that if someone bothers you, they don't live to see the next day."

"So that was all a test?" And Grey had been in on it? She'd have words with him later. Her partner was supposed to be honest with her. Tell her everything. And he'd conspired with the vampire to toy with her emotions. She could kill them both for putting her through that. How long had he been testing her? The kiss... Had that been a test, too, back at the apartment? She didn't know whether to be upset or relieved.

"You picked someone who travels in less than honest circles. There are certain expectations that come with impersonating such a person." Ice returned to Zack's eyes as quickly as it had been lost. She made note of that small detail. She'd assumed that when the beast took over, the man was lost. But Zack had just let slip the truth; he had full control to wield his darker half at will. She wouldn't let him trick her like that again.

"And you wonder why I don't trust you?" She secured the small blade between her breasts.

"I know you don't like being shown the darker side of the life you live." Zack chuckled. "Tough love is not for the weak-willed. I've accepted my place as the bad boy you don't want to admit you like...yet."

Some people never know when to quit.

"Are we finished with the games now?" Grey angled his head toward the divider separating them from the driver. "We have a job to do. Are we free to speak?"

"Yes. He has no affiliation," Zack answered.

"Good." Grey leaned forward, resting his elbows on his knees, staring straight at Sage as if the vampire sitting next to her didn't exist. "From this moment on, you are to stay in character. You are Liliana. I am Gerard."

"Fine," she agreed.

"Along with that, you're going to have to think on your feet a little. I'm not sure how many people know of the pair's apprehension. It was a silent operation. ASSET only just brought them in two nights ago."

"If anyone questions me, I could say I used my feminine charms to escape," she suggested.

"Of which you have plenty," Zack said.

"Enough with the games," Grey barked. "She needs to be serious. We've only got a few more minutes to prep before we arrive."

"She's impersonating a succubus. Using her sexuality to get her way is completely in character. It will be expected of her to act as such while we attend the party." Zack's flirtatious tone turned cold. "Perhaps, for her own safety, she should stay close to me."

Grey shifted his gaze toward the vampire, narrowing his eyes in a threatening glare. "What exactly do you mean by that?"

"She is impersonating a vixen. One, I might add, who has a known habit of driving her incubus mate into fits of jealousy." Zack turned his lusty gaze to Sage. "She'll be expected to act uninhibited. Your part is easy. Just keep acting like an overprotective prick."

"I'm her other half. Of course I would be a little possessive. Especially at a party filled with strangers."

"That's how Grey would act." Zack clucked his tongue disapprovingly. "Gerard may be a jealous mate, but he's also got needs, which he's famous for flaunting. When she's out of your sight, you need to be out there flirting with everything on two legs."

"I'm not letting her out of my sight," Grey argued. "Not there. It's too dangerous. We can just spend the night flirting with each other."

"Wrong again." Zack shook his head. "That's not believable. Not for the people you have chosen to impersonate. You two have to work the room."

"How about a compromise?" Sage suggested. "Why not let me bounce between you tonight. This way you can both keep an eye on me without ruining our cover."

"That's a smart idea," Zack said.

"Switch every five minutes. No more. This is dangerous territory we're heading into," Grey agreed. "But remember, she gets hurt, by you or anyone else while she's under your watch, I will kill you."

"I'd expect no less from Gerard Rathburn." Zack mocked him with a flamboyant salute. He turned toward Sage, scooting in close again, and whispered in her ear, "How close do you want me to follow you?" His hand found her thigh and squeezed. She fought against the desire to slap him.

"Is it wise to grope me without an invitation in front of my love?" she asked sweetly. "Surely there are more pleasant ways to get yourself killed."

Zack's hand vanished from her thigh.

"Much better."

Grey turned to look out the window. Even with his mask on, Sage could see the tightness of his jaw. Of all the magic in the world, she wished she could peer into his mind and know what was going on behind that stony expression. Did he worry for the mission? Did he think she'd be the one to screw things up?

No. She'd play her part to perfection. They wanted a sex-starved succubus, so that's exactly what she would give them. From that moment on, nerves be damned, she'd work over every man who crossed her path.

TWENTY-THREE

The limo entered through a set of wrought-iron gates and pulled into a large circular driveway. A red carpet had been rolled out. Men as large as giants greeted guests as they exited their vehicles. Limo after limo entered the circular drive, each one dropping its passengers at the red carpet before pulling away.

Their limo came to a stop, and the door opened.

"Game on," Sage whispered like a promise.

She put on her best smile and grabbed her purse before stepping a foot out of the vehicle. This was the moment where Sage would just stand on her own two feet, but she wasn't Sage. Not now. She was Liliana. Someone who expected to be pampered. Where was her greeter with an offered hand to help her out of the car? A moment passed, and no hand was offered.

She glanced upwards, locking eyes with the big brute of a man standing there. "Is this how you treat a lady?"

"Sorry." The man offered his hand to help her out of the car.

She ran her hand up the side of his arm as she stood and squeezed his bicep. "So strong. Look at all those muscles. I guess one can forgive you for being a little bit of a brute." She leaned in and whispered in his ear, "I bet you like it a little rough, don't you?"

Grey exited the car and took hold of Sage's arm. "Liliana, dear, save it for the party." He tugged her gently, pulling her from the big beast.

Sage's words had already worked their magic. A flush of warmth bloomed on the guard's cheeks.

"I'll be back for you later." She winked at him before turning to her date. "We could share him, baby. Would you like that?"

Zack stepped out of the limo, laughing as he handed over his invitations to the guard. "She's going to be a handful tonight."

"So many men, such little time tonight. Let's hurry." Sage led the way toward the front entrance.

Zack scooped her off her feet and carried her up the stairs to the first landing. "Let's see what you've learned." He stole a kiss before setting her on her feet.

Her instinct was to slap him, but she was being watched. "Naughty, naughty." Sage giggled and reached her hand out toward Grey. "Lover, what should I do with this bad vampire?"

"I have a few ideas, but they will have to wait until later." Grey chuckled. "Enjoy your snack. I think I see something enticing inside." He brushed past her, whispering, "Five minutes," as he entered the wide-open double doors to the mansion.

Zack hooked Sage's arm, leading her into the mansion. "I'll make any introductions. You keep that saucy attitude going."

"Steal another kiss like that, I'll rip your lips off," she whispered through her teeth, all smiles, nodding to the people watching them enter.

"Promise?" Zack was enjoying this far too much for her liking.

She let him guide her through the various rooms filled with people.

The house was a modern art masterpiece. Every room had been decorated around a different color scheme, using fabrics and paints to create splashes of color on what would otherwise have been a very stark, almost clinical backdrop.

But it wasn't the décor that had Sage's interest piqued. Magic was on display here. More than she had ever seen in her short employment at ASSET. Pixies flitted all around the room in their natural forms. Brownies, shadowrunners, vampires, fire elementals. All dressed to the nines but were otherwise in their natural forms.

Sage spotted a familiar-looking troll guzzling a tankard of beer in the far corner, but this was not the time to go up and speak to her old boss. As far as Sage was concerned, all those in attendance were potential criminals aligning themselves with the Order of Mystics. She made a mental note to check in on Marcy later in an official ASSET capacity.

Zack led her through room after room, keeping a keen eye around, as if he were searching for something or someone. Sage hadn't been paying attention to the time. Grey had been adamant about the five-minute rule. It would take her twice that to locate him in the crowd. She hoped he was keeping a loose tail on her.

Sage positioned herself in a corner of the room, giving her the best possible view. She noticed another familiar figure. Hair of flames danced from the top of a tiny red man's head. This certainly was the crème de la crème of the magical realm. He'd been one of the three council members at her trial, demanding she reveal her bloody hand to prove she did not have the weapon they were seeking. If she hadn't been undercover, she might give him a closer look at it now. He'd definitely get a mention in her report to Ava.

"Flame head to our left. Do you know him?" Sage asked.

"Cor Ignis. He sits on the high council of the Elementals," Zack replied.

"Friend?"

"I wouldn't call them that," Zack replied with a chuckle.

"Business associates?"

"Closer," Zack replied. "In my line of work, I come across many people."

"What do you know about him, other than his status?"

"He's not a man to cross."

"A glowing recommendation, then?"

"You're not going to find dirt on him. You don't raise to the level of class council member without earning the respect of your people."

"Those people haven't been on the other end of his fire." She remembered the way flames leaped from Cor Ignis's head when Ava had made him look like a fool at her trial, refuting every accusation he threw at her. His flames had glowed bright enough he could set the whole damn building on fire if he'd wanted.

"That's one of the reasons he's so respected," Zack replied.

Across the room, a woman dressed in black from head to toe, with hair to match, locked eyes on Zack and made a beeline toward him.

"Incoming," Sage whispered. Time to get back into character.

The woman's face was hidden like everyone else's with a masquerade mask—black, matching the rest of her outfit. But even so, she could be a dead ringer for Morticia Addams.

"Zackary, darling, I'd know those baby blues any-where." She greeted him with a kiss on both cheeks.

"Natasha, my love, thank you again for the invita-tion. This is quite a party." Zack took the woman's hand and brought it to his lips before turning to Sage. "My plus one."

Who was this woman? More importantly, *what* was this woman? Her coal black eyes were not a comforting indicator. If she were a vampire, she'd be deadly, but Sage saw no fangs. She didn't seem to be made of vapor like Sylvia, so shadowrunner was out.

She'd been silent for too long, trying to figure Nata-sha out. Eyes were on her, expecting an answer of some kind. What should she do?

"Liliana?" Zack nudged her. "Have you not fed to-day?"

"Sorry. Distracted by so many tasty morsels. How am I to survive tonight without sampling at least a few?" She licked her lips as her gaze lifted to meet Natasha's eyes. "Is there a private place a lady might enjoy a little midnight snack?"

"A woman after my own heart. Zack, you sure know how to pick 'em." Natasha playfully tapped him on the shoulder.

"He's all yours. I think I found a little bit of devil's food across the room." The words came out before Sage had actually committed to saying them, but once they spilled from her mouth, she knew she'd have to step away from the conversation, and Zack, her babysitter.

"Don't go ruining your diet yet. Let me get you girls properly acquainted first," Zack urged.

"We have all night to become best friends." Natasha chuckled. "Let her feed her desires. That's what this little get-together is all about. Just make sure you're done snacking by midnight. We've got something special planned out in the gardens."

"Ta for now. I'll find you later. Don't go gossiping about me unless you spread something super juicy. I have a reputation to maintain, you know." Sage waved in the air and sauntered away without looking back.

Her heart was pounding. She hoped she had made a convincing show of acting like a succubus. With any luck Grey was close behind.

Sage stopped in the center of the room, after she felt she had filtered into the crowd enough to be out of Natasha's and Zack's line of sight. Grey was still nowhere to be seen. She needed him now more than ever. Where the hell was he? Had he gotten into trouble, or was he just that good at blending in?

A tap on her shoulder sent Sage into a twirl, hoping to see Grey. The man she faced, unlike the rest of the crowd, wore no mask. Long dirty blond hair fell in a mane around his angular face. A neatly trimmed mustache framed full lips as it blended into an equally maintained beard that softened the sharp angles of his jaw.

"I don't believe I've met you yet. Are you enjoying my little soiree?" he asked.

Fierce as he was beautiful, the sudden shock of his approach rendered Sage silent. She struggled for words. Her mind ran a mile a minute, searching for clues to identify his magical type. Beyond his human-like appearance, she could see something else. Like the ghost of his other form, a shadow hanging around him like an aura.

"Gorgeous," was all she could say at first. Usually she could see through illusions without much effort, but his looked distorted, as if compacted into human form. If that were the case, his true form had to be massive. "Sorry, I came as a plus one." As human forms go, his was stunning. He had the most perfect face with almond-shaped amber eyes and an arrow-shaped nose. His appearance was as wild as it was tame with a hint of something deadly just below the surface. "We have not had the pleasure."

"I welcome all potential new friends to my sanctuary."

Sanctuary That word struck a chord with her. Definitely a shifter. They liked to use that word. But what kind? Shifters were people of two forms, their other half not cloaked by a trick of magic, which made it almost impossible to know for sure what they were until they chose to reveal themselves. All she could make out of his other half was distorted darkness.

She'd done it again. Lost in her own mind, forgetting to speak. He stared at her with questioning eyes.

"Thank you…ah… Sorry, didn't catch your name."

"How rude of me." He took hold of her hand and lifted it to those full, pouting lips of his. "Are you shaking?"

"Trembling like a leaf, actually. Haven't fed in so long, and you…are beyond tempting." Sage prayed she'd said that convincingly enough. She should have never left Zack. This mission was going to fail if she couldn't get her head in the game, but pretending to be someone she wasn't proved harder than she had anticipated.

"Raynor," he replied.

"Sorry?"

He'd said the magic word. Raynor was the guy they had wanted to meet. The dragon, if Grey had been right. Raynor Brurdur. Sage looked around, searching again for Grey, or even Zack. Someone to come to her rescue. Damn her luck.

"My name." He flashed her a toothy grin. "You asked before you started sizing me up for your next feed."

Even his teeth were perfectly aligned. He had to be a model. That would explain how he could afford such a place.

"I'm Liliana." Thank the gods for the mask hiding her blush. "Excuse my manners. I'm afraid my appetite has gotten the better of me. You don't seem too bothered by it."

"Never met a Succubus I didn't like." He waggled his eyebrows at her.

"I couldn't help but notice that you're the only person here not in a mask," she replied awkwardly, struggling to find the right words to keep the conversation going.

"This form is my mask," Raynor teased.

Matt's words came back to her. *Confidence.* She had great power, if she chose to use it. Raynor was expecting a succubus, so time to earn herself an Oscar.

"I think I like this form, but you have me intrigued." She reached out, caressed his shoulders, and let her hands run over his pecs, searching his face as she let her hands sink lower, wondering how far he'd let her go. "What other forms do you take?"

"I've been called a great beast," he whispered, narrowing the gap between them as her hands came to his waist.

Sage had to crane her neck to meet his eyes. He closed the connection with his lips.

An electric shock sent her nerves firing all at once. Her hands, already on his hips, moved on their own, seeking to grip his taut butt. She tried to squeeze, but Raynor was solid through and through. He pressed his body against hers, every last deliciously hot inch of him.

His hand ghosted up her back to the base of her neck. Thick, strong fingers threaded into her hair, knotting as he tightened his grip. He tugged gently, forcing her head farther back as he deepened the kiss.

The sound of Grey clearing his throat called her back to reality. She could feel his eyes boring holes in the back of her head.

"Hate to interrupt," Grey said.

Raynor broke the connection, pulling away from her lips, but his hand remained at the base of her neck, like a promise of more to come. "We're a bit busy, mate. Another time."

"I would, but that's my lady you're kissing." Grey stood arms crossed, but rather than condemning Sage for her actions, the look in his eyes was surprisingly amused.

Sage wiped her mouth and turned toward Grey. "Gerard, dear, I'm busy."

"Gerard Rathburn?" Raynor released Sage, taking a step backwards. "I didn't realize this was your Liliana."

"Excuse me?" She put on her best angry face. "I am no one's property, and I was in the middle of something when you so rudely interrupted us."

"Dearest." Grey chuckled. "We don't feed on our host."

"Oh, listen to him talk," she said, feigning aggravation. "When he was the one to leave me all alone here like a kid in a candy store."

"I offered. Its fine," Raynor assured them. "I hope you two are enjoying yourselves here tonight."

"Very much." Grey turned his gaze outward to the crowd of people. "Do you host these parties often?"

"No. Never, actually, but a few of my friends talked me into it, so I thought, why not," Raynor said casually.

"Are these friends as good as you?" Sage asked.

"I could use a few more *good* friends if you know what I mean," Grey said.

"You're hanging around for midnight, I hope," Raynor said.

"I heard there was something special happening," Grey replied. "I'd be interested to see what all the fuss is about."

"It's worth sticking around for." Raynor's smile had a devious edge. That man was up to something, but Sage didn't have a clue yet how to extract that information from him. "If you'll excuse me, it's my party. I'd be remiss in my duty if I did not continue to make the rounds and meet all of the guests."

"Will I see you again later?" Sage licked her lips, remembering her character's overtly sexual nature.

"I hope so." Raynor winked as he turned toward the crowd.

Grey snatched her by the shoulder and roughly escorted her to the back of the room. "What the hell did you think you were doing?" he growled under his breath.

"Playing my part. Keeping him talking."

"Talking? That's what you call it?"

"He's the one we were looking for, remember?" Sage pulled out of his grip. "What the hell are *you* doing?"

"You realize you could have blown your cover with that kiss?" Grey glared at her. She'd never seen him so enraged.

"What? How?" Sage felt as if they were having two different conversations.

"How do you think Succubi feed?"

"Sex?" She threw the word at him.

"Sexual energy," he corrected her. "All sexual energy. The physical connection. They drain that energy through physical touch. You had better hope he doesn't realize your kiss was dead."

"I'm a damn good kisser. I'm sure he felt something," Sage said, defending her pride.

"Where is Zack? Why the hell did he allow you out of his sight?" Grey turned around, scanning the room.

"I sort of left him. I didn't know what else to do."

"You don't leave your protection. He shouldn't have let you. Damn him."

"Well, don't go acting all crazy now. You'll draw attention to us."

"That's what we do. Fight and make up," Grey said. "I'm still in character. You're the one threatening our cover. Shit. Raynor is looking. Kiss me."

"What?"

"Pretend to feed on me. Kiss me. We need to make a little show of it." Grey met her eyes with a look of urgency that contradicted the anger he'd shown her only moments before. "Please."

She took his face in her hands and pulled his lips down to meet hers. Passion, raw and powerful, connected them. Like fire and ice when they touched, the reaction was intense and all consuming.

His arms enveloped her, welcoming her to share the warmth of his body. She melted against so much heat, and yet she wanted more.

Grey pulled away, leaving her lips with a whimper as if he had struggled to break the connection. He stepped back and swayed where he stood, looking like he might faint.

"Are you okay?" She reached out to steady him. "What happened?" Only a moment earlier, he had been perfectly fine.

Grey lifted his hand up to his head and groaned. He stumbled a few steps then turned around, wobbling. "I need a place to sit."

Raynor appeared as if he had materialized on the spot. "Sorry, mate. My fault for getting her motor running. Took a bit much from you, did she?"

It took Sage longer than it should have, but she realized what he was doing. Grey played his part so much better than her. She wiped the concerned look off her face, replacing it with a cocky smile.

"He'll be all right. Gerard is a big boy. He can handle it. But the next time he decides to be so possessive, I'll leave him in a puddle on the ground."

Raynor helped Grey to a wing-backed chair a few feet away. "Still hungry?"

"I hate to be a glutton, but perhaps some dessert later?" Sage licked her lips and blew him a kiss.

"I'll be looking for you." Raynor flashed that mischievous grin again. The one that had her curiosity so piqued but left her second-guessing his true intentions. He sounded so genuine, but there was something else going on there. Something she couldn't quite put a finger on. "If you're okay here, I'll take my leave again." Raynor bowed out and turned to his other guests.

Grey captured her attention with his pained gaze. "That was a close one. From now on, you stay by my side."

"Gladly." She came round to sit on his lap. "I'd much rather feed on you when dessert comes anyway."

"Oh, really?"

"Wouldn't you like to know?" she teased. "Let me know when you're ready to get up. We still have work to do. I've seen a few people of interest, and I'll bet we find more."

"Glad to see your head in the game. Keep up the good work, and maybe I will let you feed on me some more."

"You'd like that, wouldn't you?" She cupped his face in her hands and brought her nose up to meet his. "If only I had the power to suck every last drop of your energy."

"That's the weirdest way I've ever been propositioned, but I'll take it." He closed the gap and pressed his lips again to hers.

The world faded away as if they were the only two in existence. Their heat. Their passion. All that mattered was the connection. His lips. His body. Why had she waited so long to give in to these feelings she had for him? A mistake she would not make again.

She pulled away breathless but exhilarated, wanting more, but knowing they had to stay sharp and complete the mission. "To be continued." She panted, trying to catch her breath.

"Damn you."

"Wrong time. Wrong place."

"Rain check."

"We'll get it right one of these days."

"You two really don't understand the meaning of covert, do you?" Zack's face appeared in front of Sage. "Quite a show you two put on. I should applaud you."

"Just playing our parts." Sage wiped her mouth.

"Well, you certainly have our host's interest." Zack angled his head toward Raynor, who stole a few quick glances between speaking with the crowd that had gathered around him. "There is, however, a danger to playing your part a little too convincingly."

"He's right. Duty calls."

"Did I just hear what I think I heard?" Zack slapped a hand to his cheek with a mocking gasp. "Inconceivable."

Sage snorted, earning her a dangerous glare from Grey. "Sorry. Yes. Work. What can you tell me about Raynor and his circle of friends?"

"Let's take this conversation somewhere a little more private." Zack bent down and whispered in Sage's ear, "Meet me upstairs, second door on the left. Five minutes."

TWENTY-FOUR

Right on time, the pair entered the room as Zack had instructed, a bedroom that was half the size of Sage's apartment. One day she promised herself a luxurious room like that. It might not be as big, but it would be just as poshly decorated with the highest thread counts she could find.

Zack sat atop a four-poster bed that looked far larger than king-sized. His hand wrapped around a hand-carved wood post depicting fire-breathing dragons.

Sage pulled the door closed behind her. "What do you have for us?"

"Did anyone see you come in here?" Zack stood and crossed the room to meet them.

"I don't think so," Grey said.

Sage shook her head. "We gave up show business."

Zack reached for the door as if he meant to escape before delivering his news. "You two need to get out of here, now. I've already ordered a taxi. I'll follow later."

"What? Why?" Not at all what she had expected him to say, but she understood the worry in his eyes.

"Are you not leaving with us?" Grey asked.

A fair question. One Sage wished she'd asked first.

"I have a reputation to maintain," Zack answered.

Grey crossed his arms at his chest. He stared at the vampire, seeming unconvinced. "What are you not telling us?"

"I don't want to worry Sage." Zack gripped the door handle a little tighter.

"I can manage my own feelings," Sage shot back at him. For all their protectiveness, those boys could be pretty misogynistic when they wanted. Treating her like some fragile thing that needed to be handled with kid gloves. "What the hell are you hiding?"

Zack let his hand fall from the door and faced Sage head-on. "While you two were making a spectacle of yourself, it came up in conversation that ASSET agents are here."

"Someone recognized us?" Grey asked.

"No. I don't think so. At least I didn't hear that exactly." Zack's attempt to assure them felt hollow. The vampire had to be holding something back. "But I would rather not take that chance. They have some kind of spectacle planned at midnight, and it was implied that ASSET being here was something to make an example of."

"Well, that confirms one thing," Grey scoffed. "We're definitely at the right party."

"So we need to try and find our agents and get them out before midnight?" Sage went straight into problem-solving mode. She hadn't expected any other agents to be working this case, but nevertheless, if they had been found out, they'd need help. "What time is it now? How long do we have to move?"

"You don't understand." Zack met her eyes. "You need to leave now. No one specifically said who the

194

agent or agents were, but on the off chance you were recognized, especially after your little show downstairs, you could be in serious danger."

"I agree." Grey nodded. "We have some clues to follow up on. And Zack, you can let us know what happens tomorrow."

"I will let you know what I can," Zack said.

"Don't play games, vampire." Grey's tone darkened. "You will tell us everything. When next we meet."

"But what about our other agents?" Sage couldn't believe they were ignoring the potential for more of their people to be in danger. "If they are here, we need to find and warn them."

"If they are here, they may be undercover as we are. Shadow Ops are not public about their assignments." Grey at least had the courtesy to look bothered by what he was saying. "I'll send a message to headquarters. Whoever their point of contact is should be able to get a message to them."

"What if they are too late?" Sage asked.

"Curse your bleeding heart," Grey growled.

"Don't be a jerk. We have a duty."

"Hard to do when you're dead."

"Fine," Sage grumbled.

"We appreciate the intel." Grey held a hand out for Zack to shake.

"Appreciate later. Go now. I will wait a few minutes here before returning to the party. Reputation and all. You know how this goes. I'll be in touch tomorrow."

Grey offered Sage his arm to take. "Shall we, my dearest?"

Sage heaved a sigh and took his arm. She allowed him to lead her through the door into the hallway. They started down the stairs, the front door in sight.

Raynor greeted them as they reached the ground floor. "Are you fully sated now, or would you care for dessert?"

Where the hell had he come from? She couldn't remember seeing him as she walked down the stairs. But there he was with that perfect smile, and the dark aura of his other half bursting at the shadowy seams all around him. She almost wanted to see his true form and learn exactly how big a dragon was. But they needed to make their escape.

"You are a naughty thing, aren't you?" Sage giggled. "Gerard, dessert?"

"Pace yourself, my dearest." Grey tightened his arm around hers, tugging her toward the front door. "I have yet to see the grounds outside of this lovely home."

"Why don't I give you the grand tour? As your host, I feel it is my duty." Raynor hooked his arm through Sage's free one, matching pace with Grey as they strolled toward the door.

She kept her expression in check despite the sudden desire to make a run for it. "That would be lovely."

They crossed the threshold. A taxi sat waiting in the circular drive. Might as well be a million miles away with the iron grip Raynor had on her arm. Sage looked to Grey for guidance, not knowing how they'd manage to escape. He didn't seem to have the answer either.

Raynor guided them down the steps, turning as they hit the sidewalk, and led them down a darker path lit only by small solar lights.

"Desert landscaping can be quite beautiful if done properly," Raynor said. "Cactus does quite well here. And some produce wonderful colors in their blooms."

"Never been a fan of prickly plants myself," Grey commented.

"I wasn't at first either. But I grew to appreciate their ability to not only survive but protect themselves without having to be aggressive." Raynor chuckled.

"Passive-aggressive plants," Grey added.

"Yes, you could say that. Anything wishing to feed on them or harm them takes the risk of being harmed in the process. An excellent deterrent, wouldn't you agree?"

"Perhaps, but it is not foolproof," Sage added.

"Nothing is. Nor should it be. Survival is earned. It's how one survives that makes it worthy of appreciation." Raynor led them past all varieties of cacti down a path that seemed to end in a wrought-iron gazebo. "Tell me something… How is it an incubus and succubus can feed from one another? I always thought you two would simply cancel each other out. Isn't that why you have such an open relationship?"

Shit. He knew.

"It's very hard to explain if you are not one yourself," Grey answered. "It would be like me asking you how it is you can change forms so easily at will."

"Well, that's very simple, isn't it? Magic." Raynor laughed. "I have the magical blessing of being a creature of two bodies. I change forms as easily as breathing."

"We all have our own types of magic, don't we?" Sage politely laughed along with Raynor.

"That we do. Which is why parties like these are so important. Bringing together all kinds of magical people so we can share our gifts." Raynor stopped short of the gazebo's iron bars.

"You've done an excellent job of that. I don't believe I have seen such an eclectic bunch." Sage looked around, noticing how the gardens blocked the view toward the house. Just she and Grey against Raynor. Their odds were better here. She tried to communicate that much to Grey with her eyes.

"Eclectic, yes, but sadly not a complete representation of all the magical people. We have no Terras here." Raynor smiled. "At least, I didn't think we'd be hosting their kind."

"Why is that?" Grey asked.

"Their sort are snapped up the moment they learn of their magical lineage, are they not?" Raynor asked. "Forced into a sort of servitude."

"Are you talking about ASSET?" Sage asked, feigning ignorance.

"Yes. Do you know what that organization stands for?" he asked.

"They help keep the order among our kind," she replied.

Raynor's expression darkened. "Anonymous. As in loss of identity. Supernatural, though they lack real magic to qualify. Security. A false sense of, I'd argue. They've done plenty of things that make the magical community feel more frightened than secure. Do you know what that is?" Raynor didn't wait for her answer. "Elimination… Ah, now we come to their true mission. Removing life, magical life, from the world. Whomever they deem unfit, for whatever reason or trumped-up charge. They act as executioner with impunity. And how do they accomplish this? Task force. They are far from benevolent. ASSET is a military organization. You see, they give it a pretty name so recruits feel empowered to fight for truth, justice, and whatever else, but it is simply forced servitude for the poor creatures born into that life. They are never allowed to experience magic and spend their entire lives eliminating it at the commands of their superiors."

"I had never looked at it from that standpoint," Sage said politely. He'd all but come out and said he was the ringleader of the Mystics. Good to finally find him, but Sage had no idea how they planned on bringing him in. "You're wrong, of course, but entitled to your opinion nonetheless."

"You're so young. Youth is easily corrupted." Raynor patted her hand. "It is unfortunate. Really."

"Unfortunate for who?" Grey asked.

"I had hoped the rumor was false," Raynor said quietly.

"What rumor?" She looked down, feeling the point of claws digging into her skin as his nails shifted into talons. Green scales formed at the back of Raynor's hand. "What is going on here? Is this how you treat guests?"

"According to my information, Liliana and Gerard are in ASSET's prisons at this very moment. Taken on some trumped-up charges. Punished for nourishing their bodies in the only way they are able."

"We're standing right here. What are you talking about?" Sage tried to pull her hand from Raynor's grip.

"That kiss we shared, much as I hate to say, was seriously lacking," he said.

"Rude," she sneered. "I should have drained you dry."

"You really should have. Not that you could." Raynor's tone bordered on sympathetic. "But that is all in the past. Your being here is actually a happy accident. One I plan to make the best of. You two are my guests of honor for tonight's spectacle." He released Sage's arm, allowing her to back up as he shifted into a green dragon the size of a warhorse.

"Thanks, but we've been treated so rudely I think it's best we leave before things get ugly." Grey reached out for Sage's arm as he backed a step away from the beast.

"I'm afraid that is not going to be possible." Raynor came down on all fours and beat his wings, creating a gust of wind that knocked Sage to the ground.

Claws dug into her back, pinning her where she'd landed. Not quite breaking the skin, but dangerously close to.

"The time has come for our spectacle, and I want you to have a front row seat." Raynor scooped Sage up from the ground and tossed her on his back. "Try to enjoy it. I don't often allow people to ride on my back."

Before she could get away, Raynor beat his wings again, harder this time, and lifted into the air. Sage could do nothing but hold on for dear life. She straddled his neck, ripping the fabric of her dress as her hips settled just above his wing joints.

Raynor rose into the air, circling the house, and let out a mighty roar. She clung to him, gripping his scales but finding no security there, her nails not even strong enough to find purchase against his armor.

Everyone within miles would be able to hear him. How long before someone spotted the great big fire-breathing beast? Just as the thought came to her, she felt warmth rising up from his chest, into his neck.

Raynor's house sat at the edge of a mountain. They circled once, twice, and on the third time, Raynor unleashed a stream of fire aimed at the side of the mountain.

Heat burned under the dragon's scales but did not burn Sage where she sat. She was lucky, if she was allowed to use that word in this circumstance. But what about the people below her? Had he roasted them alive? She couldn't turn to look, not that she wanted to see people roasting alive. Any sudden movement might cause her to lose her grip. Falling to her own flaming death really wasn't the way she wanted to end this night. Sage clung to Raynor's scales for dear life as he banked for another turn, coming round to face the mountain he'd just set ablaze.

The fire began to take shape. Not merely burning brush. Spectacular indeed. A flaming Tree of Life scorched the mountainside far above the cheering crowd below. Sage had no doubt the symbol was also clearly visible for people in the valley to see. For those close enough, they'd have video of a dragon circling in the sky as well. The Mystics were out for blood. No doubt about that.

Sage had no words. What could she say? Ask why? She'd already heard the company line. The Mystics wanted to end the ASSET organization. And with a stunt like that, they might have just gotten their wish.

Raynor roared once more as he let his wings rest, gliding in a spiral toward the ground.

She might not be able to force an answer from his lips, but she'd be damned if she let him bring her back to that house filled with Mystic supporters whooping and hollering at the charred symbol left smoldering on the mountainside.

Sage threw herself off his back as soon as she was close enough to the ground.

She hit the rocks hard, and scrambled to her feet.

Wings beat the air behind her, and Raynor let out another mighty roar.

Sage didn't dare look back. She hobbled as fast as her legs could take her toward lights in the distance, hoping to take refuge behind the walls of another mansion until she could get word to Grey and escape.

TWENTY-FIVE

Smoke's acrid stench filled the air. The dragon's roars faded as it disappeared from the sky, replaced by the sound of approaching sirens and the thundering chorus of helicopters heading their way. Sage hobbled through the rocky terrain, following the fence line of a large estate, until she saw streetlights.

She couldn't be more than a few houses away from Raynor's mansion, not that she'd dare return. But with luck, she'd find Grey nearby, alive and well.

The street came into view. Sage hid in the shadows watching, listening, and wondering if the Mystics were searching for her. Dogs aggressively barked, threatening Sage as she followed the stone wall border of their property. Nerves already frayed, Sage nearly jumped out of her skin. She slapped a hand over her mouth to stifle her surprised screech.

Devon's training came back to her, and she'd give anything to see the smug expression on his face. He'd warned her, and as always, the ogre was right.

Of all the ways she had imagined this evening going, traipsing around in the desert with a broken shoe, hiding from unseen enemies in every shadow, had never crossed her mind. Even in her worst case scenario, Sage had expected Grey to be at her side. Alone, with her anxiety cranked up to twelve, she realized how much she needed her partner. Just having him around gave her strength.

But she didn't have him. All she had was herself, at least for the moment. She refused to think of the alternative. She'd find Grey soon enough. She had to keep her head about her.

Helicopters were the first to arrive on scene. Like a second sun, their spotlights highlighted the ground. Two of them working in tandem circled overhead, scanning the neighborhood and inspecting the aftermath of the blaze.

Deep in enemy territory, she couldn't let the Mystics find her. Nor could she risk the police bringing her in for questioning. There was a way out of this. She could find it.

Deep breaths.

Find a point of contact. Make connection with ASSET and request extraction.

The dogs continued to defend their home, loudly, possibly giving away her positon. She couldn't stand there any longer.

Two options lay before her. Go forward, cross the open street, keep walking, and find where the posh neighborhood ended. The alternative was to go back into the desert toward the mountain, cut off from everything, and risk the lights of the helicopters landing on her.

Which way would Grey go?

Movement in the shadows answered her question. A blur at first that could have been nothing more than a trick of her eyes. Sage crouched low, and watched the shadows across the street. Unseen eyes were there. She felt the weight of them. Someone was watching her, just as she was watching them. She held her position, staying as still as she could, balancing on her good heel despite the burn of her thighs.

Any of the Mystics who might have chased after her wouldn't hide. They'd taunt and tease, attempting to draw her out with lies.

It happened again. A flash. No more than a blink, but she'd seen it. Purple. Moving from one shadow to the next. Disappearing as quickly as it had appeared.

This was a man trying his best to not be seen.

It was him. It had to be.

Hope gave Sage strength. She pushed her legs as fast as they could carry her, keeping just out of reach of the streetlight's glow as she clip-clopped across the asphalt. She came to the other side in time to meet the streaking shadow of Grey as he sprinted between pockets of darkness.

"That was a close one." Sage panted, catching her breath. "I thought we were both goners."

"Are you okay?" His words came on a shaky breath. Grey's eyes glistened with tears. He patted her down frantically, checking for injuries before gripping her hard at the shoulders. Crazy as he looked, Sage wasn't sure if he planned to throttle her or hug her. She held still either way, allowing him to see she was fine, all except for her shoe. "What the hell possessed you to throw yourself off the back of a dragon?" Concern morphed quickly into something like anger. He let his hands fall from her shoulders, but his eyes remained fixed on her face.

Had she heard him wrong? It sounded as if he was angry at her for trying to escape. But that didn't make sense. "Uh, the fact that worse would happen if I landed at a party filled with Mystics' supporters on the back of that very dragon."

"You could have killed yourself."

Had he not heard her? Landing back at that party was ten times more dangerous than the leap she'd taken. Bruises covered both knees, her right hip, and elbow. Could have been worse, sure. She had thrown herself off the back of a dragon in flight, but that was nothing compared to the alternative. She'd love to see him make a better choice in the same situation, scared shitless, clinging to the back of a great flying lizard. She was lucky to have held on for as long as she had, not that she would admit that out loud.

"If I'm going to die, I'd prefer to go out on my own terms."

"Don't act all tough. You slipped, didn't you?" Grey chuckled like a madman.

Fear. That was it. He wasn't angry at her. Angry at his own helplessness. She'd give him that. Only a few moments prior, she was freaking out. But now they were back together.

"If my arm didn't feel like it was about to fall off, I'd smack you right now," she teased, combatting his attitude with snark.

"Seriously, are you okay?" With the sirens closing in, they didn't have the luxury of time to joke or rest.

"No blood. No breaks. I'll be fine." She'd be sore in the morning, but at the moment, she was ready to do whatever it took to get the hell out of there. "Murphy's

Law at its finest." She pulled her broken shoe from her foot and held it up for him to see.

Grey's brow crinkled, his eyes shifting from the ruined shoe to her face, as if he didn't know how to respond. "Can you still walk?"

"Wouldn't be the first time I've had to do the walk of shame with a flat tire." She pulled the other shoe from her foot, opting for bare rather than breaking her ankle should they have to move quickly.

"We can't stay here."

"You think the dragon is coming back?" Sage asked.

"No. They accomplished their mission. They made an even bigger statement against ASSET than last time."

"But they know we were ASSET agents. You don't think they'd want to silence us?"

"Absolutely not. They want word of what they did spread far and wide. And especially when they were able to do it right under our very noses."

"Or on the back of their dragon." Sage hung her head in shame, her cheeks burning with embarrassment. She reached up to her face, realizing her mask had come off, but couldn't remember when that might have been.

"You can't be blamed for that. How could you have known what was going to happen?" Grey pulled her into a hug. "We were both outed. Luck of the draw that you were thrown on the back of the dragon. Could have just as easily been me."

If only she could stay there, in his arms. Even with his heart thundering against her ear, she felt at ease clinging to him. His warmth comforted her as much as the kindness of his words. But the truth was, they were in for it when Ava learned of their adventure. She probably already knew. No doubt the images of a dragon circling around the mountain were being broadcast on the news.

"You think Ava will accept that excuse?"

"We've got more things to worry about right now, like getting back to headquarters."

"If we make it back there."

"Hey now." Grey pulled back and met her eyes. "Where's your positivity?"

Sage plastered a fake smile on her face and chirped, "I hope we make it back."

"That's the spirit." He dropped his arms and spun around slowly. "Now, let's figure out where we can go. Somewhere safe to call for extraction."

He took off almost as soon as he spoke, leaving Sage no choice but to sprint after him. They danced around the lights, keeping under the cloak of shadows, heading, much to Sage's dismay, back in the direction she had just come from. The desert at the base of the mountain.

Damn her luck. As the first rock bit into her heel, she regretted taking her shoes off.

Grey moved swiftly, a man on a mission, while she struggled to keep pace. She caught her toe against a rock and tumbled ungracefully, shredding her dress into sparkly ribbons as she hit the ground.

Grey stopped in his tracks, kicking up dust, and turned around to face her. "You okay?"

Her pinky toe stung like a hot dagger had been shoved under her nail. The truth was she'd probably sheared the damn thing off. But there was no time to sit and inspect it. She kept her mouth closed, refusing to let the sounds of pain escape.

Breathe. Accept. Get up and keep running.

Grey returned to her side and offered his hand. She took it and rose to her feet, keeping her painful whimpers hidden behind her lips.

Soon as we get far enough away from this neighborhood, we can call for a pickup, she recited to herself for motivation as Grey took off again, heading into the darkness of the desert.

TWENTY-SIX

A car came for them, as promised, once they had made it far enough away from the three-ring circus, and whisked them off. Helicopters still circled the mountain, though the blinking red and blue lights from the police vehicles had ceased. How long would the charred symbol of the tree of life remain? ASSET would already be working on removal or some kind of cover-up. With any luck, by dawn's first light, it would be gone, or at the very least rendered invisible to human eyes.

Sage finally allowed herself to relax when the car pulled into the ASSET headquarters parking garage. Despite the way the night had ended, they had a definite finger to point at the Mystics. Ava had demanded a name, a head to put on the proverbial pike, and they had it. That had to count for something.

Sage walked with Grey, ready to deliver the good news to their boss. Raynor Brurdur. After making such a public show of his true form, they had probable cause to bring him in as well. All they needed now was to send in the cavalry.

"I should have known better than to send you two." Ava beat them to the punch the moment they crossed the threshold of her office. "You were too green for an assignment like this." She slashed a manicured fingernail in Sage's direction.

Sage exchanged a nervous glance with Grey. She'd expected a little anger about the dragon sighting, but the way Ava had begun the conversation sounded as if she blamed the entire evening on Sage.

"And you, Mr. Maddox." Ava turned her icy glare in Grey's direction. "Why the hell would you let her out of your sight? You two should have been attached at the hip."

Despite their few moments of separation early on, and the little incident with the dragon, they had spent the bulk of the night attached at the hips. Sage wanted to explain herself. To offer up what they had learned, but the words stuck in her throat.

"We were unfortunately identified early on." Grey lowered his eyes. "We attempted to get out the moment we learned our cover had been blown."

"Am I supposed to just accept your complete and utter failure?" Ava wasn't falling for his reproachful look. "You obviously don't understand the first thing about being undercover. As is evident by the fact you were ID'd…at a masked ball. You're both off the case," Ava said with finality.

"Don't," Sage blurted out without having a concrete defense in mind. If only Ava would give her a moment to organize her thoughts she would surely see that their mission had been a success. But she was on the warpath.

"Excuse me? Miss Cynwrig, when I want your input I will ask for it."

"You're the boss, of course." Sage lowered her head respectfully as she softened her voice. "We have the name you want. We got the head of the organization. It wasn't a complete failure." That information had to count for something. At the very least, it should make up for the way things had ended.

"No. Not a complete failure," Ava responded with a heavy dose of sarcasm. "Only a few people recorded you riding a damned dragon." She spun her laptop around so Sage could see the sparkly blur of her dress caught on a camera phone on the back of a dragon, flying circles in the air.

On balance, the darkness had worked to her advantage. Sure, the argument could be made that the incriminating figure in the video was Sage, but to the causal viewer who did not know what she was wearing, Sage appeared as little more than a shimmering blob. And that was with the brightness turned up to the max on Ava's screen. Sage wanted to say that. She meant to form the words into a coherent string to give her argument some strength. But her brain short-circuited the moment she opened her mouth.

"No one knows it was me." A far cry from the excellent defense Sage had been trying to mount. She cringed at the way her voice betrayed her, making her sound like a petulant teenager.

Grey was no help. He glared at her as if she'd grown an extra head.

"What I mean is…" Sage took a breath to steady herself. She clenched and released her hands, getting the blood flowing to her fingertips, and started again. "I never lost my mask. No one was able to see my face. So my identity should remain secret."

"That's wonderful for you, Miss Cynwrig," Ava replied coldly. "However, the world isn't as concerned with you as they might be with a damned dragon flying around their city setting mountains ablaze."

Sage pleaded with her eyes for Grey to help. She was striking out hard. Why the hell was he just standing there, allowing her to take the brunt of Ava's anger?

"No. You're right, of course." Sage kept her tone calm, level, despite the cold chill of dread trickling down her spine. "I was just trying to point out that ASSET hasn't been implicated here. Our cover remains—"

"They lit our symbol on the side of the damned mountain," Ava fired back sharply, cutting straight to the heart of her point. "How exactly has our organization avoided any implication here?"

"It was not all Sage's fault," Grey offered with nothing further to explain himself.

"I never said it was. You two are partners. You both share the blame for the failure of this mission." Ava turned her laptop back around and sat down to face it.

"But we didn't completely fail. Let us bring Raynor in. He's the head. It was his party. We don't need to be undercover any longer. We can go in with the full might of ASSET behind us," Sage said.

"Storm the castle and take Raynor prisoner. Simple as that, eh?" Ava threw the words back in her face.

Defending herself against a boss like that required the kind of mental acrobatics Sage didn't have the energy to perform. She turned to Grey hoping he might have a better approach, but her partner stood with his head down, pinching the bridge of his nose. He had the measure of things. His silence wasn't due to any lack of information. He'd just realized nothing he could say would help dig him out of the hole they'd gotten into. One of these days, Sage would learn that lesson herself.

"I appreciate your desire to go after the bad guy, Miss Cynwrig, but Shadow Ops does not operate that way. We're trying to mitigate damages not stir the pot more. These Mystics will do anything to paint our organization in a bad light. As is evident by the guerilla tactics they are using to discredit us to the whole of the magical community. Any perceived force without proper backup will only serve their purpose."

"We have backup. We have a dragon flying around the city, lighting fires." Sage was grasping at straws, but surely this was enough to bring Raynor in. "As you pointed out, evidence is there, online for all to see."

"And we have unauthorized ASSET agents' party crashing," Ava fired back without missing a beat. "And riding said dragon. We're really not in a place to go accusing high-level members of the magical community when our people are just as culpable."

"But Raynor..."

"Is no longer your concern. You two are off the case," Ava said.

"That's not fair," Sage groaned.

"Dismissed, Miss Cynwrig." Ava waved her hand, shooing Sage out of the office. "Mr. Maddox, I need a word in private."

Sage trudged away, exiled to the hallway, wondering why she was being ostracized.

TWENTY-SEVEN

She waited in the hallway for her partner to emerge from Ava's office, and practically pounced when he came out, tail tucked between his legs like a beaten dog.

"What the hell was that back there?" Sage released all her pent-up frustration. He had hardly said two words back there in Ava's office. Just let their boss run roughshod all over them as if they had purposely screwed up the mission.

"There was nothing I could say." Grey shrugged, the look on his face unrepentant. "You know how Ava operates. Her word is final."

"Bullshit!" Sage refused to give up. That couldn't be it. One little screw-up and they were off the case? No. She'd screwed up way worse than this in the past, and Ava hadn't benched her. Or Grey for that matter. Why now? What hadn't she understood back there in Ava's office? Something subtle. Some subtext. This was most certainly not the end of their case. "Her tone might be final, but her word is always open to interpretation."

"You lost me." Grey's face scrunched in confusion.

"How many times has she told us no, knowing we would do something anyway, and we were right to do the thing?" Sage asked.

"Was that supposed to be English? Because I didn't understand a word of what you just said."

"We need to put a team together and go get Raynor," Sage said.

Grey rolled his eyes as he blew out an exasperated sigh. "You have a death wish, don't you?"

"If you don't want to go, I completely understand."

"Oh no." Grey shook his head. A mixture of shock and disbelief twisted his expression. "You're not doing this to me again."

"I'm not doing anything to you. In fact, I'm releasing you of all obligations. You should be happy."

"We're partners." Grey said the words like a plea, as if reminding her of their relationship would be enough to change her mind.

"Don't worry. I'll make sure Ava knows I did this on my own," she assured him.

"Stop it. Please. For once, just let it go." His voice cracked. Concern? Fear? Some mixture of the two? Either way, he sounded firmly against her plan. "There will be other cases."

"No. There won't. We have to prove ourselves worthy of being in Shadow Ops. Don't you see? We have to do this on our own. Outside of ASSET's official permission. Off the books."

"You're insane. That fall must have knocked you harder than I thought. Let's get you checked out at the infirmary."

"Stop it. You're not listening. I'm fine. But this…" Sage waved her hand in the air. "Ava is testing us."

"Ava gave us a direct order."

"How long have you been an agent?"

"Longer than I care to admit," he sighed.

"So why bench you for such a small thing?"

"Because we are partners, we are both benched until you get a little more training," Grey said. "That's what Ava wants. She didn't want to hurt your feelings."

"Bullshit." Ava never cared about feelings. What the hell was Grey playing at? "She needs to make the paperwork look good because our cover got blown. She knows you're well trained. And thanks to our little escapade in Phoenix, she knows we can handle ourselves working outside of ASSET jurisdiction. We've just been warned not to go in flashing ASSET badges, but we're far from benched."

"You are reading way too much into this."

"Which is why you don't have to follow me." She didn't believe for a second that he would let her go in alone, but she made her statements nice and loud, on the off chance anyone else was listening. "No harm. No foul. You did exactly what Ava said."

"You want me to drive you home?" Grey looked at her as if she had lost her mind.

Something was wrong with him. She hadn't been able to hear what was being said in Ava's office. It must have been bad. This was the guy who had been willing to throw his whole career away a few weeks back to ensure her safety. And now he was passively accepting their dismissal when they had a clear suspect. It wasn't adding up.

She glared up at Grey, searching his face for any sign of truth. "That's it? You're not going to argue with me?"

"What's the point?" He shrugged again, utterly defeated, complacent. So not like himself. "Your mind has already been made up."

"Okay." *That's a first.* "Yeah, I'd love a ride home," she replied.

"I need to make one pit stop before we can head out." Grey led the way toward the elevator. "You can go with me or hang here."

She wasn't clear whether or not Grey had just agreed to come with her or if he was just giving her a ride home. She wasn't going to press for clarification at that moment. Nor was she going to let him out of her sight. Not with the strange way he was acting. Like something had snapped and he had given up the will to fight completely.

A little sleep. A clear head. Things always looked different in the morning. She'd broach the topic again with him then.

They took the elevator down, exiting on the prison level.

"What are you doing down here?"

"Ava wants me to confirm that the people we were impersonating were actually here," Grey responded slowly. "For my report."

"Why wouldn't they be?" She followed him down the long corridor.

"Dotting my Is and crossing my Ts." Grey spoke almost as slowly as he walked. He reached a door requiring key-card access and swiped his ASSET badge. "Ava will be reading the report, and I'm already on her bad side." He opened the door and held it for Sage to follow inside.

"You live on her bad side. I don't see why you care so much this time." Sage hadn't meant to make the offhand comment out loud. She might as well have slapped him. Then at least she'd deserve the look he gave her.

"I didn't mean it like that." She tried to backpedal, but the damage had been done.

"Just wait here." Grey took off down the hallway, moving swifter than he had moments before.

Sage chased after him. No way was she letting that man out of her sight. Not until she figured out what was wrong. "C'mon, now you know I didn't mean it like that." She followed as he opened one of the cell block doors. It closed behind both of them with a loud bang.

Grey continued wordlessly past one empty cell after another, until he reached the one he had been looking for. He stopped and punched a code into a small keypad next to the door. Grey stepped inside as it opened.

"Are you going to talk to me?" She followed him in, wondering what the hell he was doing.

"What is there to talk about?" Grey turned around to face her. "You're being obstinate. You refuse to listen to direct orders. And attacking me for trying to mitigate the damage by toeing the line with our boss?"

"That's not fair," she started to say, but stopped, realizing he was right. She was mad at him for all the wrong reasons. But at the same time so desperate to prove herself to Ava. To prove herself to herself. She could do this. She and Grey both could make right what went wrong this evening, if only they had the chance to try.

Grey filled the sudden silence. "You like to use that word. Life is not fair. Our job is not fair. Get over it, or you'll end up getting yourself killed."

"I'm trying to do what is right." Sage suddenly realized the cell they were in was empty.

Grey circled around her, putting himself in the doorway, blocking the way out. He faced her, but didn't meet her eyes. "I know. And I want you to understand that I'm doing the same thing." He stepped backwards and closed the cell door, locking her inside.

"What the hell," Sage screamed and beat her hand against the door. "Let me out!"

Grey stared at her through a tiny window in the door. "You are bound and determined to go against our orders. I'm doing this for your own good, Sage. I don't want to see you get hurt."

She turned her back on him. She couldn't look him in the eye at that moment. How dare he? How could he double-cross her like that? He was supposed to be her partner. They had made a pact to always be honest and open. More lies. More bullshit and manipulation.

"You've already hurt me more than anyone else, partner."

The outer door to the cell block closed with a final, heavy *thud*. Grey was gone. Leaving Sage more alone than she had ever been.

TWENTY-EIGHT

Her phone had been rendered useless in the prison, leaving Sage with no way to contact the outside world. No use screaming or beating her hands bloody against the walls either. No one would hear her frantic pleas to be released. She couldn't remember seeing anyone in the cells when she followed Grey down here. Nor did she see any guards posted. He'd been crafty, that bastard. Put her into the deepest, darkest place where only he would know her location, and only he could come to release her. How long would she be kept in this tiny cell, locked safe behind windowless concrete walls?

Grey claimed he'd done this to stop her from getting hurt. Protecting her from herself. A weak excuse after all they had been through together.

No. Worse than weak.

Insulting.

Grey had proved how little faith he had in her. All their time together accounted for nothing. So much for being partners. All that bullshit he'd fed her about being honest. Not having secrets from each other. Being a team.

The next time she laid eyes on him... He'd better be wearing protective gear when that cell door opened. She'd have more than strong words waiting.

Rage kept her company in the long, lonely hours, whispering reminders of Grey's betrayal in her ear. Each time she calmed enough to recognize the call of fatigue.

Hours passed before Sage finally gave in to the nagging need to sleep. But just as she'd begin to drift off, she caught the sound of a door opening.

The outer cell door.

Footsteps confirmed it. Someone was coming.

Sage balled her fist, ready to strike, all her anger ready to unleash.

The cell door opened. Bright light streamed in from outside, casting her warden into shadow.

"Do you want to explain to me why you're here?" Devon spoke before Sage had the chance to let her fist fly.

Grey hadn't told him. The coward. What other secrets was he keeping?

Sage unclenched her fist and took a breath. "Wish I could say. You'll have to talk to my partner."

"Any idea where he is?" Devon asked. "What he'd planned to do?"

"No. I was kind of hoping you'd tell me so I can find him and teach him a thing or two about faith and courage." She collapsed down on the bench and rubbed the aches from her back.

"Then we are both at a disadvantage." Devon sighed and joined her on the bench. He handed her a small strip of paper. "Ava headed up a special mission this morning. She hasn't returned. I assume Grey joined her. You too until I found this, presumably from your missing partner, shoved under my office door."

Sage is in time-out. Cell block 23.

"That jerk!" She jumped to her feet. "He told me not to go after the dragon, and he went with Ava?"

"If she was leading a mission is something of great significance," Devon said thoughtfully.

"Our mission didn't go exactly as planned, but we learned Raynor Brurdur was firmly on the side of the Mystics, possibly their leader. He all but outed himself taking me for a ride on his back."

Devon chuckled at her revelation, but quickly regained the control he had over his expression. "That was you in the video?"

"You saw it?" She cringed. It had been bad enough for Ava to point it out, but if the video was still making the rounds on the internet, ASSET's reputation was in a far worse place than she had expected.

"Unfortunately, we can't control everything on the internet here," Devon replied. "We can, however, spin things. Like a new fantasy movie being filmed in Vegas."

As far as cover stories went, it was pretty thin. But Sage had seen the willingness of people to believe what they wanted rather than what was right in their face. Media crafted more beliefs than truth ever did. Politics was proof of that. So, if it worked, great!

"What about the mountain?" Sage asked hopefully. "Is our symbol still there?"

"That has been erased, thanks to a few of our elemental friends."

Thank the gods for small miracles. That meant ASSET still had some friends left in the magical community. "Who?"

"What?" Devon stared at her as if she had grown an extra head.

"The elemental we called on for help. Was it Nyx?"

"Unimportant." He shrugged off her question. "What we need to know, right now, is Ava's location, and why she and her team have not reported in."

"We find Raynor…" Sage stood, ready to head for the door. "We find our people."

Devon took hold of her arm before she could take a step. "If that is what Ava intended to do and didn't return, do you really think that is the best course of action?"

He had a point. But with little else to go on, all they could do was start at square one.

Sage pulled free of his grasp with a groan. "Raynor is a dragon. Dangerous, sure. But he could have killed me when he had the chance. Instead, just took me for a ride. That had to count for something." She might be a newbie, as everyone loved to point out, but her intuition was as sharp as any of the more seasoned agents at ASSET. "If Ava went to apprehend him and something went wrong, he's the first person we need to speak to. Benefit of the doubt here. Just give me this for a minute."

Devon crossed his arms and stared down his nose. Not the look of confidence Sage was hoping for, but at least he wasn't denying her this opportunity to discuss theories.

"Okay, so they go after Raynor, right? Let's say he didn't hurt them. He might know where they were heading next. Assuming they approached Raynor and someone else was there to do the deed, whatever that is." She silently prayed that wasn't the case. Grey and Ava needed to both be alive and well. Sage would not be denied her opportunity for payback on her jerk of a partner. "If Raynor did do the unthinkable…well then, he'd probably be gone. Vacate the scene of the crime. We can search his property for clues to follow and learn the fate of our missing people."

Devon remained silent the whole time she'd been speaking, his expression unchanged. Unconvinced. She might as well have been talking to a brick wall for all the feedback she'd gotten from him.

"What do you suggest, then?" Sage took a breath, and prepared for the worst.

"Information," Devon answered calmly. "We need to arm our minds before we head into battle."

She couldn't argue that point, though she still suspected that all roads were going to lead her to Raynor. But information was something she might be able to get with ease. "Zack attended the party with us." She and Grey had planned to meet with him once everyone was safe. "I haven't spoken to him yet."

"Where did you arrange to meet him?"

"We didn't have a specific place in mind. But if I go home, my roommate will know how to contact him."

"Then that is where you must go. I will do what I can here. When we have a plan, we go together. No vigilante crap, you understand?"

"Scout's honor." She saluted him.

"This is not a joke," Devon replied sharply. "You understand Ava is not available. The head of ASSET operations is not available."

"Yes…I know." She'd never seen Devon like this. He yelled at her all the time in training, but this was different. His voice carried a double edge of anger and anxiety that demanded strict compliance. "I'm sorry. I was just trying to lighten the mood a little."

"Not the time." Devon shook his head slowly. "Not the place."

What was he trying to convey to her without saying outright? He'd been avoiding saying the word 'missing' when referring to Ava. That much she understood. But there was something else. Something much more important she was missing from this conversation.

The problem with being a newbie, Sage found herself always needing to ask the dumb questions. "What happens with Ava out of the office?"

"Officially…her whereabouts are above our paygrade. We continue business as usual until other orders are sent down." Devon glanced up at the ceiling, his eyes darting around, looking for something. He shifted his body, forcing Sage to adjust where she stood as well.

She followed his path and saw a tiny pinhole in the ceiling. A camera probably.

Devon stepped in closer and whispered in her ear, "She should have never gone. Field work is not her place."

Sage whispered, "Then why did she go?"

"It is my belief that the Mystics have specific targets at this time."

Sage understood immediately. The trial. There were so many unknown faces in the audience. They had seen the crafty way Ava had an answer for all the council's questions. Never revealing anything as she refuted all their accusations with no small amount of attitude. The Mystics had been committing small acts of terrorism. Nuisances really. Nothing major. Nothing that resulted in violence or death. These weren't the kind of actions that would bring down the entire organization, but could easily take one person out. One very important part of the organization. Ava. They were calling her out. And she'd answered.

"Why the hell would she..."

Devon slapped a hand over her mouth before she could finish that sentence. "We don't need to know the reason. That's not your job right now. Understand?"

Sage nodded and Devon released her.

"Go see Zack. Learn what you can." Devon stepped aside, releasing Sage from her cell. "And when you are ready, meet me at the dojo."

TWENTY-NINE

The moment Sage arrived at her apartment, she stripped off the ruined leftovers of her dress and made a beeline for the bathroom to wash away the failure of the last twenty-four hours in the hottest water her shower could provide.

Bruises had bloomed in deep purple on her hip and knee, but her cuts and scrapes were beginning to vanish. Thank the goddess for Terra healing.

If only other things fixed themselves that quickly, but reality was like a vengeful GM who set the board full of impossible tasks, and rolling a natural twenty was the only way to accomplish them. Sage never had that kind of luck in games or life.

Still, she had to try. There was no rage quitting in life, though she couldn't promise she wouldn't flip a table or two along the way.

Showered and changed, Sage emerged from the bathroom ready to tackle her next challenge. She sauntered into her living room, and had to do a double take. It was her apartment, but no longer the empty shell it had been when she'd last looked. She'd breezed through the living room in a fatigued stupor on her way to the shower, but the fact she had missed all that had Sage questioning her sanity. Couches, television, coffee table, side tables, and curtains. Even framed movie posters hung on the wall.

Matt's bedroom door opened behind her. "What do you think?"

"When did you have time for all of this?" She stood blocking the hallways, stupidly gawking at the room. Tears welled in the corners of her eyes as the word *home* formed in her mind. This was exactly what she needed.

Matt pulled her into a hug. "Hope you like it," he whispered against her ear as he lifted her up in the air.

She didn't fight the crush of his arms, or the tears falling down her cheeks and landing on his shoulder. "Yes. This. So much this!"

He carried her all the way into the furnished room, set her down in front of the heavy wood coffee table, and took a step back. "Josh helped…a lot."

"The table was his idea, wasn't it?" She bent down and ran her hand along the smooth wood surface. "You two doing better?"

"We're good." He grinned mischievously.

"Finally some good news."

"Rough night at the office?" Matt asked, but his tone betrayed his attempt to play ignorance.

"Like you don't already know." Sage collapsed on the couch. Much firmer than their old one. Rather than enveloping her in its cushiony embrace, its firmness resisted her, nearly sending Sage back to her feet. She'd break it in soon enough. "I need to talk to Zack."

"Guilty." Matt sighed. "He told me to call the minute you came home. He's on his way."

"Anticipating every one of my questions and needs." She smirked. Of course he knew. He'd have blown up her phone if he hadn't been getting a play-by-play from Zack. "Why are you so perfect?"

"If I told you, I'd have to kill you."

"That would just spoil the evening, so I guess you can keep your secrets." Sage reached a hand out toward Matt.

He took it and let Sage pull him down to the couch with her. "Smart choice."

"I have been known to make those from time to time."

Matt gasped in shock. "Stop the presses, really?"

"Shut up." She slapped his shoulder.

"Fine. But only if you tell me how *he* reacted to the dress."

Damn him. They were having such a nice conversation, and Matt had to bring Grey back into the picture. And as much as she wanted to gush about the look on her partner's face and the kiss, all of the kisses, those memories had been ruined when that bastard locked her away in a prison cell at ASSET. That sent her spiraling back down into the pit of stress that was her mission. She had to get Grey and Ava back.

Matt stared at her, waiting impatiently for her to unload, but she wasn't ready to hit him with the heavy stuff. That would wait until Zack arrived.

"The dress… What can I say?" She forced the smile back across her face. "You created a masterpiece. All eyes were on me. Damn near blew my cover I was so sought after."

"I knew it would be a hit. I mean, how could it not? We were starting with such an attractive base."

Had he caught on to her strained tone? Deflecting with compliments was his go-to method of diffusing things.

"I am a ten, right?"

"Well, when I dress you," he teased. "Yes."

The doorbell sounded, a death knell for Sage's good mood. No more holding back; it was time to continue her mission.

Sage answered the door, ushering Zack in quickly. "I'm happy to see you survived."

He stormed into the living room like a man on a mission, no perky attempt to flirt, and took the couch opposite the one Sage claimed. "It was quite the evening. Why did it take you so long to make contact?"

"I can't get into that right now."

"As you wish." His well-chosen words, though restrained, gave her a small sense of hope.

"I need to know everything about the dragon."

Zack narrowed his eyes, staring across the coffee table at Sage. "The dragon is not who you think he is."

"I'm not interested in thoughts about his character." She hadn't meant to cut him off so rudely, but she needed to get him on point. "He's a fire-breathing dragon. He flew me around his home. Videos are all over the internet. He's clearly allied with the Mystics."

"That point is questionable," Zack noted quickly.

"What?"

"The dragon... Raynor...seemed to be unhappy when he came back. I'm not so sure—"

"Of course he was unhappy." Sage couldn't help her annoyed reply. "I escaped, and so did Grey, at least for that moment."

"Hold on." Zack leaned forward, resting his elbows on his thighs. "If Grey made it out alive with you…where is your gloomy partner?"

She chewed on her cheek, not sure how much truth she should reveal. "That's what I'm trying to figure out. He disappeared shortly after."

Matt let out a soft gasp before slapping a hand over his mouth.

"That doesn't make sense." Deep lines etched across Zack's brow. He sat quietly for a moment, tapping his lips with his index finger.

Sage quietly waited for his next words, hoping they would be something helpful.

"Raynor shut the party down pretty quickly after his return."

"No surprise since police were swarming all over the place." Sage scoffed. The conversation had yet to provide any real help. She began to wonder if talking with Zack was wasting precious time.

"No. You're not understanding me." Zack grunted in frustration. "He really seemed bothered when he got back. Came through the front door and told everyone to get out, then stormed off himself, practically smoking."

"He is a dragon." Matt chuckled.

Sage would have laughed, too, if she weren't two seconds from leaving. If Zack didn't have anything helpful to give her on Raynor, she'd have to reach out to her other resource.

"Please listen," Zack urged. "He'd been all smiles moments before. The shift in his personality was noticeably odd."

"Raynor knew he stirred the hornets' nest." Sage had seen that firsthand with Ava. And the fact her boss went personally to apprehend the dragon was proof of how important it was he be brought in immediately. "He had to know ASSET would be coming."

"Exactly. Why do something so blatantly stupid? Dragons are rare enough as it is. Why risk outing yourself? Even if you have a vendetta against ASSET, that's the worst way to try and exact revenge."

Zack's questions were similar to the ones Sage had asked herself during those long hours of silence spent in prison. It didn't make sense for someone to make such a show, knowing they would become ASSET's number one target. That fact alone reinforced Sage's belief that, dangerous as it might seem, she needed to speak to Raynor. She needed the other side of the story.

"Well, that's where Grey was most likely headed when I lost him." Sage leaned back into the stiff couch cushions, letting the full weight of her revelation fall on Zack's ears.

"You're not suggesting he went back to face the dragon himself, are you?" His eyes widened in shock.

"What if I am?"

"No." He shook his head. "I really hope you aren't."

Those two weren't exactly best buddies, but they shared a mutual respect for each other's positions. If Zack had thought Grey was being stupid, he'd have eagerly mocked him with plenty of laughter. She'd have welcomed that. She wanted to give her idiot partner a good swift kick in the balls for locking her away in time-out. But without the laughter and mocking, all that remained was the very real possibility that she might never see Grey, or Ava for that matter, again.

Sage lowered her gaze, not willing to acknowledge the fear on the vampire's face. "You think he would get rid of an ASSET agent coming to bring him in for questioning?"

"I don't know what he would do, only what he is capable of. Dragons are as powerful as they are temperamental."

"I need to know for sure. I need to speak with Raynor myself."

Matt shifted uncomfortably next to her.

"No. Please don't," Zack replied sharply. "Have you not heard a word I just said?"

"I have." Sage stared straight into Zack's angry eyes. "And I'm not planning on going in as a hostile. Threatening a dragon is clearly a bad move. I just want a conversation. I need to know the truth of what happened that night."

"Don't ask much, do you?" Zack's outrage turned to sarcasm. "And how exactly do you think that's going to happen?"

His attempt at playing dumb wasn't going to deter her. She softened her approach. One last try to get him to be helpful before she found other means. "You have connections everywhere. You can do this. I know you can."

"While I would love to be your knight in shining armor," Zack offered, "there are things even I am not capable of."

She kept her gaze locked with his. "Zack...please."

"Don't do this." He turned away. "You don't know what you're asking."

"If it were me who was missing...and Grey came to you with this same request...would you deny him?"

Zack balled his fist and slammed it down on the coffee table, shattering the wood, sending splinters out in all directions. "For you, I would in a heartbeat. Grey…can handle—"

"Don't you dare pull that misogynistic crap on me," she replied, unleashing every ounce of her pent-up frustration.

Her tone sent Matt retreating to a safer place on the other side of the couch. "Not the best choice of words, man."

"I'm not trying to insult you." Zack spoke slowly, as if carefully choosing each of his words. "This is a point of fact. You have so much to learn. Have I not shown you this? If you can't handle me, how do you expect to handle a dragon?"

"Because, you egotistical asshole, I don't plan on dealing with him as if he were a blood-lusting vampire who can't distinguish between his brain and his…" She turned to Matt and mouthed the word *sorry* before redirecting her anger at its intended target, Zack. "I'm a damn newbie. Have we got it all out of our systems now? Because I'm sick to fucking death of everybody and their brother reminding me. I'm a Terra. I'm an ASSET agent. Shadow Ops. This is my job. You can either help me do it, or I will find someone else who can."

Zack turned his focus to the shattered table. "I'll replace that. Sorry."

"I don't give a crap about the damn table," she barked. "The dragon. Can you arrange a meeting in a public place, or not?"

"I'll see what I can do," Zack growled. "But know that I don't like this plan."

"I'm not going to attack him. I just want to talk. Tell him whatever you need. I was fired from ASSET or whatever. I'm not there in any official capacity, just to find my friend."

Matt nudged her with his shoulder, and took her hand in his. A small show of solidarity, unasked for, but definitely needed. Without her partner, Sage needed all the help she could get to unravel this mystery. Matt gave it willingly. Zack reluctantly. Maybe between the three of them, and Devon, they could pull this off. The alternative was unthinkable.

THIRTY

Waiting sucked. Waiting while worried with no actionable information was pure torture. Zack had left assuring Sage he'd let her know the moment he could arrange a meeting with Raynor. Even Matt had abandoned her, though she couldn't argue his motive. Once Josh had arrived, it was inevitable. Still, lonely hours passed with all the speed of a slug on a salt lick. Sage paced her apartment like a caged animal, anxiously awaiting a call that would probably not come, but there was no way she could get sleep.

She needed to plan and be ready the moment she got the call with the location of where to meet Mr. Dragon.

Devon and Zack had both warned her how dangerous a dragon could be. But with Grey and Ava's lives at stake, what choice did she have? To face him alone was admittedly foolish, but if Sage hoped to get any information from him, she couldn't make him think she was approaching in any formal ASSET capacity. A problem of logistics that needed a real solution. How could she work alone without actually working alone?

Sage sprinted across the apartment complex as the sun began peeking over the horizon, and took the stairs two at a time up to her favorite ex-Djinn's apartment.

"Luke, I need you." She pounded on his door.

After the third consecutive round of knocks, he opened it. Luke stared at her with heavy-lidded eyes as if still partially asleep. "What time is it?"

"I don't know. Morning-ish. I haven't slept much. Crazy last couple of days. I need you." All her anxiety came rushing out in the flood of words, leaving her gasping for breath as she finished. "Will you help me?"

His soft, sleepy expression hardened into cold determination. "Do I have a choice?" Luke stepped aside and let her into the apartment.

"Well…um…" Not the greeting she'd hoped for. Then again, if she'd been woken up at the crack of dawn by a crazy person babbling about problems and favors, she wouldn't be instantly receptive either. She gave herself a moment to collect her thoughts and breathe. "I guess we are even…so you're free to say no. But…if you do…some very important people might die."

"Flair for the dramatic much?" Luke turned toward his kitchen. "Is this about the magic school bus or the burning bush? Hilarious video of you on the dragon by the way. How did you manage to hold on?"

That video was going to haunt her for the rest of her life. Embarrassment burned like dragon's breath against her cheeks. Forget all the good work she'd done at ASSET. Sage would forever be labeled as the dragon rider. Only the actual name would be something ten times crueler.

"Are you going to help me?"

"With which part? The dragon?" he teased. Luke opened the refrigerator and pulled out an energy drink. He held it up, giving her the universal sign for *you want one too?*

She nodded. Not having slept in who knows how long, she could use all the caffeine she could get, even if that meant drinking what tasted like battery acid.

"Like you don't already know."

"Humor me." He handed her a can and cracked open his own.

She'd been close-lipped with the others, but Luke dealt in information. Honesty and trust were the only way she'd get his assistance. "Grey, Ava, and a few others at ASSET never returned from a mission to bring in members of the Mystics."

"Are you serious?" He sputtered and covered his mouth before he could completely drench Sage with his drink. "Do you know if they are still alive?"

"No." Saying it out loud made it feel real. But she didn't want it to be. She had to hold on to some hope that they were alive. They were hostages. She still had the chance to get them back. "Which is why I need to set a plan in place, like now."

"And that is?"

"Fight fire with fire." She cracked open her can and took a sip. Definitely battery acid, with a hint of citrus. The taste alone was enough to give her a jump-start.

"You and the dragon an item now?" he teased. "I can't believe they tried to pass that off as movie studio BS. No one is going to actually believe that nonsense."

"You better hope they do. ASSET looks like a bunch of damn fools letting crap like this happen." She forced down another chug, cringing as the sour flavor washed over her tongue. It was doing something. She could already feel a rush of renewed energy. "Which is why I have to talk to the dragon. I think… I hope… Look…I don't know what to imagine right now, but Raynor is my key to learning the whereabouts of our missing people."

"You are hearing yourself, right? I just want to be sure you understand how ridiculous you sound."

"Okay, yes, I'm kind of reaching here. But hear me out. Raynor might be a big bad dragon, but he didn't strike me as totally evil. I think he might be something like…evil adjacent." She wasn't entirely sure how that word popped into her mind, but it fit. Caffeine was clearly starting to kick in. "Kind of like you when we first met."

"Hey now." Luke bristled at her accusation. "I had reasons."

She stared him down, crossing her arms, and waited for him to get over himself. Whether he had a master or not, when he'd been a full-fledged djinn, he deserved that title and more.

"Sure. Evil adjacent. Whatever."

"So…since I don't think he's totally evil, I've requested a friendly little one-on-one where I can feel him out."

Luke's eyebrow lifted suspiciously, but he didn't open his mouth.

"Mind out of the gutter," she warned him.

Luke smiled innocently. "You do have a thing for bad boys."

"I'm talking about a meeting. In public. Where I can assess his true intentions."

"Alone?"

"That's where I need your help."

"You're going to explain yourself, I'm assuming, any time now, right?" Luke chugged the entire can, without puckering or cringing, then crushed it in his palms before throwing it away.

"The Mystics have been playing a dirty game, trying to make ASSET look bad. They're using propaganda to show us as evil overlords who are totally inept at doing our jobs."

"Yeah, they have a good smear campaign going," he agreed a little too eagerly for Sage's liking.

"So if we want to win, we need to play their game. And you know me, I love to play." She could feel the surge of caffeine. Her brain was alive. She slammed down the rest of her drink just as Luke had, not even tasting it as she gulped every last drop. "And I'm going to beat them. The magical community will soon see the Mystics for the fanatics they are."

"And you came to me, why? I have no magic."

"Oh, but you do. The best kind of magic, really." She pointed to the four computer screens mounted to the far wall in the living room above his desk. "Surveillance and hacking."

"Someone's going super spy." He chuckled but the look on his face clearly said he was impressed.

"If I want to get information out of the dragon when I meet him, I have to be sneaky. I'm going into this meeting as a private citizen. Not as ASSET. If he suspects what I'm doing, things could get ugly, even in public. We've already seen he's willing to go full dragon even at the expense of normal humans seeing him."

"So what do you propose?"

"For starters…do you have any tracking devices? Small ones?"

"I can get some gear together if you give me a couple of days."

"I kinda need things now-ish if possible. This meeting could happen anytime. I'm literally waiting for my phone to ring."

Luke's brow furrowed. He stalked over to his desk. "I might have a few things that could work in a pinch." He opened a drawer and rummaged around inside. "They're a bit unconventional, but if tracking is all you need…"

"And maybe some recording too," she added hopefully.

"You're lucky we're friends." He glared at her as he crossed the room again, heading back to the kitchen and another set of drawers. "I want these things back, you understand."

She knew she'd come to the right guy. Thank the goddess above she hadn't been forced to kill him back when she had the Seed of Destruction. Despite their rocky start, Luke had become one of her best allies. She'd owe him big time, assuming she lived to see him after the meeting with Raynor. "I really appreciate this."

"I'll send you my bill after I see you return safely…with my things."

She saw through the tough-guy act. He wasn't really worried about his things. But she wasn't going to call him out on that. Maybe if she could work her own brand of magic, she could get him a position in ASSET. He would make a valuable addition there.

Luke crossed from the kitchen back into the living room, hooking a sliver paw-shaped key chain onto what appeared to be a set of car keys. "This is a tracker." He pointed to the paw charm. "It's meant to keep track of pets. It has its own SIM and it's Wi-Fi enabled. As long as you have the input code, you can track it anywhere through an app on your phone."

A dog tracker. She wanted to laugh, but the utter simplicity of it was genius. "Would you mind tracking me? Just in case things go south. Then you'll at least know where to find your things."

"Good idea," he said with a playful wink.

"And I guess it's probably safer if a separate party had eyes on me. You know. Accountability and all."

"Sure." He chuckled as he held up a set of keys. "Now pay attention. This is a personal favorite of mine."

"You're letting me borrow your car?"

"Are you crazy? No. It's a personal recorder."

"What?" He had her attention now for sure. That was exactly the kind of thing she needed. Discrete and utterly ordinary-looking. She thought for sure it was a real set of car keys with the key fob alarm clicker. "Talk about super spy gear."

"Have no fear, Double-o. No one will suspect a thing. It doesn't make any sounds or have any visible lights. Once you hit the record button" — he pressed the unlock button on top of the key fob — "it will vibrate twice to let you know it's powered on. To stop recording, hit the lock button. It will vibrate one time to confirm it stopped recording. This baby has a fifteen-hour battery life, plenty of storage space thanks to the added SD card, and can record clearly even if you have it sitting in your purse on the table. Or in a pocket." He flipped it over and stuck his fingernail in a small seam, revealing a hidden compartment. "There's a USB port here so you can connect it to your computer and access the recording."

"Perfect." She couldn't hide her enthusiasm as she took the key chain and examined it herself. Her plan was beginning to come together. She'd solved the logistical angle at least. "This will definitely help me gather the information I need. Between you keeping an eye on my whereabouts, and the public setting of our meeting, I should be safe enough to meet with Mr. Dragon man."

"Tracking doesn't ensure your safe return. I'm sure you know that, right?"

"True. But it does provide a bit of leverage in case he gets any funny ideas."

"A bit, yes, but you have more up your sleeve, don't you?" he teased. "That can't be all you need."

She hesitated to ask, not wanting to press her luck. On the off chance she didn't get anything useful from the meeting with Raynor, there was another possible way to find out what happened to her people. "There is one more favor I could use help with. But this one requires expert-level skills and might be too much. I didn't want to bother you with it."

"Wow." Luke stepped back, his jaw dropping in stunned disbelief. "I give you all the tools you ask for, and this is how you butter me up for the big favor?"

It was her turn to tease him. "Working like a charm, isn't it?"

"I should take back my equipment right now."

"But you won't." Sage stuck her tongue out playfully. "You know I'm just messing with you."

"First, tell me what it is you want me to do. Then I will decide if I like your teasing."

"I've got Raynor's information, address, phone numbers, stuff from his file at ASSET. I need someone to gain access to his home security systems and cameras. Just in case he's not totally forthcoming with information at our meeting, I would love to see what happened following the party, from whatever angle his cameras could capture."

Luke's brow furrowed as he listened to her needs. His gaze darted from her face to his computer as if mentally working out what he'd need to accomplish her request. "You were better off when you were telling me I wouldn't have the skills."

Couldn't all be winners. She sighed, forcing a half-hearted smile across her face. He'd already given her plenty to work with. "It's okay if you can't. That one was a long shot. My backup in case he didn't spill his guts Oprah-style in our meeting."

"Never said I couldn't," he said confidently. "It's just going to take me a bit of time."

"So you'll try?" She couldn't tell if he was teasing or serious. Damn him and his trickster ways. "You're the best."

"We'll see if you still think so when you get my bill."

"Whatever it is will be worth it." She threw her arms around him, putting all her energy into thanking him. Even if he couldn't pull off the second half, he had given her everything else she needed. "You're the best." She pulled away, smiling as she headed for the door. "I'm going to email you everything I have on Raynor as soon as I get home."

"And?" he called after her.

"What?"

"You'll tell me when you're heading to this meeting so I know when to start tracking your movements."

"Right. Yes. Thank you." She waved goodbye and headed back to her apartment, feeling more excited than anxious about her meeting with the dragon.

THIRTY-ONE

An unfamiliar number flashed across Sage's phone screen. She typically let those go to voice mail, but intuition compelled her answer. The voice seemed foreign at first, but it only took a moment for Sage to recognize the southern twang of Travis's accent. He gave her an address to a coffee shop, in a very public outdoor mall, where she could meet with Raynor and then hung up before she had the chance to ask any questions.

Not that she needed to. That was the information she had been waiting on. She took off, praying that meeting with Raynor would not be the last mistake she'd ever make.

He was already there, sitting outside at a table, sipping from a steaming cup when she arrived. Just as handsome as he'd been the first time she'd seen him, but out in the open and in broad daylight, the dark shadow of his other half was more visible. A dragon stuffed into a human-sized container. Lacking true form, his shadow appeared to bulge at the seams, as if at any moment he might explode out in all directions. She wondered if it felt as painful as it looked.

Questions for a better time. At that moment, she had to focus on her mission. She reached into her pocket and pressed the small remote on the key chain recorder, and waited for the vibration to confirm it was ready before she let it go.

Raynor stood as she approached, a gentlemanly move she'd not expected. He circled round the table and pulled out her chair. "I must say I was a little hesitant when I heard you wanted to speak to me."

She smiled awkwardly as he held the chair for her to sit, and then he scooted it in before rounding back to his own seat. "Thank you for meeting with me."

"Why did you seek me out so vigorously?" Raynor spoke with an air of nonchalance that matched the expression on his face.

"I have questions," she answered honestly.

"I'm sure you do." He stared, holding her gaze longer than Sage was comfortable. She turned away at first, but he called her back with his words. "What makes you think I have the answers you're after?"

"I'm one of those people who goes by their gut."

"I have to wonder if those you consort with find that an annoying liability?"

She allowed a smile to spread across her face. "Do you read minds, too, as well as fly and breathe fire?"

"When you've been around as long as I have, you read body language better than minds."

Did he know she was recording him? Had he seen her hand or heard the vibration from the key chain before she had closed in? She gulped at the lump forming in her throat. Even if he had, there was no turning back.

She leaned forward and folded both hands on the table, trying to not so subtly show her eagerness to continue the conversation. "So tell me, in your great wisdom, what should I be doing?"

"If your gut says you should ask me something, all you can do is try." Raynor picked up his cup and took a sip.

"Why didn't you just kill me when you figured out the truth that I was not who I was pretending to be?"

His eyebrows arched sharply. "Should I have?"

"I'm glad you didn't." She chuckled. "But I was under the assumption that Mystics and ASSET were enemies."

"Opposing viewpoints more than enemies, I'd say."

"Do you really believe all that rhetoric you spouted?"

"I believe both sides have their points."

Only a short while earlier, he had been so confident when spouting the party line. But this time when he'd answered, Raynor sounded less convinced. This was usually the point Grey would add in some tactful words. Just the thought of him caused her heart to ache. Was he okay? Was he still alive? He had to be. And she had to get her damn head in the game! Be tactful. Diplomatic. Not exactly her strong suit, but if she hoped to see Grey and Ava again, she couldn't fail.

"On that, I think we can both agree. No one is perfect."

"Wise words. You impress me…"

"Sage," she answered his implied question.

"Pleasure to finally learn your true identity." His easygoing expression was disarming, even as his words had her wondering if there might have been some double meaning behind them. A flash of realization glinted in his eyes as if he, too, realized her negative interpretation. "I wish we had been able to meet under better circumstances that night. You played your part to perfection. I want you to know that. It wasn't your kiss that gave you away. That was maybe the highlight of my evening."

Heat rushed to her cheeks. Damn, he was charming. And with the looks to match. No. She couldn't fall for the smooth-talking. No matter how good he was at it. She slapped a hand over her mouth like a shield and looked away.

"Do you want to know what clued me in?" He reeled her back in with his soothing voice.

"Sure."

He snatched her hand before she could resist and pulled it toward him, revealing her scarred palm. "I was there. At the trial. I saw the bloody ruin. A Terra's ability to heal is legendary, but there is no mistaking these scars." He traced the line from her palm out toward her fingers.

Despite the chill rushing through her body, Sage held perfectly still. "I hadn't thought of that."

"Your disguise was lovely." Raynor folded her fingers forward, closing her hand into a fist before letting it go. "I do apologize for the dress. I only meant to take you for a ride."

"And what would you have done with me when we landed?"

He chuckled at her nervous question. "You were smart to jump when you did."

"Fall, you mean," she admitted, hoping to keep the levity of their conversation going.

"Hope you didn't hurt yourself too badly. You don't look much worse for wear. I will, however, replace the dress."

"No need. I doubt I'd ever have occasion to wear something like that again."

"Please, I insist." Raynor took another sip from his coffee, eyes peeking over the rim of the cup, keeping his gaze locked on her face.

The meeting had gone so far from what she had expected in such a short time. Raynor had shown himself to be charming and charismatic, nothing less than a perfect gentleman, and yet he had conspired with the Mystics. How could this be? There was no hint of animosity in his eyes, nor had she heard a single note of disdain in their conversation. Of course, she hadn't gotten to her true reason for being there. She almost regretted having to sour the mood with business.

"Have I said something wrong?" he asked after the silence between them had gone stale.

"No. Not at all. It's just… I don't need another dress. What I really need is" — she took a deep breath, forcing back the ache in her chest, and sighed — "my partner back."

"Has he disappeared?" Lines formed at his brow. His expression seemed to match the tone of his question.

She wanted to believe he was genuine, but how could he be? "He came to see you shortly after the party."

"The last I saw of your date was him scurrying away from my property, shortly after I took to the air." Raynor's tone remained perfectly neutral, a little too controlled for Sage's liking.

"This would have been later in the evening," she clarified, "after the police and all left."

"I could not have seen him then, as I made my exit during the hullaballoo." Raynor leaned back in his chair, distancing himself as he crossed one leg over the other.

His excuse seemed too convenient, though it matched what Zack had said about the dragon returning agitated and demanding the party end that moment. But there was something else. The odd shift in Raynor's body language. He held his hands clasped together in his lap as if he were guarding himself. Protecting himself. Hardly the posture of a dangerous enemy.

"Can you tell me where you went after the party?"

"Something of great value was taken from me. I was mourning its loss." Raynor turned his eyes to the sky, then down to the ground, looking everywhere but at Sage as he spoke.

She'd used that tactic more times than she could count. It made sense now why he'd so easily accepted this meeting with her. He was ashamed of something. "You were used?"

"Now who's the mind reader?"

"You make it look easy."

"I didn't kill you because that is not my way. People think dragons are mindless beasts. We're actually very intuitive. Well, usually." His shoulders slumped. "I saw the arrogance of your leader at the trial. She refused to share any real or helpful information. She seemed extremely defensive and had a snappy retort to any questions about ASSET and its operation. It left a very bad taste in my mouth."

That certainly sounded like Ava. Sage couldn't argue with that fact. But her boss always had a reason behind the things she did.

"ASSET comes across as rulers without impunity. The trial, a mockery of our system. The council was created so that the four branches of magic could work together. But we don't really. The real power resides with ASSET. A fact that has caused unease among the other magical clans."

Sage looked around as people meandered by, making sure no one was really paying attention to them. "ASSET protects magic, at great costs to our own people." She opened her palm again, resting the back of her hand against the table so her scars would be seen.

"I do not dispute the travesty that befell you in service of your duty. It is a shame that one so young should have been put through so much pain. In the past, ASSET at least made an effort to pretend the council had a voice. They shared the burden of policing our people with the leaders of the council."

"This was an extenuating circumstance, I assure you."

"I wish that it were," Raynor replied solemnly. "But that is the downfall of so many secrets. One never knows where the truth lies. So when I heard rumblings among my associates, I started to listen. I chose to believe the convenient lie that we didn't need to have ASSET dictating to us any longer. That maybe it was time we stopped living in not only the shadows of your organization, but hidden away from the human world as well. Our people deserve to have the same freedoms as anyone else belonging to the earth."

Sage's mouth gaped open. Humans would never be ready to deal with the realities of this world, knowing how much magic surrounded them.

Raynor spoke before she could say as much. "I was supposed to share my magic with the world. The headlines would read 'Dragons Are Real.' What else is out there? Magical beings could come out of hiding and assimilate into society. Usher forth a new age in history." He scoffed and shook his head. "And then I saw the symbol burning on the mountainside."

"How could you not? You lit it." She hadn't meant for the words to come out so sharply.

"I did not!" he snapped back. "Fire comes from within me, yes, but not at that distance. Someone else lit that symbol." He turned away from her as if trying to hide the shame in his eyes. "But I wasn't a champion of my species, bravely taking the first steps to allow our people to come out of the shadows. It didn't occur to me until after I had outed myself to the world that I was simply serving *their* purpose, revealing magic through minor acts of terrorism, to create trouble for ASSET."

"So why didn't you confront them when you landed?"

"With police sirens in the distance? No. Letting myself be seen in the air was bad enough. I was not about to let the police find me. And I didn't trust that those so-called associates who'd convinced me to do this wouldn't just throw me to the wolves to further their interest. A dragon, behind bars, the freak show for all to see. For ASSET to have to find a way to get rid of… No."

"But you have your human form," she suggested.

"The damage had already been done. And, as I told you at the party, this is my mask. It's uncomfortable to hold this tiny form for long. My wings need to beat free."

"Sorry. You're the first dragon I've ever met."

"Not many of us around."

"So these associates who convinced you to reveal yourself. Did they stay?"

"It's possible. But as I removed myself, I do not have an accounting of what happened."

"How long were you gone for?" Sage asked.

"In truth, I have not yet returned."

"Where did you go?"

"Away!"

"Okay." She softened her approach. "So you're gone. A few hours go by. Let's say my partner came to visit your home in an official ASSET investigation. Would he have found anyone of importance at your place?"

"I had arranged for overnight guests due to the nature of the party. Yes, it would stand to reason that some might have stuck around."

"I think you know what my next question is going to be." She stared at him, hoping he would be forthcoming. "I need to know who these people are."

"Planning to storm the castle alone and save your friend?" He chuckled.

She'd do that and more if she thought it would work to get Grey back. "We're more than friends. We're partners."

He arched an eyebrow sharply as he met her eyes again. "Work partners?"

"Am I that obvious?"

"Just a little." The hint of a smile returned to his face. "But before I throw any potential associates under the bus, let me ask what ASSET plans to do?"

"I'm not working under official ASSET orders right now. This is a personal mission to find *my* missing partner."

"But after, when you learn of the people involved, what happens to them?"

She found it interesting that even as he admitted they betrayed his trust, he had not come right out and done the same. Was that his way of showing nobility? Why was he being so guarded with their identities? It wasn't quite adding up.

"ASSET is not without rules. We may operate in secret for some missions, but ultimately we serve magic. As my partner has told me many times, we protect magic and the community of magical beings. How are people in our community supposed to feel safe when there are others actively trying to cause chaos and harm? How does breaking the system affect real positive change? It can't. You know this, or you wouldn't have agreed to meet me here."

"I'm happy to hear you say that." Raynor nodded. "I believe you. But this situation would have never happened if ASSET had operated with all the dignity you just described. The magical community you serve and protect needs to see this as well."

"If I find my people and bring them in safe, I will do all that I can to see those who have caused all this trouble receive a public trial."

"I will hold you to that, Sage."

"So you'll help, then? Give me the names of people to investigate so I can locate my partner?"

"If I give you names, how do you plan to get your friend back? One girl against the Mystics hardly seems like even odds."

He was right. She hadn't really planned past learning the identities of who had her people. If they were higher-ups in the community or well connected, they would not be easy targets to take out. She needed to be smarter and more prepared. A level playing field was what she needed. Neutral ground like the meeting she had requested with Raynor.

"Oh, I don't plan to fight... Not yet at least. That's what they want. The Mystics want nothing more than to see ASSET as the big bad, coming in force. That's what their propaganda is all about. Isn't it? So instead, how about I propose something a bit more civil? A negotiation."

If she could get members of the Mystics to talk as she had with Raynor, she could learn so much more than just the whereabouts of her missing people. Information was more deadly than any single weapon. With luck, she might learn enough to dismantle their organization. But only if she could get them to talk.

"Interesting." Raynor picked up his drink and drained the cup. "I'm assuming that means you have leverage?"

"Let me worry about that part. Instead of names, can you arrange a meeting? At your place? Familiar ground to...discuss our opposing viewpoints."

"You think they can be won over as easily as I've been?" He chuckled.

"I do have my charms."

"No one can deny that. However, I fear you're setting yourself up for failure."

"I have to try."

"I understand and respect you for that." He reached across the table and took hold of her hand. "I'll honor your request. Come to my home later this evening. Drinks at ten? I will arrange for my…associates to be there."

"Thank you."

"Don't." The light seemed to fade from his eyes as he met her gaze. "I will do my part, as requested, and I hope your plan works out. But please, take some advice… Bring friends…for your own safety."

She nodded, feeling a bit awkward with him still holding on to her hand. "I plan to. I'm not going into the lion's den unprepared."

"And should things not go the way you plan?" he asked.

"My associates will be on our best behavior while in your home. That I can promise."

He smiled but the light never fully reached his eyes. Raynor lifted her hand and kissed the top of her knuckle before letting go. "I do hope that by facilitating this meeting for you that ASSET will look kindly on my transgressions when this is all over."

"I'll do what I can. See you tonight." That didn't leave her much time to rally support, but at least she had gotten one step closer to finding her people. With any luck, they would still be alive.

THIRTY-TWO

With only a few hours to rally the troops, Sage headed straight to the Sortilege Staffing Solutions office. Not that she could afford to owe any more favors to her so-called friends, but desperate times called for desperate measures. If only there was a coffee shop nearby. Favors are best accompanied by caramel-sweetened lattes.

"Three times in one week. This is beginning to become a regular occurrence," Sylvia snarked as she welcomed Sage in from the waiting room at Sortilege. "Though I am surprised to see you use the front door. Does this mean you need a job?"

"I don't have time for a verbal sparring match," Sage replied with blunt honesty, hoping her tone would convey the seriousness of her visit. "I need your expertise."

Annoyance flared across the shadowrunner's face, but she held her tongue as she ushered Sage out of the reception waiting room, saving her words for the privacy that followed the closing of her office door. "Two visits without Mr. Maddox. I think I understand."

"He's gone." Sage collapsed onto the chair in front of Sylvia's desk. She'd been holding it together all day, but hearing his name roll off Sylvia's lips with such condescension put a crack in the dam she'd been using to hold back her feelings. "I'm not even sure if he is alive."

"Dealing with dragons is tricky business." Sylvia's expression shifted, annoyance fading into something resembling sorrow. "But that's not their way."

"What do you know of them?" Sage struggled to keep her voice steady. "Are they trustworthy?"

"Being a dragon does not predispose one to a specific side. Every person has the capability of good and evil. You know this."

"Sorry… I know, newbie questions. I just… I'm used to having my partner to say these things to." Dammit. She was losing the fight. The dam had been breached, and all her anxiety was spilling out whether she liked it or not, revealing just how truly vulnerable Sage felt. "With him gone…I just can't."

"I had wondered when you two would finally acknowledge your feelings. Bad timing it seems." Sylva patted Sage's hand, a motherly kind of affection. Odd coming from the domineering shadowrunner, but at the same time, comforting.

She wasn't alone. Not truly. This was the mission she'd set for herself. If she could see it through.

Sylvia gave a little squeeze of solidarity before pulling away from Sage's hand. "If it's any consolation, I think you two are a matched set. If for nothing else, you temper his rough personality."

In better circumstances, Sage would have laughed at that. And if she somehow did manage to get her partner back, she'd make sure to rub that in his face. But that was still a long shot that rested squarely on how good or bad this meeting went.

"The dragon may be able to help me find out if he is alive. If I can trust him."

"Well, that is something. Let's focus on the positives here. I'm assuming he is not the one who took Grey?"

"He claims not to. But right now, I am not very certain who I should trust."

"You came to me. I assume that means you trust me?"

"Yes." Sage met Sylvia's coal-black eyes. "As you trust me, right?"

"I'm honored to know you value my trust. That is very reassuring." Sylvia rounded to her chair on the opposite side of the desk. Her posture stiffened as she sat firmly in her chair and folded her arms on the desk. "You have my trust as well. And that line of thinking, if I'm not mistaken, means you're assessing your resources. Which I can also assume I'm counted among? The question remains, what kind of plan could Miss Cynwrig be concocting that includes a dragon?"

She didn't seem shocked by the possibility of helping Sage. The ease with which she'd revealed her own importance felt like she'd expected Sage to come to her with this request. Did she know something she wasn't admitting? Sylvia always had her finger on the pulse of the magical world. Not unlike Zack. Only where he regularly dealt with the underbelly of the magical realm, Sylvia's connections were far more respected. Sage wanted to press on that point, but at the risk of insulting her would-be aide, she chose discretion.

"I do need support. Well, maybe not active support. More like witnesses." Sage stumbled over her own words. She hoped that their meeting would be as peaceful as the one she'd had with Raynor earlier, but reality never went the way anyone expected. "I wouldn't ask if I didn't think it was necessary, but I need support. It won't be just the dragon who I need to see to locate Grey."

"He is acting as emissary for the Mystics?"

"In a manner of speaking, yes. And I don't want to walk into a potential bad situation alone."

The corner of Sylvia's lip twitched, momentarily betraying her poker face. "Where is your boss? What does Mrs. Masters say about all of this?"

Sage fidgeted in her seat, wracking her brain for a plausible answer. "I'm deep undercover, acting outside of ASSET jurisdiction right now for this mission." The excuse had worked for Ava in the past. She hoped the shadowrunner would believe it now. "Please do not let anyone know."

Sylvia's gaze narrowed on Sage's face. Smoke began to rise around the shadowrunner. She evaporated and re-formed as she held the room in suspense. Despite the desperate urge to turn away, Sage held still, letting her eyes glaze over, refusing to lose the silent game of chicken. She couldn't let on, not even to Sylvia, that the head of ASSET had gone missing. Not yet at least. Not here, with the potential for so many others to hear. She couldn't afford to lose Sylvia by being caught in this lie, but revealing the truth had far worse consequences.

"You are truly alone?"

"Not if I bring friends. I'm hoping to recruit a few people I trust to join me for this meeting. As witnesses."

"Witnesses only?"

"That's what I am hoping. I would like to present a counterpoint to those insisting ASSET is an underhanded organization lacking in…uh…people skills."

"You mean a faceless organization lacking in empathy for kindred beings."

"Can I borrow that line?" Sage chuckled.

"You do have a gift for diplomacy. It needs cultivation, but it's certainly there." Sylvia nodded thoughtfully, but the smoke rising around her gave away the unease of the shadowrunner. "Have you recruited others to join you in this... What are you calling it?"

"Meeting." Sage shrugged.

Sylvia let out an impatient sigh. "Do you need more allies to join you?"

"I need all the friends I can get."

"I'll call Nyx if you like." Sylvia picked up her phone and began thumbing through it.

"I would love that. Thank you!" Sage jumped to her feet, excited to have secured the shadowrunner. "Do you think she could be ready quickly?"

"You can count on me. I cannot, however, vouch for Nyx. I will relay the importance of speed in this case. How soon will you be needing us?"

"This, evening...around ten-ish." Sage cringed as she said it. So soon. And she still had more contacts to reach. "I have to chat with Devon. I need him too. Covertly," she rambled on before she realized her inner monologue had more volume than it should.

"That does put a rush on things, doesn't it?" Sylvia's eyes swelled with surprise. "I'm assuming you have yet to secure transportation, given that Mr. Maddox did not lend you his keys before he disappeared?"

Touché. She deserved that little jab for failing to reveal how quickly this was all supposed to go down. "Yes, ma'am."

"You do need all the help you can get." Sylvia sighed and pulled a pad of paper from her desk drawer. "I will pick you up in my car at nine, so we have plenty of time to reach your meeting place. Put your address down here and go."

Sage took the paper and quickly scrawled her information on it. "Thanks!" She rushed out the door before Sylvia could possibly change her mind. Two down, three more to go, though those would be much easier sells than Sylvia.

THIRTY-THREE

Sage spent the entire bus ride home exchanging emails and text messages with Devon. ASSET agents were beginning to ask questions about Ava's disappearance. Sage relayed all she had learned and the time for their meeting. So far so good. Devon had agreed to be her wingman. She could check one more witness off her list. But though she was tired and hungry from her travels, she still had more work to do. Soon as the sun set, her roommate would wake.

She showered, changed, and had just begun to make herself a sandwich when Matt emerged from his cave-like room to greet her.

"You don't look crispy, so I'm assuming your meeting went well?"

"Two steps forward, one step back." She slathered a heaping dollop of peanut butter on her bread and slapped the two halves of her sandwich together.

"That good, eh?" Matt stared longingly at her food.

How long had it been since he'd eaten real food? Poor thing. Eternity on the slim-fast diet was a definite downside of being a vampire.

"It wasn't all for naught. He's a charmer. And not bad-looking either. Want to meet the dragon?" Sage set her sandwich aside, choosing to wait to eat it when Matt wasn't drooling.

"Why are your dates always more exciting than mine?" Matt teased.

"Hey!" Josh's voice sounded before Sage could continue easing the conversation toward the impending meeting. Josh rounded the corner, coming into the kitchen with a look that had Sage backing up a few paces. "What the hell did you mean by that?"

"I didn't mean it like that." Matt lowered his gaze and looked appropriately ashamed of his words. "I was just teasing our resident spinster. I mean, who passes up on a dragon?"

Poor guy. Matt would have fared better if he'd kept his mouth shut. The more he spoke, the madder it appeared to make Josh.

"Last night was more than thrilling," Matt continued. "You…are all the thrills I could ever need."

"You're a terrible liar." Josh huffed. "You're mad about the…the…" His hand flew to his neck.

"Please… I'm sorry. I'm still getting used to things."

Josh gave him a scornful look before returning to his room.

"Anything you want to tell me about date night?" Sage shook her head.

"Nope. Nothing to tell." For all his good qualities, that man was a terrible liar.

"Well, whatever it is, remember to apologize, be sincere, and tell him how much you love him"

"Yes, we do love each other," Matt said a little louder than necessary.

"But before you get busy with the making up part of this fight…" She cringed, knowing she was asking her best friend to follow her into a potentially dangerous situation. "I need you tonight. Zack too."

"So we're not simply meeting your new beau? What haven't you told me?" Matt crossed his arms. "Am I going to like this plan?"

"Nope."

His shoulders slumped with a heavy sigh. "What do you need?"

"Witnesses."

"You're being oddly cryptic."

"I have to be. I need genuine reactions from people."

"People? Does Zack know?"

"The plan? Nope." She hadn't had the time yet to talk to him. "He's got to be in the dark just like everyone else for it to work."

"And if it doesn't work?"

"I don't want to think about that bit."

"Sage." He stared down his nose at her. "Tell me you thought this through."

"Okay, I did."

"You're a worse liar than he is." Josh appeared again fully dressed and marched straight toward her.

"Look. I'm working alone. My boss along with her elite team who went after the Mystics are all MIA right now. I don't know if any of them are alive. There has been no word of ransom or anything. I'm flying blind, and the only way I can hope to get them back is to beat them at their own game."

"That I believe," Josh said, then turned to Matt. "And I believe you love me too. But you're going to have to let me be mad and figure out a way to make it up to me."

"I will," Matt promised, the smile returning to his face.

"Until then, I need to go. I can't be around all this" — Josh waved his hand at the both of them — "right now. I need some normal."

"I totally understand." Sage came in for a hug before Josh could reject her. "Believe me. I really understand. I wish I could escape too. Just don't be away for too long. I need you too."

Josh struggled at first but eased into the hug. He nodded as he tightened his arms around her. "I'm not going far. I just need to breathe." He pulled free of her arms and turned to Matt. "Be safe."

Sage bashfully averted her eyes as they shared a goodbye kiss, her mind turning to the last kiss she shared with Grey soured by the way he'd tricked her into a prison cell. When she freed him, he'd be getting a smack across the face before she kissed him like that again.

"How many people have you recruited as witnesses?" Matt asked after seeing Josh out the door.

"A handful. No more."

"And what are we going to be walking into?" Matt asked.

"Just a meeting."

"Mystics?"

"Who else?" she admitted.

"Why are you meeting them with witnesses? And don't give me this honest reactions BS."

"Because I need to show them the error of their way." She could never keep secrets from him. "I need them to see I come without force. To talk openly. And formally request the return of my people."

"And you think you will get that?"

"I'll get a meeting. That's all I can hope for," she said.

"You won't get your people back that way," he said.

"Will I?" she asked.

"What aren't you telling me?"

"You just have to trust me. Please. Don't ask for more," she said.

"You know I will do whatever you ask. I don't care about my own safety, but I do need to know you are not putting yourself in danger. Just give me that, and I won't ask any more."

"Normally I go charging in alone. That is dangerous. This time, I bring a team with me. Trust that if nothing else."

Matt gritted his teeth and nodded as he turned away.

She couldn't blame him for being upset with her. She didn't keep secrets from him. She'd already said more than she wanted in an attempt to ease his worry. If this worked out, she'd owe him and everyone else big time. But first she had to get her people back. Her plan had to work.

"Can you call Zack while I run a quick errand? We need to be out of here like ASAP."

Matt grumbled quietly but nodded and grabbed his phone.

Sage snatched the sandwich from her plate and scarfed it down as she rushed over to Luke's apartment, praying he'd had enough time to accomplish his mission.

He opened the door on the first knock as if expecting she'd show up. Small win, but she'd take it.

"You have a few more of these?" She held up the little paw-shaped trinket Luke had given her earlier. "Like two or three more?"

A sly grin crossed his face as he ambled over to his desk. "Dog trackers are so convenient, aren't they?" He chuckled as he handed over three more.

"I'm hoping so. Oh…and the recorder worked perfectly. At least I think it did. I haven't had time to download. But video would really be good this time around. Have any other super spy gear for that?"

"Remember, I'm on a budget." He picked up a pair of glasses. "I want these back! These can record continuously for fifty minutes once activated." He brought them over and showed her the hidden buttons in the arm of the frame. A space at the edge of the frame opened revealing a tiny memory card. On the other side a charging port.

"That's genius."

"Thank you."

"And for the hacking bit?" She held her breath, waiting for his answer.

"I was able to gain access. He has pretty extensive security systems in the house. No audio unfortunately."

"Will he know when you're inside his system?"

"Doubt it." Luke shrugged. "And I can download all the video, in real time, from his cameras here and make you a disk."

"That's exactly what I need. Recorded proof in case things don't go as well as expected. If I don't come back for the recordings in twenty-four hours, release them to the public."

"That's a bold move." He blinked at her as if unsure of how to take her words.

"Not one I want to have to make, but better to have something up my sleeve, even if it is only used as a bargaining chip."

"I've got your back. Way. Way back." He chuckled but there was no real amusement there.

"Thanks! Eye in the sky is better than nothing. And you have already done more than that."

"Go. Get out of here, before you make me blush." Luke ushered her toward the door.

Sunset had come and gone. Sylvia would be on her way. Devon and Zack too. Game on.

THIRTY-FOUR

Sage took the stone steps up to Raynor's mountainside mansion, keeping her head held high, doing her best to hide the fact she was one slipup away from crumbling. No matter how fast her heart raced, she couldn't let anyone see her sweat. Not the dragon, or the Mystics, and especially her witnesses Devon, Nyx, and Sylvia. For her plan to work, she had to project confidence. Easier said than done, especially with half her team still unaccounted for. The vampires had promised they'd be along in good time. Dinner before social calls and all. She'd laughed that excuse off back at her apartment, but now as she waited for Raynor to answer the door, she really wished she had Zack there to crack a joke or employ some of his usual carefree charm to lighten the mood.

"Welcome, honored guests." Raynor greeted them with an uneasy look from Sage to the trio accompanying her. "Is this all in your party, or are you expecting more?"

"Two more would like to join us. Their dinner ran a little late. Sorry," Sage replied.

"We'll make introductions out on the back patio." He ushered them inside the foyer and led them straight through the house, keeping his tone conversational. "I don't believe you were able to see the back gardens when last you came here."

Outside, Sage recognized two familiar faces seated around a large stone firepit. One was a gaunt man with a balding head partially ringed in shaggy white hair. He'd been one of the council members at her trial, though she had never learned his name. Sitting next to him was the little flame-headed elemental, Cor Ignis. She could have predicted his involvement.

A few other men stood around acting as sentries, but none of their faces were familiar. She made sure to get a good long look so the camera in her glasses could record them.

"What is the meaning of this?" Blue flames danced on Cor's head as he aimed his angry question at Raynor.

"The handling of Mabon left me with many concerns about the true intentions of the Mystics," Raynor answered calmly as he pointed out the open seats to Sage and her guests. "It seemed logical to discuss the issue among those of differing viewpoints."

Cor glowed an unearthly shade of blue. "So you bring ASSET here to what? Have us arrested?"

"No one is here to make arrests." Sage spoke slowly, fighting against the warble in her voice.

The little man looked as if he might explode with all that unchecked rage on display. His partner, the gaunt man sitting to his right, however, seemed less bothered by this new development. Between the two of them, he seemed more dangerous.

"I'm here to listen, and provide alternate opinions."

"And them?" The gaunt man pointed to the trio behind Sage.

Sylvia placed a hand on Sage's shoulder and stepped up. "Lord Malcolm, I am greatly disturbed to see you here…given the circumstances."

Sage made note of his name as Malcolm bristled in response to being outed. "These are my friends," she said. "And as you can plainly see, representative members of the various families of magic. They are here to listen, for now."

Raynor offered them seats opposite the Mystics' party, leaving the firepit as a buffer between them. Sage took her seat as the two men across the flames exchanged glances.

The corner of Cor's mouth quirked up deviously, as if they had played right into his hands. "Why are you here without your people?"

Openly baiting her? That was a low blow. Sage wanted to reply in kind, but she bit back her snarky reply. Playing into his taunting might feel good, but it would kill any chance she had of making her plan work.

She allowed herself a deep breath before responding. "In a case such as this, it seemed more prudent to come with the support of other pillars in the community rather than a show of Terra force."

"Pillars?" Cor huffed. "We are members of the high council. What claim does your…group have to consider them pillars?"

"Let me ask this." Sage clenched her fists, fighting to keep her anger in check. "Why is it that members of the high council are…associating…with the Mystics?"

"Our jobs require that we work for the betterment of our people," Lord Malcolm replied as casually as if he'd been asked about the weather. "The Mystics have been cast in a dark light by ASSET, but their mission statement aligns better with the ideals of our own families."

"And that is?" Sage asked.

"Magic is a gift to our people. Maybe not yours, so I understand your disdain for it," Malcolm added politely. "But the use of our magic is limited by the rules set down by your ASSET organization. How can we, the families of active magic, realize our full potential if we are not allowed to use the gifts we are given?"

Sage could hardly believe what she was hearing, and at the same time, didn't have a proper response, or at least a diplomatic one ready to counter him.

Sylvia placed her hand on Sage's thigh before she broke the awkward silence. "My lord, pardon me, but what exactly are we prevented from doing with our magic?"

Shadows in the distance caught Sage's attention. She spotted Zack and Matt at the side of the house skulking around the corner like deviants. Not exactly the entrance she'd planned for, but having a few more people on her side gave her the confidence she needed. She waved them over as she awaited Malcolm's reply.

"A good example has just presented itself." Lord Malcolm looked on eagerly as Zack and Matt came into view. "Your vampire friends here."

"Good evening, my lord." Zack paused and nodded respectfully.

"Go on, please explain," Sage urged. All the bowing and scraping was a little over the top, not to mention annoying. So much respect for people actively trying to tear apart the balance of their society.

Malcolm shifted his gaze from Zack to Sage. "Vampires exist on only one form of nourishment. But they are limited to how and when they feed or risk ASSET raiding their places of residence or business."

"Zack," Sage said just as his butt hit the cushion on the patio chair.

He bounced right back up to his feet and turned to face her. "Yes?"

"What is it you told me about your consumption of blood?" She fought to hide her cringing at the topic.

"You mean my comparison to beer?" Zack elbowed Matt next to him. Both vampires shared a laugh. "Yeah. Just like with a nice cold one, back in the day, we prefer ours a pint at a time."

"So, would you say that you feel put upon by ASSET to alter your diet?" Sage asked, bringing the two boys back on point.

"Not at all. Death is not a necessity of a feed. Over-indulgence is what leads to deaths." The laughter faded from his voice as Zack took his seat. "And if I'm being honest, ASSET doesn't exactly care if the odd human doesn't survive feeding, as long as we clean up our own messes. That's the only bit they care about. The human population finding out about all the others living around them and freaking out."

His sobering statement had just the right ring of truth to it. ASSET might not be perfect, but they at least had the magical community's best interest at heart.

Sage turned her attention to Raynor. "What is it that attracts you to the Mystics and their mission statement?"

Raynor sat thoughtfully for a moment. "I suppose it was the desire to not have to hide my true self. It's painful at times, compressing myself into this form. But necessary to live among humans."

"We should not have to be hidden. To cower. To glamour or take on other forms to appease the lesser creatures of the world," Cor added. "We were born here. Our people predate the humans. This is our world."

"I agree." Sage forced a smile across her face, satisfied in the knowledge that all of the little flame-headed man's words were being recorded. "You shouldn't have to."

Cor's flames burned brighter. "But ASSET—"

"Living among humans who outnumber you, however… It would be stupid not to do all you can to remain anonymous." Sage spoke louder, ensuring she would be heard. "You have magic. Sure. And so do they. Only theirs is in the form of weapons of mass destruction. Scare humans and what do they do? Retaliate. That's why ASSET works so hard to keep them blissfully unaware."

"That is the party line we've been fed for centuries," Cor sneered. "Even before the humans had the technology to rise en masse against us. It's weakness. Fear. Used to control the wrong people."

How that little hatemonger rose to the ranks of high council member Sage wasn't sure, but he had a voice, and clearly wasn't afraid to use it. If nothing else came from this meeting, she'd have enough evidence to extinguish his flames, at least in the court of public opinion. But that wasn't going to help her find her missing people.

"If the wisest among our kind felt it was the right choice back then, it is even more so now." Devon spoke before Sage had the chance. "Peace is the only option.

Between our great families, and the humans, with whom we share this world."

Sage picked up the thread, turning the point back to her new dragon friend. "Raynor, you choose to live among humans. But you could easily live alone somewhere unpopulated and maintain your true form without worry."

"Life would not be as comfortable or fulfilling alone," Raynor replied.

"Which is why you choose to live within a human society. By doing so, you have accepted that you must adapt to the norms of that society in order to participate in it." Sage directed her words at Cor, speaking as clearly as she could while making her point. "The same goes for anyone who moves from one place to another. Transition requires adaptation. Small changes that allow one to fully experience and enjoy that new home."

"You have a splendid answer for everything." Lord Malcolm praised her, his tone more than friendly, but the way his eyes narrowed on her face, married with the subtle crease in his brow, all but shouted the truth—she'd just made herself his personal target. "ASSET trained you well. But did they prep you for the harder questions?"

Hairs stood on the back of her neck. She couldn't lose her nerve. Not now. She forced herself to hold his gaze even if he looked at her like a predator ready to pounce. "What questions would those be?"

"Why does ASSET hoard magical artifacts"—Malcolm snorted in derision—"when they cannot possibly use them?"

Every instinct she had screamed for her to look away, but Sage kept her eyes forward, unblinking as she answered. "Without specifics, I'm afraid I cannot say."

"You see?" Cor pounced on her answer. His sharp reply caused her to flinch.

Sage lost the battle of wills, breaking eye contact with Malcolm, but kept her voice in check as she replied, "How can I speak about a particular item if I don't know what this item is?"

Cor's flames flickered excitedly. "You were rumored to be in possession of the Seed of Destruction."

"Hearsay!" Sylvia shocked Sage with the sudden volume of her voice.

Sage reached out to her and whispered, "Witness," as a reminder before turning her attention back to Cor. "Yes, and I paid dearly for that rumor." She held out her hand for Raynor to see the scar as emphasis. "Because of it, I had my hand sliced in two. And what came from that? Nothing."

"You touched one of our people and stole their magic." Cor all but shouted the accusation.

Nyx sprang up from her seat, little wings fluttering like a hummingbird. "She was exonerated from those false accusations."

As nice as it was for her friends to literally jump to her defense, Sage needed them to remain calm. Between the glasses recording everything Sage saw, and the pocket recorder getting the audio, not to mention the eye in the sky hopefully there for backup recordings, Sage would have all the evidence she needed to take down these two pillars of the community. The last thing she needed was a fight to break out.

"My friends love me. The feeling is mutual, of course, but I think you'll want to have more than rumors to throw at me if you want to tarnish my reputation as a Terra with ASSET. Let me ask you this... Are they dead? The person who I allegedly touched with the Seed of Destruction?"

"No," Malcolm answered calmly.

"Can they still wield their magic?" Nyx clarified, her tone almost as sharp as Cor's had been.

Sage reached up and waved Nyx down to her. The little pixie landed weightlessly on Sage's scarred palm. The two made eye contact quickly, before Sage turned her attention back to her accusers.

"With some difficulty," Malcolm replied.

The pixie flew back to her seat, allowing Sage to take the lead again. "Well, I can't speak to magical impotence, but if I had stolen their magic using this Seed of Destruction, wouldn't it have rendered them powerless or dead?"

"Perhaps not." Cor sounded less sure of himself. "You only touched him."

"You're telling us..." —Sage gestured to all in attendance—"that me, a Terra, with no ability to wield magic, was able to not only use this seed, a magical artifact only rumored to exist, but also me, again a Terra...was able to control it enough to prevent it from destroying a creature of magic when it touched them?" She waited for the reality of all her words to marinate in the minds of those who were listening. She'd lived through all of that, true, but even as she'd spoken them, they sounded ludicrous. "Would that I had that kind of power..." She laughed. "I might go mad with it."

Raynor joined her, chuckling in response. "I think just about anyone with that kind of power would go mad."

"Which is why I was maimed. Blood lust… No offense," she said to Zack and Matt. "Madness. All because of a rumor." Sage speared Cor with her most dangerous glare. "And since we are on the subject of rumors, why is it that the Mystics, who claim to be about reaching full magical potential, are working to undermine the very agency who protects it? The magic school bus incident? The burning bush? All symbols that Terras bear. However, none of the magic that caused these things is possible for a Terra to do."

Blue flames dimmed, turning grey and smoky atop the little man's head. "None were harmed in those calculated revelations of magic."

"I beg to differ." Sage gave herself a breath to keep control of her voice. No good would come from her losing her cool in front of all these people. She shifted her gaze between Cor and Malcolm. "You admit to participating in these acts of terrorism? You sent a very powerful message to the magical community. All to undermine the community's trust in ASSET. You created chaos. Calculated, definitely. But harmless. No."

"If all it takes is a simple act of levitating a bus to undermine the credibility of your organization, then how good is your organization to begin with?" Cor chuckled confidently.

Would that count as admission? She'd accused him directly. In no uncertain terms called both Cor and Malcolm members of the Mystics. And neither had denied it. She had that on camera. But would it be enough?

"You can drop the pretense here." Devon commanded their attention with his booming voice.

Sage realized she had left the conversation quiet for too long.

"It's been established that whisperings from on high have been working to undermine the reliability of ASSET," he said, continuing the thread she had started. "The floating bus. Convincing a dragon to take an evening flight. Those were just the last nails in the coffin you've been building."

"Whisperings from on high?" Cor laughed even harder.

"Did you not just proudly proclaim yourself as pillars of the community?" Sage countered. "It stands to reason that you have the ear of your people. Spin your propaganda in whatever way you like in a position like that."

Cor's laughter stopped abruptly. "I have always carried out the duties of my office to the letter."

"Which duty is it, please remind me, that puts children in danger?" Sage asked.

"No children were harmed to my knowledge." Cor's flames ignited again, burning brilliantly blue. "So please present us with actual facts before you lob accusations my way."

Devon leaned forward, resting his elbows on his thighs. He locked eyes on the little burning man. "ASSET was thankfully able to retrieve the Terra child aboard the bus you floated and branded with the same symbol he carried on his arm."

"Without the quick response of my people, yes, a child could have been harmed thanks to your actions," Sage added.

"Terras' symbols are not clear when they are young." Malcolm waved his hand dismissively.

"That is the best you have? The symbol isn't clear? You risked a child's life and ruined a family's home in your little calculated act of magical terrorism." Sage regretted the tone of her reply the instant those angry words left her lips.

"No need for hyperbole." Malcolm maintained his cool tone. "There is no proof of your accusations. All the Mystics did was float the bus and mark it. You make it sound like they actively engaged in ruining someone's life."

Cor might not have openly denied his association, but Malcolm was certainly keeping a professional distance in this conversation. Sage needed him to admit his membership to the Mystics.

"Wouldn't be the first time," she said. "And whether or not you take responsibility for it, you have actively ruined that poor child's life. Our people are left unaware of our lineage until it becomes necessary. With your admittedly calculated act, you singlehandedly scared the community and gave them a symbol to associate with that new fear. You tore a child from the only home they knew, and from the bliss that is ignorance of the life he might not have had to take part in. The innocence of a child is a precious thing. How dare you sit here smugly after destroying it." Sage sneered as she stared down Lord Malcolm. After a silent moment, she turned to Raynor. "I hope I have given you the understanding you asked for."

Raynor nodded. "Yes. I appreciate your willingness to speak plainly tonight. You have given me much to think about. I hope you…both of you…understand I will need time to consider all that has been revealed tonight."

"You have been most gracious in allowing us here to speak plainly." Sage's smile faded as her gaze shifted from Raynor to Malcolm and Cor. "And now that the pleasantries are over, I demand the members of my team you took. Alive and well, if that's not too much trouble."

"We were unaware that members of your team had gone missing. A shame, really. But it does account for your apparent sensitivity this evening. You have my condolences." Malcolm's face was a mask of indifference. "If there is anything my people can do to help you in your investigation, do not hesitate to ask."

"Raynor, I must ask a favor of you. I require your security records. If you don't mind. Any video feeds pertaining to the night of your flight up through the morning after." Sage dug a tracking paw from her purse and held it concealed in her hand as she reached out for Raynor.

He stood, took her hand. She nodded toward Malcolm and mouthed the word "tracker," shaking his hand as she made the exchange.

"Certainly. Just give me a moment to make sure our guests get off okay." He accepted the tracker and moved on around the firepit to Lord Malcolm. "Do you want to wait here or take your leave?"

Lord Malcolm stood and offered his hand to shake, but Raynor pulled him into a hug instead. Patting his back firmly, he slipped the tracker into Malcolm's coat pocket as he pulled away.

"I want you to know I have the utmost respect for your position as member of the high council," Raynor said. "I do hope this does not affect my standing with you."

"No, of course not. I appreciate your open-mindedness to listen to all sides," Lord Malcolm replied before turning to Sage. "And you…have provided quite the interesting representation of your people. I'm glad we had the chance to meet."

"Let us all go our separate ways in peace, then." Raynor waved a hand toward the door.

All in attendance stood.

Sage stepped up to Cor, but had to lower herself to meet his eyes. "I hope you understand there is no need for such animosity between our people."

"You are so young." Cor reached for the strap of a bag next to him.

"Let me help you." Sage grabbed the bag before he did, slipping the tracker inside while Cor jumped down from his seat.

"I wish I could say it was a pleasure. But it certainly was interesting." Cor snatched the bag and followed Lord Malcolm inside.

Sage turned to her group. "Thank you all for being witnesses. I know this was unorthodox, but I needed to record everything they were saying." She tapped her glasses for effect.

"You showed great restraint today, and no small amount of class." Devon beamed with pride.

"She's got a head on her shoulders, that's for sure," Sylvia added. "I've always said she had potential for great things."

"You did not." Nyx laughed.

"When she is not being a pain in my ass," Sylvia clarified.

"Thanks for the vote of confidence, you guys." Sage's cheeks burned with embarrassment, but their praise gave her the courage she needed to continue on to the next part of the mission. "Ready for phase two? Shadow Ops time." She pulled her phone out and opened the tracking app. "We need to follow them. Quickly. To see where our people are."

"You think they will lead us?" Devon crossed his arms at his chest.

"Not willingly. But now that they know that we know they have them, they are likely to get rid of the…evidence." Sage hoped she was wrong about the getting rid of them part, but knew their mission was at a critical point. "And the sooner the better, so we have to go now."

The tracking markers moved away from their location, each beacon slowly splitting into different directions.

"I think we need to follow Lord Malcolm," Sage suggested.

"Not Cor?" Zack asked.

"He's a Mystic Order fanatic for sure, but I don't think he's got our people," Sage answered.

"He'd be at the top of my list," Zack replied.

"Mine, too, at first. But then I thought about it. Our people were taken quietly. No spectacle made of their disappearance. That doesn't fit with Cor's blazing personality."

"What if he killed them?" Devon asked. "No need to make a spectacle. Just get rid of them. Burn the bodies and be done with it."

"That is a thought I don't want to entertain." Sage cringed.

"But you must," Devon said. "If you're thinking of all possibilities…that is one."

"But how would that serve the Mystics?" she asked. "They want to make an example, but they want to do it when the time is right. That's calculated, cold, and Lord Malcolm fits that to a tee."

"We can't stand here debating," Sylvia reminded them. "They are already on the move."

"She's right. There is no time to debate this. We need to move now," Sage said. "Devon, you and I will go follow Lord Malcolm."

"Nyx and I will follow Cor," Sylvia said.

"Zack. Take Matt back home and talk to Luke. See what he got on the surveillance tapes. We may need them. Especially if we don't come back. If either of you finds the missing ASSET agents, let the others know." Sage marched off before anyone could argue with their assignments.

She prayed she'd made the right choice in following Lord Malcolm. Being wrong meant sending her friends into danger.

THIRTY-FIVE

"What do we know about Lord Malcolm?" Devon asked as he drove the car, following the little blip on Sage's phone.

"I didn't have time to research him. I know he sits on the Shade branch of the great council." He'd been one of her accusers at the trial. That had been the only time she had seen him prior to the meeting at Raynor's.

"He's a dark elf. That much I know. Elves are a different sort of enemy. Especially dark ones. How's the hand? You sure you're up to fighting form?"

She'd all but forgotten the pain of her wounds. The scar was still there and would be for the rest of her days, but her hand felt good, strong. "I'm more than ready for a fight."

"You'll need more than faith and courage to defeat him."

"I thought you said I was best fighting with my own two hands." She chuckled. Hand-to-hand combat was good and all, but she'd come prepared with her daggers sheathed at her back.

"Combat is a primary part of their education. They're raised knowing how to wield weapons from the moment they can hold them. And, if you hadn't already noticed, they're exceedingly clever."

"Should I give my daggers names, then, too?"

"As long as they're with you, I don't care what you call 'em. Keep those blades ready."

Up to that moment, she'd been overwhelmed by anticipation, hoping to finally find her missing people. But after Devon's revelation, she realized as close as she had gotten, she was still dangerously far from the finish line. "Glad I have you with me!"

They followed the path of the tracking beacon as it took them back into the city, heading for an area Sage knew to be filled with industrial buildings and storage yards for construction companies. Warehouses and storage facilities dimly lit and empty of all but security personnel gave the area a deserted feel. But if Sage were going to keep people prisoner, that certainly felt like the right place to do it.

Malcolm's tracking beacon stopped at the largest of the warehouse buildings, with no signage on the outside. Other cars sat in the parking lot, too, average four-door sedans and a couple of motorcycles. Nothing out of the ordinary. All the shipping bays had been closed for the night. Lights on each corner of the building were all lit. People concealed by shadow came out to greet Lord Malcolm as he stepped from his car.

Sage counted quickly. "I see six people."

She spotted what appeared to be the front office doors. Lights on inside confirmed it, and Malcolm appeared to be heading toward them with the people he'd just met in the parking area.

Devon circled around, hunting for a place to park. "We'll go in on foot. Scout the exits first before going inside."

Sage looked at the tracking beacon. Cor's had stopped as well in what appeared to be a master-planned community. Home most likely. Another hopeful confirmation she'd made the right choice to follow Malcolm. Though, if it had been Cor, he probably would have kept prisoners captive in his home. But she couldn't let herself think about it too long. Sylvia and Nyx were heading his way. She said a silent prayer, hoping they'd check in soon, preferably with good news.

Her heart pounded as Devon parked the car. She held her breath as she stepped out into the warm night air. The target in sight, she focused. All that mattered was getting her people back. She *had* to get them back.

Devon took off and she followed.

At the side of the building, just beyond the glow of the lights, Devon stopped and held his finger to his lips. She tried to listen, but the pounding of her heart flooded her ears, drowning out the silent approach of footsteps. She hadn't heard them, but Devon signaled for her to duck.

A shadow lengthened from just beyond the corner of the building. Devon crouched, ready to spring. The moment the shadow took human form, Devon took hold of the man and tackled him to the ground. A quick strike to the head rendered the man unconscious.

"There will be more." Devon peeked around the corner of the building and then waved her forward to follow. Together, they made one full round of the building, noting every door, and finally stopping at the rear of the building. A small door with a burned-out light looked promising. Cigarettes littered the ground next to an overflowing concrete ashtray.

"You lead, I'll follow," Sage said, unsure of what to expect inside.

They slipped in, and Devon closed the door just as quietly as he'd opened it.

Shelves ran from floor to ceiling in rows in front of them, boxes and equipment piled high on each shelf. Camouflage for the moment. Somewhere beyond, Sage could hear voices. Men were talking. She remembered the count. Six including Malcolm. They had already taken out one. That left five. And by the sounds of it, they were about to face two more.

"Boss says they need the package moved offsite. We need the truck," a man with a gravelly voice said. He sounded like he was responsible for the litter of cigarettes they'd passed on their way in.

"Great. Just great!" another voice replied. That one sounded younger, and a bit frantic. "Driver is halfway to LA. You want me to just have them turn around?"

The two men walked in step two aisles ahead of Sage. She crouched down behind the piles of clutter on the lower shelf and listened.

"When the boss gives an order, we don't have a choice," the chain smoker replied.

"But..." Junior squeaked. "It's going to be at least two hours before they get back. And that's assuming I can get ahold of the driver."

"As long as we get the package moved tonight." The pair of footsteps stopped briefly. "Make it happen."

Devon and Sage exchanged glances. No words were needed. They had to take out the two men talking. Sage ducked down, slipped through a gap in the lower shelf, and came out in the next aisle.

Two pairs of legs in the next aisle over began to move in separate directions. Sage took a quick peek right, and then chose to go after the one moving to the left. Moving swiftly to match pace, she stalked her target on the other aisle, looking for another opening she could sneak through to make contact.

A gap appeared between pieces of large crusted drill heads and a collapsed box filled with small parts that looked like it had finally burst under the weight of all the things that had been tossed inside.

She spotted him, taller than she expected. Older too. A long grey ponytail hung down his back. He walked with his head up, scanning the shelves as if looking for something. Easy pickings. Sage came up behind him, taking out his left knee. He went down, crumpling to the concrete floor with a shout.

She sent her foot out again and kicked him in the head.

His eyes rolled back and his body went slack. Sage stared for a second, making sure he was still breathing. A quick scan of the shelves, and Sage found an open bag of industrial strength zip ties. Just what she needed to make sure Sleeping Beauty didn't try to follow her when he woke up. She made quick work of rolling him over and securing his legs and arms then pocketed the remaining ties for later.

A shadow came up behind her. A man. He cleared his throat. Jumpy as she was, Sage turned with her fist cocked to strike before she realized it was Devon.

He caught her hand in mid swing. "You do understand how to be silent, right?"

"I could say the same to you," she countered, her heart beating so hard it ached.

"If we're lucky, no one heard your guy take his fall. Don't make that mistake again." He pointed down the path he'd just come from. "Other than the odd shipping containers, there is nothing out of the ordinary. The office is that way. And with luck, we've only got three more people here to deal with."

Sage followed, keeping her eyes peeled for signs of movement in the racks or video cameras watching them, until they reached the office they'd seen on the way in.

Devon placed his ear against the door. "When I open the door, you stay to the other side. If anyone comes out, disable them."

"Disable?" Not exactly what she had expected him to say, but she balled her fists all the same.

"Yes. Dead people don't talk. And since we need a location for our missing people, we need to talk to someone. Got it?" Devon pulled the door open, facing the unknown.

"Visitors typically use the front entrance," Malcolm said casually from the office in front of them.

"You know what we are here for," Devon replied.

One of three more left. She didn't like those numbers. She'd have rather heard the order from their fearless leader telling henchmen one and two to attack. The others were somewhere. Sage had her eyes wide open, scanning around the warehouse for signs of movement while keeping her ear trained on the conversation between Malcolm and Devon.

"ASSET barging into my place of business, uninvited, casting aspersions? Whatever should I do to respond to such an insult?" The *zing* of blades being pulled from their sheaths followed Malcolm's cocky words.

"Put the weapons away unless you are prepared for the consequence of using them," Devon warned.

"Aligning yourself with them, ogre. I expected better from someone of your caliber." Malcolm's voice grew louder. "Stand aside. My fight is not with you."

"You brought the fight, Lord Malcolm," Devon countered. "You're smarter than this. Why join with the likes of the Mystics?"

With no sign of henchmen in the aisles, Sage turned her attention to the door just in time to see the dark elf stroll forward toward them.

Sage lowered her hands toward the daggers sheathed at her back.

"You have two choices. Leave now by the door you came from, or you will be removed with the rest of the garbage." Malcolm's gaze shifted between Devon and Sage as if determining who to attack first.

"Return my people, and I will leave with them," Sage answered.

"Your people are not here. But then, I think you already knew that." Malcolm lifted the slender blade in his right hand, pointing it straight at Sage's chest.

She pulled her daggers and deflected the blade away from her body. The clang of metal on metal echoed in the warehouse.

Devon released the door and threw his weight into the dark elf's body, knocking him off balance. Lord Malcolm found his footing and trained his blades on the ogre. They circled each other. Sage stood with her heart in her throat. Two blades versus none was not a great position to be in, but her trainer always had a trick up his sleeve. Too bad he didn't have a sword there. At least for the moment, he kept just out of reach.

"Is it worth it?" Sage hoped talking might distract Malcolm. "You do this now, you sign your own death warrant."

"Words like that are what put ASSET in the place it is now." Malcolm twirled his blades as he stepped forward, forcing Devon backwards to avoid being cut. "But I commend you for your bravery in the face of death."

Cocky. She hated cocky bastards.

He maneuvered Devon back again. The ogre had no defense against the speed of the dark elf's blades. Longer and more slender than Sage's daggers, they reminded her of katanas in shape but lacked the curve or the length. The dark elf moved with them like perfect extensions of his hands.

Devon scooted back again, but one more step and he would be against the racks.

Sage flipped the dagger in her hand and prepared to throw it at the dark elf. If nothing else, it might distract him enough for Devon to get away.

The ogre backed against the rack. He grabbed hold of a length of metal pipe behind him and used it to deflect Malcolm's strike. With a new weapon in hand, Devon immediately shifted the direction of the fight. He wielded it with practiced efficiency like a staff, taking the offensive, forcing the dark elf to deflect each of Devon's strikes.

Metal against metal clanged like a broken metronome. Devon gained more ground, pushing Malcolm back. Sage, too, to remain a safe distance from their fight.

One of the bay doors opened, and three men came running in to join the battle. She must have miscounted on her way in. One more than she expected, and with Devon busy, there was less assistance cleaning up this new mess.

"Incoming," Sage warned, daggers at the ready.

A body dropped to the ground with a thud. Sage chanced a glance.

Lord Malcolm lay at his feet, no signs of blood, but unconscious all the same.

Devon picked up Malcolm's blades and stood ready as the new horde approached.

The first of the three men came down the aisle toward them.

"I got this one." Sage sprinted towards the enemy, a willowy man with the same elf-like features as Malcolm. He had one slender-bladed weapon in hand, striking the moment she was in range.

Sage spun away, scant inches from the path of the blade. Her daggers poised, she struck hard with her right hand as she came out of her turn to face him.

A frustrated growl confirmed contact as her blade sliced through fabric.

He faced her, eyes turning as red as the blood blooming though his shirt. He attacked with frenzied speed, his blade twirling and slicing ribbons through the air.

Sage blocked and deflected as best she could, but each strike sent her backwards with no room to gain ground.

Behind her, another battle raged with the staccato beat of multiple swords.

Her attacker kept pushing her back, using his advantage to keep her daggers from striking distance. She ducked, dodged, all the while continuing to back up, searching for her opening.

He overreached with a strike that stole the button from her shirt.

Sage sprang into action, maneuvering around him, using all her strength to punch both blades into his torso. As fast as she plunged them in, she removed them, keeping her momentum going as she spun to face his back.

He gasped, swinging his blade wild and sloppy. She deflected it easily, using the opening to stick him again, this time right between the ribs. She met his eyes when her blades found their target. He gasped and let his weapon fall.

Slowly, she pulled her daggers free of his chest. He dropped.

No use wasting a good blade. Sage retrieved his and turned to see the fight behind her. Devon had already felled one dark elf and was quickly finishing off the second.

Two bodies lay on the ground. But there should have been three. Lord Malcolm had taken off.

The last of the dark elves fell. Devon faced her, the thrill of battle adding a wildness to his eyes she had never seen before. He panted, and as he caught his breath, he wiped the blood from his newly acquired blades.

"We've got a problem." Sage pointed to the spot where a body should have been. "Malcolm's gone."

"Take care of these three and let's go," Devon said. "He's probably long gone now."

Sage pulled out the zip ties and bound their hands and feet. On the off chance they survived their wounds, she didn't want them following any time soon. As soon as she finished, she and Devon headed back to the car to find her phone. With any luck, that tracking beacon was still on Malcolm.

THIRTY-SIX

Sage tossed her new blades in the back seat before strapping herself into the car. Her phone sat in the center console. She said a silent prayer as she picked it up and opened the tracking app.

Devon brought the car to life, ready to take off as soon as she gave him a direction.

"He's on the move." Sage watched the little blip representing Lord Malcolm, wondering where he was heading. Another blip on the screen was on the move too. Cor.

Had Nyx and Sylvia gotten to him? Was he escaping from them, or had he done something terrible…? That frightening thought had her immediately sending messages to everyone on her team, telling them to check in.

Switching between the map and her text messages, she guided Devon turn by turn, following as they tracked the movement of their prey.

"You did pretty good back there," Devon said.

She appreciated his words, kind as they were, but the truth was, if Devon hadn't been there with her, she'd have been dead. There was no way she'd have survived facing off against Lord Malcom. Not with him dual wielding. Even with all her training, he moved too damn fast.

"You were amazing too."

"You will be, too, once we get you up to speed on your new toys." Devon laughed. Sage caught the split-second movement of his gaze as he peeked up, looking through the rearview mirror at the weapons lying in the back seat.

"I think those just might be my new favorites." She turned around fully to appreciate the light elven blades.

"Don't get attached. They are not yours yet. You haven't truly won them from your enemy."

"Is that a thing?"

"The warrior's code," Devon clarified. "To claim a weapon, you must best its owner."

"Makes sense. So let's go best ourselves a dark elf."

The two blips of Cor and Malcolm started to head in the same direction.

Sylvia finally replied to her message.
He ran the moment we got there.

Zack's message followed immediately after.
Luke has your video feed. And the security tapes from when ASSET failed to apprehend. Someone knew they'd be watched. Cameras were blocked.

"Raynor's security footage was inconclusive. Cor's on the run now. I have a really bad feeling about where we are heading."

"You think Raynor is part of it all or innocent and being used?"

"Honestly, I don't know. My read on him is good, but there are too many questions left unanswered."

"Like what?"

"Why was his security footage tampered with at the exact time our people would have been by? Why was he so willing to meet with me and set up this meeting?"

"Maybe he is just as in the dark as you are and wants answers."

"I'd love to believe that, but what if this is some elaborate web of lies leading us all to our doom?"

"Doom? Is this a game or some epic fantasy? Who speaks like that?"

"I do, dammit. It's the best word I have right now."

"So use your gamer instincts. When faced with tough…situations, how do approach them?"

"I'd roll the dice to see what my chances of success were," she scoffed.

"Do none of your choices matter in these games? Everything you do is based on the roll of dice?"

"No…not really. The roll affects your advantage."

"So then, what else do you have besides luck?"

"Character attributes, weapons, armor… That kind of thing."

"Assets, you mean. Good. Focus on those. What do we have in our corner as we head into this unknown situation?"

Dammit. He always found a way to teach her something. Even now as they were heading into battle, Devon found a way to make it another one of his training sessions. He was right, as always. Looking at it like prepping for a rescue campaign with a new DM was the best way to keep her nerves at bay. It wasn't like they were going in as noobs in cloth armor either. She had a freaking ogre at her side. Best meat shield she could hope for in combat. And once Nyx and Sylvia arrived, she'd have two spell casters at her back. Sage couldn't ask for a better team to raid a dungeon with.

"You're right. We got this. Roll the dice!" Sage said confidently.

They followed the tracking beacon until it stopped in a rural neighborhood. Houses were spread apart by tons of land and hidden in the dark by the sparse street lamps. The house they came upon had three cars parked in its gravel driveway.

"Do we wait for reinforcements or recon?" Sage asked as she sent the address to both Sylvia and Zack.

Devon parked far enough away to avoid being seen but still allowing for a view of the front door. People were outside. A couple, smoking and chatting. "Recon. We need to know how many people are inside before we attack."

"Recognize those two?" Sage pointed to the dark-haired woman. She'd seen her somewhere before, but couldn't quite put a finger on where that was. Not without a closer look.

"The woman, yes," Devon answered. "Natasha. Watch out for her. A Ker is not someone you want to fight with."

"I'd prefer to avoid fighting, but…you know… It's kind of part of the mission," Sage joked, hoping to cover the unease in her voice.

"You've heard of Valkyries?" Devon asked.

"Yes."

"Same thing, only rather than Norse myth, these are Greek," he explained. "Makes sense now how someone overpowered Ava."

"So we're definitely bringing the blades." Sage tried again for levity. It was either that or lose her nerve completely. "And maybe the dragon."

"You've decided you trust him now?" Devon's eyebrow arched sharply as he turned on her.

"Not yet, but I'm willing to if he shows up and fights for us."

"And what if he is already here? You're telling him we're coming?" Devon asked.

"You're right. Better to check first."

Sage hopped into the back seat of the car and grabbed her new blades. She double-checked her daggers sheathed at her back. The elven blades were too large to fit her sheath. She'd have to carry it for now. If she survived the night, she would find a belt or sheath that would allow her to carry these regularly.

"Stop drooling." Devon chuckled. "Send some up this way. I'm going to go out for a quick scout around."

"Wait. What? I thought we were going to do this together."

"Not until the others get here. We go in as a team. I'm not going far. Just want to get my bearings with the roads so I can plan an exit strategy."

She didn't like the sound of that. Splitting up now while they sat waiting for the rest of their team felt like the worst thing they could do in that moment. But before she could argue, Devon ducked out of the car and disappeared into the shadows.

Sage's phone went off, buzzing in her hand. She checked the message. Zack, confirming he would come. That had her feeling a little more confident.

A fist knocked against the car's window. Startled, Sage jumped in her seat, and looked up to meet the cold black eyes of Natasha staring down at her.

Shit!

She was busted. And Devon had left her. Sage had no other option. She rolled the dice, sending off one last text message before Natasha yanked open the door and pulled Sage out.

THIRTY-SEVEN

Natasha dragged Sage into the house. "Look what I found skulking around outside."

"I was wondering how long it would take you to arrive. Bad traffic?" Lord Malcolm teased. "Where is your friend, the ogre?" He held up the little paw-print tracker she'd had Raynor slip into his pocket. "Did you think I wouldn't have noticed this?"

"What are you talking about?" Sage feigned ignorance.

"I took you for a cunning agent. Coming here alone… Not quite up to par." Malcolm clucked his tongue, mocking her.

"Cunning agent. Such high praise from someone in your position. I'll take it," Sage snarked.

"One should always appreciate one's enemy. Show proper respect for those who are about to die," Malcolm replied.

Natasha closed in behind her. Hairs prickled at the back of Sage's neck. No sign of Devon or the rest of her team's arrival. Her prospects were not looking good.

"You could kill me. I'm outnumbered, alone, vulnerable. It's true. But before you decide to make that very bad mistake, ask yourself why am I standing here? If you think me truly cunning, what reason would I have to be here, knowing death is the only possible outcome?"

Malcolm smiled. A frightening sight Sage wished she could un-see.

Next to him, Cor's head burst into flames. "She's stalling for time. ASSET is on their way. Just kill her and be done with it."

"ASSET is not coming," Sage said calmly.

Cor's face contorted in confusion. "She's lying."

Lord Malcolm stared down his nose at Sage. "Is she?"

"We don't have time for games," Cor said.

"Just be done with her. We have other places to be," Natasha said.

"I can't stop you." Sage swallowed hard and fought to steady her voice. "But whatever your plan, wherever you go, you will be hunted down. Your faces are known. Your deeds as well."

"Strong words so weakly spoken. I'd call your bluff, but I don't think you are bluffing," Lord Malcolm said. "Either way, you don't want to die. You still think there is a chance to get your people back. But where you have failed to account was your value. A foot soldier is not a worthy exchange as hostage."

"And what would be worthy of such an exchange?" Sage grasped for the thread, hoping to prolong the conversation.

"We are not in the business of taking hostages."

"And yet you took my people." She threw the words at him with all the anger she'd had building up inside her.

"How do you know they are not already dead?" Cor added.

"You haven't made an example of them yet," Sage replied, praying she was right. "That's been your mission, has it not?"

"She is a smart one. I'll give her that." Natasha's voice came from behind her, so close Sage could feel the words brush past her ears. "But she's stalling. We need to get moving."

"I've been paying close attention. I have this habit of needing to be shown before I can learn. Drives my partner crazy. Well, it used to. I don't know if I'll have the chance to do it again. But that's a conversation for a different time," Sage teased.

Natasha gripped her arm tight, long nails like talons digging into her skin.

"You've done an excellent job making ASSET look bad. I specifically enjoyed how you managed to do it without bloodshed. That was brilliance on your part. I was paying attention."

"Shut up," Natasha said.

"I wondered how I might be able to do the same. Reveal the Mystics to all without resorting to violence." Sage turned to look at Natasha. "But I guess I'm just not as good at that part, yet."

"What the hell are you talking about?" Natasha asked.

"I don't need glasses." Sage snickered. "But they are a clever way to disguise a camera."

Natasha released her arm and snatched the glasses from Sage's face.

Sage held her ground, fighting against her nerves to keep her face expressionless. "You can destroy them.

The damage has already been done. Your faces have been sent to ASSET. You. Are. Known. Kill me if you want. You will never escape their hunt."

"Quick study." Malcolm's lips parted in a smile that would haunt Sage's dreams, if she lived long enough to have them.

Sage steeled her courage and took a breath before delivering her demands. "My people will be returned. Unharmed."

"If we were to entertain your request, then what?" Malcolm asked. "We have no assurances of safety. When you negotiate, there must also be something to offer. Otherwise, you give us no reason to do as you say. If in fact you have sent our images and recorded video to your people, we will still be charged and tried by ASSET. We gain no benefit at this point."

"Your fate is far better in cooperation. I cannot offer what I do not control," Sage answered honestly.

"You offer nothing," Cor shouted. "You want a deal. I'll give you one. You will be the last to die after we make an example of destroying the rest of your team. Natasha, bring her with us."

Natasha snatched Sage by the arm again and pulled her roughly toward the door.

She opened it. Devon stood on the other side, waiting. Sage flung herself to the floor. Devon attacked before Natasha could react, wielding the twin elven blades he'd collected earlier.

The two erupted into combat.

She rolled to her belly and pushed herself up, searching for the little flaming man. He had vanished, but Lord Malcolm stood defiantly.

"Are you going to use my own weapons against me?" Malcolm said.

She'd left those back in the car. And Natasha had seen to the removal of her daggers before bringing her inside.

"I wouldn't dare." She smirked.

"And I thought you were clever," he taunted.

"I fight with faith and courage." She balled her fist and set herself into fighting position.

Natasha and Devon fought only a few feet away, effectively blocking the front door as an exit.

Malcolm dropped low to swipe Sage's leg. A dirty move she'd not expected from the well-trained dark elf. He wanted to fight dirty? She could do that. Sage maneuvered out of his reach toward a wall lined with bookshelves; projectiles just begging to be used.

She sent a book sailing past his head. Malcolm ducked and Sage used the distraction, sending her foot out to connect with his chest. The kick didn't land as hard as she'd hoped, but it stunned him long enough for her to recover and resupply with projectiles.

Tchotchkes of all kinds went flying through the air. Some connected and earned her a grunt of pain, others shattering on impact with the floor.

The more she pelted him, the madder he got.

"This is how ASSET teaches its people to fight?"

"I fight with the weapons available." She sent a volley of porcelain cherubs at his head.

"You fight like a child." He lunged.

"I could say the same for you." She spun out of his reach. "I had heard you were a warrior." She closed in, striking his nose with her palm. "But you seem useless without your blades."

Malcolm howled as blood erupted from his nose. His hands went up to shield himself.

"What a disappointment." A punch to his gut with a roundhouse finish sent Malcolm to the ground.

When the dust settled, Devon stood above Natasha, blood dripping from the claw marks across his face. She lay with two blades through her chest.

Lord Malcolm rested below Sage, his face mottled with bruises. She had wanted to end him, but couldn't. She still had to get her people back, and even with all the evidence she had against Malcolm, she needed to bring him back to ASSET alive if she hoped to make any accusations stick.

Cor had evaded them again.

A car pulled up. Doors slammed. Feet rushed up the rocky drive. Sylvia and Nyx appeared at the open door, their expressions a mixture of shock and awe at the scene.

"Sorry we are late. Traffic," Nyx joked.

"Cor is missing, and we still don't know where our people are being kept," Sage said. Malcolm twitched and moaned at her feet. She kicked him in the head. "And I need someone to secure this one so we can bring him in."

"Did Cor come by car?" Sylvia asked.

"Probably," Sage said.

"We didn't see any driving away. He's still here somewhere. Hiding," Sylvia replied.

Nyx took to the air. "He could be using a glamour."

Sage pulled one of the blades from Natasha's chest and looked around. "I'd see him if he was."

She worked her way around the room, slowly, inspecting every corner. A hallway led toward the bedrooms. Three of them. She walked toward the farthest door and opened it, looking for blue flames. Nothing. The second door opened to darkness. She tried the third. A small glimmer of blue emanated from under a bed in the center.

"It's over, Cor. Tell me where my people are and you live. Any more tricks and I swear to the mother I will enjoy killing you."

The light of the blue flame grew brighter as the little man came out. He looked her smugly in the eyes. "Your people are dead."

"If that is true, I have no need of you." She held her blade ready to strike.

His flames grew brilliant, as bright as she had ever seen. Cor charged at her with his blinding light. She had no choice. She brought the blade across, slashing it through the air. It connected with flesh. Cor cried out. The room went dark.

Cor's body lay in a heap; his blood spilled out, staining the carpet. Sage couldn't tear her eyes from it. He would have killed her. He was her enemy. But he didn't have to die. Not like this. Not yet. Not when she was no closer to learning the location of her missing people.

Nyx fluttered in behind Sage, her pinkish glow casting more light on the unsightly scene at her feet. "How will we find them now?"

Sage stood, numb, her fingers clenched tightly around the hilt of her weapon. "We still have Malcolm."

THIRTY-EIGHT

Her blade still dripping with Cor's blue blood, Sage stood, arms trembling with anticipation, ready to deliver the killing blow to Lord Malcolm.

Devon had bound and gagged the dark elf, leaving him helpless, and more importantly, silent, while he awaited Sage's justice.

Her blood boiled. She wanted nothing more than to strike him down for all the problems he and his team of Mystic enthusiasts had caused. But since he was the last one alive, she had to keep him that way. He was the only remaining proof of the case she was making against the Mystics.

Standing behind her, the team waited silently to see what she would do. All of them had their reasons for wanting the dark elf dead. None had lifted their voices in defense of this madman. Sylvia, Devon, and Nyx stood silently as Sage forced back the bile in her throat so she could speak.

"You have one chance," she warned. "Tell me where my people are, or I will end you. I'm done with games."

Malcolm's coal black eyes lifted slowly as he drew them up to meet Sage's. His nostrils flared with a deep breath. Even helpless as he'd been rendered, the dark elf was still trying to lord over them. Sage stared him down, refusing to allow him to feel high and mighty. He had been defeated. He was nothing. She'd make good on her promise to end him eventually. The more of a prick he acted, the more she'd enjoy it when the time came.

The dark elf finally lowered his eyes and nodded.

Sage released his gag, anticipating his answer.

"Death comes for us all, eventually," Malcolm replied.

"Asshole!" She bashed him in the head with the pommel of her sword, knocking him out, and stuffed the gag back into his mouth. He wasn't going to give them any information, and she couldn't risk another Cor situation. As much as she wanted to kill him, he had to remain alive. At least until ASSET got ahold of him.

"There are no other places in this house to hide our people." Devon's tone echoed the fear plaguing Sage's mind. Without some clue, some direction, information of any kind… How were they ever going to find their people?

This couldn't be it. Just a dead end. After all they had done? No. They had missed something.

She thought for a moment. "No garage? Basement?"

"We're in Vegas, honey… Basements aren't really a thing," Sylvia answered. "Garage is empty."

"Attic? Crawlspace? Makeshift bomb shelter." Sage was grasping at straws but had nothing else to go on.

Nyx circled around the room. "They are not here. I'm sorry, hon."

"You went through Cor's home? Checked everything?" Sage asked.

Nyx fluttered down and perched on top of Malcolm's head. "You want me to work my magic on this guy? I could try to extract some information."

"Magical torture?" Sage didn't want to admit how tempting that idea was. "Probably wouldn't help. I think I scrambled his brain with that last hit."

"We're here for you." Nyx giggled.

The little pixie had never sounded so devious. Sage had seen her darker side. She rarely showed it, preferring to use the pink aura and small stature to lull people into a false sense of security. Sage knew better. That little creature packed a powerful punch that made Sage appreciate her magical immunity.

"You can have him after ASSET is through. How's that?" Sage joked.

Lights from a car pulling into the gravel driveway briefly glowed against the wall of the living room.

Better late than never, Sage muttered to herself, expecting to see Zack or Matt show up now that all the excitement had passed.

Devon positioned himself near the door, his fist balled and ready to strike in case it wasn't their wayward vampire friends.

"We didn't see any signs of additional guests at Cor's home. I don't believe he kept them there." Sylvia stepped in closer to the unconscious dark elf. "Just going to have to make this one talk."

"He'd only stall us until it was too late." Every moment they wasted debating what to do, her people could be dying. She had to find them. She'd lost so much time already hunting leads. She'd been all over the city, chasing the damn dark elf from his warehouse to... "Dammit! This was a diversion," Sage groaned, realizing the truth. She could have found her people hours ago. "Devon, what did that guy say earlier? At the warehouse? How many hours for the truck to arrive? A package that had to go tonight…"

"What?" Devon asked, but his eyes lit up with the same realization. "Malcolm was leading us away. Stalling for time."

"We need to get back to the warehouse," Sage said.

"We don't have enough time to get there by car," Devon said.

"Then you need a dragon." Raynor appeared at the front door.

Not the person she had expected. Quite the opposite, but welcome all the same. Sage had wondered if the text she had sent him had been delivered.

"I can be there in minutes if I fly."

His timing was impeccable. And the fact he'd showed up proved she'd been right to trust him.

"Let the whole city see a dragon flying…again?" Devon crossed his arms and planted his feet firmly on the ground. "We just continue to play into the Mystics' hands if we do that. Rescue or not, Ava would never condone that."

He was right. They couldn't be seen. Even if they saved their people, it would effectively drive another nail into ASSET's coffin.

"Not if you have shadows on your side," Sylvia suggested, allowing her body to shift between solid and smoke to emphasize her point.

"I can shield you from all sight," Nyx added.

Sage's heart swelled with pride. She really did have the best of friends. Unlikely as they all were, they made one hell of a team, and if they were right, they still had a chance to beat the clock.

"There's only one problem with that," she admitted, realizing she was the flaw in their plan. "I can't go with you."

All eyes in the room shifted to Sage. She felt the weight of them, each and every one. They didn't want to agree, but it was the truth. Magical immunity meant that all their shielding would be void if she went with them. But she couldn't be left out of the loop. This was her moment. This was her rescue. She had to be there.

"You can meet us there." Raynor broke the awkward silence and tossed his keys at Sage. "Not a scratch, you hear?"

Better late than never. That settled it.

"I'll drive the prisoners, or what's left of them, back to ASSET. And make sure this one is processed and appropriately restrained," Devon said. "I will make sure everyone at ASSET knows you, Sage, were responsible for his apprehension."

"I don't need recognition. We're all a team here." Sage retrieved the recorder from her pocket and the glasses she'd used to record their adventure. She handed both to Devon. "Take these as proof. I'll message Luke to send over the other files to complete the case against the high council."

"Text me the moment you have our people," Devon replied.

"Sounds like a plan!" She pulled Devon into a good-bye bear hug. "I couldn't have done this without you."

"We still have work to do. If there is a truck, then there will be more henchmen. Bring the sword." Sylvia gave the order to Sage like an overprotective mother.

"Remember. Not a scratch!" Raynor warned again before transforming into his magnificent dragon form. He allowed Sylvia on his back.

Nyx floated into the air, casting magic like confetti all around them as Sylvia's body disappeared behind a growing cloud of black smoke.

They took to the sky.

Sage waved them off, before clicking the remote to unlock Raynor's car—a purple Jeep Wrangler. "Because of course he would have a beast of a car." She smiled to herself, thinking of Mark's Jeep. She'd affectionately called it Beast.

Time was of the essence. Her party had already flown off out of sight. She had no time to waste to meet them there.

THIRTY-NINE

Raynor was still in his beastly form when Sage pulled into the parking lot. Looking more puppy than dragon, he rolled a large sixteen-wheeler around the parking lot like a toy.

"Are we afraid of being seen?" Sage asked as she came up to her group.

"My cloaking spell is still going." Nyx laughed. "Just look at him go. He looks like he's having so much fun."

"Raynor," Sage called out.

The dragon stopped the moment he saw her. His body began to contract, growing smaller. Wings disappeared, green scales turned to skin, and in a moment, a man stood where the dragon had been.

He came toward her. "The truck arrived a few minutes ago. Two guys took off the moment they saw me." He shrugged, feigning innocence.

"Did we get an ID on who they might have been?" Sage asked.

"You can probably pull footage from the warehouse security cameras for that," Sylvia suggested. "Right now we need to get in there and see if we can find your people."

"Round back, there was a door. Smoking section. Unlocked when we were here last. Probably still is," Sage said. "I'll go in and open up one of the bays here in the front for everyone."

Aside from a few men who had been left hog-tied and moaning on the floor from their previous visit, the warehouse had been left empty. Sage made quick work of getting in and opening up the bay door.

She remembered seeing the shipping containers earlier but had not thought to consider her people might be in there. Now it seemed the obvious choice, and she felt stupid for not checking hours ago. Though if she had, she would not have had Malcolm in custody or learned that Natasha had been part of the plan all along.

She opened up the large metal container. While it appeared to be set up to transport people like a mini prison cell, there was no one inside.

Sylvia, Nyx, and Raynor made their way into the warehouse. They looked hopefully at Sage.

She shook her head and turned away from the container. "Only one other place I haven't checked."

Sage took off toward the main office. From the outside, it appeared to be a simple one-room office with a door leading to the front parking lot and the side door leading into the warehouse, but once she made her way into the space, she saw it was only the front of a much larger space. Another door led into a hallway with a bathroom, kitchenette, and breakroom, and beyond that, a set of double doors had been secured with a chain binding the handles.

Sage searched for a key.

Behind her, the patter of boots on concrete signaled others were coming into the warehouse.

"We've got company. I think our henchmen have returned," Sage said.

"We've got this." Raynor turned around and headed into the warehouse, his skin already taking on a rough, scaly appearance.

Sage continued to look for the keys. She found them buried in the pocket of a coat hanging on the wall.

Her heart raced as she fumbled with the key to unlock the chains. "You guys okay in there?" Sage shouted.

"We've got this," Sylvia replied.

Not the person she'd been talking to but she was glad for the confirmation.

The lock clicked, and the chains dropped. Sage flung open the door. Light streamed into the dark space, revealing four people.

Ava sat against the wall. She moved to push herself up to her feet, groaning with the effort it took. Beaten and bloody, her clothing dirty, hair disheveled, she was a pitiful sight, but still Ava. "I had wondered when you'd find us, Miss Cynwrig."

"You knew I'd be the one?" Sage asked, shocked as Ava made it to her feet and hobbled over.

"I had no doubt." Ava smiled. A real, genuine smile. "But I had hoped it would have been a little earlier. I could have sworn I heard you causing a ruckus hours ago."

She deserved that. Sage had been kicking herself ever since she'd made that realization. "Better late than never though."

Ava stumbled barefooted toward the door leading to the warehouse. Sounds of the fighting had died down, but there were still the odd sounds of groaning coming from that direction. "Who have you brought with you?"

Sylvia appeared at the doorway. She came face-to-face with Ava. "Oh... You found... Hello, Ava."

Sylvia sent an angry glare at Sage. She deserved that as well for not letting on that Ava was one of the missing people.

"Sylvia?" Ava greeted the shadowrunner louder than was necessary. "I did not realize I had you to thank for assisting Miss Cynwrig in this matter. Seems you and her have quite the relationship built up."

"If you're not careful, Masters, I might have to poach your girl. She's quite resourceful. You know how hard it is to find good people," Sylvia replied.

Both ladies turned to face Sage. She'd never felt so scared and proud all at the same time.

"Sorry. This one is all mine." Ava's eyes shifted from Sage to something behind her. "Well, maybe not all mine. Miss Cynwrig, I believe someone has been waiting to talk to you."

Sage turned her attention to the dark room. Three people remained, though only one had made a move. Grey hobbled into the light, looking just as beaten as Ava.

"Everyone okay in there?" Sage asked.

Two more people were laid out on the ground, unconscious in the tiny room.

"We're alive. That's what counts." Grey's voice sent her heart racing. "Severe dehydration among other ills, but we'll live thanks to you."

He came closer into the light. She stared, caught between wanting to slap him and at the same time desperate to throw her arms around his neck and never let go. She'd dreamed of this moment since their last kiss, but she still owed him for betraying her.

Sage closed the gap between them and struck hard. The sound of her hand connecting with his cheek echoed around all the office walls.

Grey let slip a groan as the impact sent his head jerking sharply to the side.

Eyes watering, Grey turned to face her again, his hand smoothing the sting from his cheek. "I deserved that."

"There's more where that came from." She reached up again, this time with both hands, and pulled his face down to hers. She met his lips with an urgency born of all the anxious days spent worrying. He was a jerk. The root cause of all her worries. Liar, betrayer, and supreme pain in her ass. He'd locked her in a goddamned prison. Left her screaming, alone in the dark. But if he hadn't, she would never have had the chance to save him and the others. Between hatred and love, she couldn't sort her feelings out for him. They both warred for dominance as she clung to him, digging her fingers into his matted hair. He was alive. Nothing else mattered at that moment. She could punish him later. At that moment, he was all hers.

Grey broke their connection, pulling away, his eyes still watering.

"No." She fought to hold on, not wanting to let go of him again.

"Let me explain… You have to understand."

He had to open his mouth?

"I don't want to hear it."

Anger sent her hand flying again. Sage slapped him before another round of stupid words could escape from his mouth.

Ava cleared her throat. "Miss Cynwrig, perhaps it would be best to let Mr. Maddox heal before you break him further?"

Heat bloomed in her cheeks. "Sorry." She turned to Grey, narrowing her eyes threateningly. "I mean it. Not another word!"

He nodded, rubbing the sting from his red cheeks.

"The other two are going to need medical attention. I'll put the call in to ASSET." Sage pulled her phone and sent a message to Devon letting him know she had the missing people and requesting backup.

"Miss Cynwrig." Ava waved her over. "This was a Shadow Ops mission to infiltrate the Mystics. I cannot be officially listed in the rescue. Understand?"

"Of course. You were the direct target. We had to keep you in a secure location while we infiltrated their ranks," Sage answered. "But once we knew where our missing people were, we called you in for the takedown."

"Very good! Devon was wrong about you." Ava's laughing eyes matched the amusement in her tone. An impossible sight Sage didn't think she'd ever see again. "I think you are perfectly suited for this job."

"He wasn't all wrong," Sage admitted freely. The sting that accompanied the honesty of that statement had been given plenty of time to fade over the last few days. Devon spoke the truth, and had never attempted to hide that fact from her. He'd done it like he did everything else, turned it into a lesson she would not soon forget. "I have a lot to learn. But I can do that on the job."

"Humility is not a quality most agents have. But you wear it well." Ava's praise was its own brand of magic, causing Sage's heart to swell with pride.

Raynor returned in his human form. "We're all clear out here now. Rounded up all the men Sage left earlier and the two we just picked up."

"Thank you," Sage said. "You've more than cleared your name in my book." She turned to Ava. "This was the dragon who'd been tricked into that unfortunate midnight flight by the Mystics a few days ago. Without his help, we would not have found you."

Ava glared at Raynor as if sizing him up. Small as she was next to his human form, she still managed to appear intimidating. "I suppose that means he wishes to be kept free of the official report."

"If possible." Raynor bowed his head respectfully. "I've come to understand that the Mystics' mission statement is not quite as in line with my own as originally presented."

"You'll see that in my report as well as the audio and video footage taken," Sage explained. "The Mystics were empowering otherwise innocent magical citizens to do their dirty work. Keeping themselves blameless for the act itself."

"Audio and video is good, but ASSET senior management will want actual heads to put on spikes. You understand that?"

Sage beamed with pride, having exactly that and more to provide. "We have plenty of heads to put on spikes. One in particular should interest you, I think."

"Only one?" Disappointment soured Ava's voice. "I had hoped for a whole council's worth given the time you've had to investigate."

Sage's cheeks burned as she turned her gaze to the ground.

"She and Devon got a little too excited with their new dark elven blades," Sylvia offered with amusement. "Trimmed the fat so to speak."

Ava's eyebrow arched sharply. "May I see?"

"I can show you in the car, on our way back to ASSET, if you like." Sage remembered her boss's appreciation for special weapons. "Its owner still has his head. My offering to you, along with all the evidence I've collected."

"If you won the weapon in battle, it is yours," Ava replied. "I, however, will enjoy taking up arms in the courtroom. Too bad this isn't the old days. I'd have loved swinging the axe at his execution. Killing his future with the Mystics will have to suffice. If you've accomplished even half of what you have promised, we'll have enough evidence to weed out the remaining Mystics in our city." Ava turned her gaze to Sylvia. "And possibly call for a vote on who should take the vacant seats on the high council."

"You thinking of making nominations?" Sylvia asked.

Her boss had never looked so devious. "I might know a few people for the job."

Sylvia, Nyx, and Raynor... New high council members? Perhaps not all of them, but it would be nice to have people in power she knew she could trust. Of course that kind of stuff was well above Sage's paygrade.

"Take your team and Grey. Call it a night. You've more than earned a rest," Ava ordered. "I'll meet with backup when they arrive."

"Are you sure? We can wait," Sage said.

Grey hobbled up behind Sage and put an arm around her shoulder. "You can finish beating me up."

"Oh, you'll get yours, don't you worry," Sage replied. "I'm just not sure we should leave before backup gets here."

"In an effort to keep your team members out of the spotlight, and official paperwork, it would be best if they were not here when others arrive." Ava's point was clear. Especially where the dragon was involved.

Raynor nodded in agreement. "I would be happy to provide a lift in my car, if you need. It's the least I can do."

"You have done plenty," Sage replied.

"Get home. Get some rest. We still have a lot of work to do. We've taken out one head, but the Mystics are like a hydra, I'm afraid. They will have more. Our work has just begun. Tomorrow, my office. Be ready to hunt." Ava cocked her head, turning her eyes to the front door. "Dismissed."

MORE MAGIC TO COME

The Agents of A.S.S.E.T. will return
with

Let Sleeping Magic Lie (2020)

PLEASE REVIEW

Your opinion matters! When people first look at a book, beyond the description and the cover, they pay close attention to what others **like you** have to say.

If the book is getting overwhelmingly good or bad reviews, it can weigh heavily on that readers decision whether or not to click that purchase button.

It does not have to be a book report.

It does not have to be 5 stars. *I would never ask for any special favoritism.*

A book review is simply sharing what you thought of the book. It answers two very simple questions:

Did you like it?
Would you recommend it to someone else?

That's it. Your opinion matters. Most importantly to me, because I want to ensure you are enjoying the books I write. But beyond my hope for your satisfaction, the review you write caries great weight in the publishing realm as well. It can quite literally make or break a book.

So, here I am, groveling at your feet.

If you have read one (or more) of my books, would you do me the greatest of honors and leave a review?

ABOUT THE AUTHOR

Katie Salidas is a best-selling author known for her unique genre-bending style.

Host of the Indie Youtube Talkshow, Spilling Ink, nerd, Doctor Who fangirl, Las Vegas Native, and SuperMom to three awesome kids, Katie gives new meaning to the term sleep-deprived.

Since 2010 she's penned four bestselling book series: the Immortalis, Olde Town Pack, Little Werewolf, and the RONE award-winning Chronicles of the Uprising. And as her not-so-secret alter ego, Rozlyn Sparks, she is a USA Today bestselling author of romance with a naughty side.

Facebook
http://www.facebook.com/pages/Katie-Salidas-Author/214780936916

Web
http://www.katiesalidas.com/

Twitter
http://twitter.com/QuixoticKatie

SpillingInk
https://www.youtube.com/c/spillinginkshow

Join the Paranormal Posse
Connect directly with Katie and get exclusives and up-dates.
https://www.facebook.com/groups/ParanormalPosse/